P9-DWW-375

Inch by Inch

Inch by Inch

A Novel of Breast Cancer and Healing

Geoffrey Norman

The Lyons Press
Guilford, Connecticut
An imprint of The Globe Pequot Press

The Lyons Press is an imprint of The Globe Pequot Press.

10 9 8 7 6 5 4 3 2 1

Printed in the United States of America.

Designed by Lisa Reneson

ISBN 1-59228-197-4

Library of Congress of Cataloging-in-Publication data is available on file.

How poor are they that have not patience
What wound did ever heal but by degrees?
Othello

The plane was crowded and late, which was nothing new. But I had been either flying or waiting around airports all day and I was ready to get off this airplane and get home. The recirculated air had made my mouth dry and foul, my skin felt faintly greasy, and I wanted a long hot shower and a cold beer. I had been on the road almost three weeks.

My seat was against the bulkhead, way back in coach, so I waited while the rest of the passengers wrestled luggage from the overhead bins and then crowded the passageway. When the congestion cleared, I made my way toward the front of the plane, where a weary flight attendant thanked me for flying with her airline. I thanked her for having me and smiled—it wasn't her fault—and walked up the long tunnel into the terminal. Leslie was waiting there behind security.

"Why don't I get the car out of the lot," she said after we were through with the greetings and the hugs, "while you're waiting for your bags. Then I'll meet you out front."

"Sounds like a plan," I said.

Twenty minutes later we were on the road. The drive home from the airport takes a little less than two hours and we usually talk the whole way. But now, there was a silence; not the kind where you are trying to think of something to say, but the kind where you know what has to be said and are trying to think of a way—or find the nerve—to say it.

Even I could sense this and my thought was, *Oh God, she's going to ditch me.*

That's what happens when you come home from three weeks on the road and your wife has something she needs to talk to you about. She's tired of it and she's leaving.

"Jack," she said, and drew in a deep breath.

"Yes," I said, thinking *Here it comes.*

After another, much shorter silence she said, "There just isn't any good way to tell you this . . . "

And then she blurted it out.

"I have breast cancer."

The air seemed to go out of the car and things got darker and felt smaller, almost as though the physical distance between us had suddenly increased. When I reached across the seat for her hand, it seemed like a long way. She drove like that for a while, one hand on the wheel and the other holding mine, which was suddenly both sweaty and cold.

After a while, she started to tell me about it and I listened. I wanted her to tell me one thing only—that the doctors could fix it. But she didn't say it.

Then again, I thought, maybe it wasn't as bad as it could have been. She didn't tell me the doctors *couldn't* fix it, either.

So I listened to the medical talk and it was like finding yourself suddenly attending an advanced seminar in college when you haven't gone to the introductory courses. She told me that it was an "estrogen-fed tumor," and I pretended I understood even though I'd thought all tumors were pretty much the same. Or, rather, that there were only two kinds. Malignant and nonmalignant. Very bad and not-so-bad.

I didn't ask, at first, about the surgery and how bad that would be. I knew enough to know that I didn't want to hear the word *radical.* When I didn't hear it, I didn't press.

But there was a surgeon and surgery was scheduled for early the next week. Monday to be exact. This was Friday night. Things seemed to be moving very fast. I took that as a bad sign and said so.

"No," she said. "Not really."

It occurred to me, then, that I had been gone a long time.

"When did they find this thing?" I said. I couldn't make my mouth form the word *tumor*.

"They didn't find it," she said, "I did. So much for all the mammograms."

"When?"

"A couple of days before you left."

And she hadn't told me, I thought. It was something we both did; something, for all I knew, that all married people did. You keep the bad stuff to yourself as long as you can. Maybe you don't want to add to your partner's problems if it's something you can handle yourself. Or maybe it's a way of saying that you don't think your partner can handle it, so you might as well deal with it yourself.

"I didn't know for sure," she said. "I didn't even really believe it at first. You know what I expected them to say, when I went in?"

"What's that?"

"I thought they'd laugh and say, Oh, *that*. Don't worry about that. It's nothing."

She paused and shook her head.

"But they didn't," she said. "They didn't laugh at all. They got real serious."

About halfway home, on the side of a nondescript stretch of highway, there was a bar where we sometimes stopped after one of my business trips. It was called the Earl of Kent, and the owner had a weakness for English pubs. He served bitter by the pint and pickled eggs and somebody was always throwing darts.

"Wanna get drunk?" Leslie said.

"Are you serious?"

"Absolutely."

"Are you sure you ought . . ."

"What am I supposed to be worried about?" she said. "That I'll get cancer?"

* * *

When we were at the front door, about to go in, she looked at me and said firmly that she didn't want to talk about it anymore.

"Not tonight, anyway," she said. "I'm sick of it. We'll talk about it in the morning. I expect we'll talk about it until you're sick of it, too. It is one unbelievably dreary topic of conversation, believe me."

So I drank a pint of Watney's and she had a glass of white wine and we listened to Diana Krall who was playing on the sound system. When she sang, "Why Should I Care," Leslie said, "I think I'll make that my anthem."

The light in the bar was low, the way it should be in a bar at that time of night, and there was some smoke in the air. She looked good, across the table from me, in that smoky light. It was the sort of sultry, dark, mature look of those actresses from the '30s and the '40s who could make smoking a cigarette and taking the first sip of a cocktail look unbearably erotic. Joan Crawford or Lauren Bacall or one of those.

The music helped, too.

She didn't look sick. She looked healthy and desirable, which seemed all wrong. Wrong as a fact and wrong for me to notice. I was supposed to be looking at her with compassion, I thought. Not lust.

She was aware that I was looking at her. Not even "looking," actually. More like staring.

"What?" she said.

"Nothing. Just that you look great."

"Sweet of you to say so."

"No. I mean it. You really do look great. You look especially beautiful tonight."

She reached across the table and covered my hand with hers.

"Thanks, sailor," she said. "But if you like me now, just wait until you see me without my hair."

I eased out of bed after lying in the dark for a couple of hours, listening to the dogs breathe and watching the numbers roll over on the face of the digital clock. It seemed impossible, but Leslie was sleeping soundly and her breathing did not change when I slipped out from under the covers.

I didn't want to turn on a light, so I was careful leaving the room. I didn't knock over any chairs or bump into the dresser. The dogs—Rufus and Silas— were sleeping on beanbag beds and they raised their heads. Curious, but not enough to get up and follow me out of the room.

I wasn't sure what I had in mind. Something from the refrigerator, for starters.

I found a plastic jug of milk and poured a tall glass. I couldn't remember the last time I'd done that. Milk was what babies drank. But just then milk was what I craved. Maybe, I thought, because I felt so helpless. I finished half the glass in one long swallow, then refilled it.

I left the kitchen and wandered into a little room that we called, a bit grandly, our study. We had bookshelves and an overstuffed chair in there. Also a desk and a computer. No globe and no trophy animal heads, though we had put up some dark paneling that looked pretty good.

I turned on the light and sat in the overstuffed chair. I thought about reading something, some old book that might divert me. Instead I got up, sat down at the desk, and turned on the computer and checked my e-mail.

Nothing important. A couple of jokes from a friend of mine who sent out dozens of them, all bad. He liked those top-ten lists and I could see that the subject of one of his e-mails was "the ten worst things to say in an argument with your wife." A discount travel company had something for me on late-summer bargain airfares. And there was an offer to refinance my home at a favorable rate. We weren't there yet, I thought, and hit DELETE.

I went to the Web, for some reason. Ordinarily I don't use it, except to check the market and the ball scores. I opened the bookmarks and scrolled. The last dozen sites, the ones most recently marked, were all about cancer.

I was still having trouble with the word, and seeing it there, in eerie digital type, over and over, down the list of bookmarked Web sites, made me shudder. It is a loathsome, repellent word, and when I imagined Leslie sitting in this room alone, carefully typing the word so Google could scour the entire World Wide Web, looking for sites, a wave of compassion broke over me. I felt awful that she'd had to be alone when the computer announced that it had found three hundred thousand, or three million, matches and ranked them according to relevance.

What made a "relevant" cancer site, anyway?

I imagined her alone in this room, with a cup of tea, taking a deep breath and then typing the dreaded word with flying fingers. She was a demon when it came to keyboarding. Her mother had believed that you needed certain basic skills to survive in this world and that one of those skills was what they used to call "touch typing." She'd also made sure Leslie learned to cook. And play tennis and golf.

She died of breast cancer before Leslie and I ever met. Leslie almost never talked about it.

I opened one of the bookmarked sites. Some outfit that sold wigs and "prosthetic devices" to women with breast cancer. There were pictures of wigs and turbans on the home page. The models were photographed with and without wigs or turbans and they were smiling for the camera. They looked like professionals and I wondered if these models actually had cancer or if they had been paid enough—and it had to be a lot—to shave their heads.

But it wasn't so bad, looking at the photographs of the women with bald heads or wearing the utterly phony-looking wigs. I didn't draw back from the screen or close my eyes or suck in my breath. I looked at the pictures and figured I could deal with that when the time came. Certainly I could deal with it if Leslie could, and she didn't have any choice. Which meant that I didn't either.

But I couldn't make myself open the pages about prosthetic devices. Not yet, anyway. Not tonight.

I turned the computer and the lights off and went back to bed, back to listening to the dogs breathe and watching the glowing numbers on the face of the digital clock until I finally fell asleep sometime near dawn.

3

Early the next morning, I sat at the kitchen table, drinking coffee. A bird feeder hung from a branch a few feet from the window and it was crowded with chickadees. I kept the feeder loaded with sunflower seeds so there would always be a lot of activity there.

"You couldn't sleep?" Leslie said, startling me a little. I hadn't heard her coming down the hall.

She was wearing a terry cloth robe that some hotel had given her when we stayed there. It wasn't as dazzlingly white or as thick and plush as it had once been. We needed to take another trip.

She had brushed her hair but she wasn't wearing any makeup. She looked pale and weary in a way that can't be fixed by just one or two nights of sleep, but there was no dread in her expression and she still had her dark, vaguely mysterious looks. Her face was mobile and animated, with good cheekbones and large eyes. You could see a lot of things in her face, including a temper. She was from North Carolina and when she was growing up, people told her that she looked like Ava Gardner, who was still a scandal down there. And Leslie did, in fact, look a little like her. You could see in Leslie the same arrogant good looks that had driven Frank Sinatra crazy; the same looks that caused a New York cab driver to say to me one night, under his breath, "You're a lucky guy, buddy."

That had been a while ago. We'd left New York, moved here to the country, and raised two kids since then. But Leslie still looked good. Even sitting at the breakfast table in her old bathrobe, knowing she had cancer, she looked good.

"I was up and down," I said. "I always have trouble sleeping when I come home off the road."

"But that's not the reason."

"No. Probably not."

She smiled. Vaguely.

"How about you?" I said. "I mean, how can you sleep at all?"

"The first night," she said, "I didn't. Not a minute. That was after you'd gone and the biopsy came back. I just lay in bed and looked out the window or up at the ceiling. There was a full moon and I could probably have read a book without turning on the lights. I was still awake at dawn. I thought I would never sleep again, but ever since that night, whenever I put my head on the pillow, I go right out and sleep like a baby. Go figure."

"Well," I said, "It's probably a good thing."

"I guess. They always say that rest is good for you. But right now sleeping seems kind of pointless. I mean, when you're short on time, why spend it sleeping?"

That made sense in a kind of brutal way. I didn't know what to say, so I just nodded.

"Anyway, I wake up feeling good and that counts for something."

"How do you feel the rest of the time."

"Great."

"Really?"

"Yes. Really. And isn't that the pits. Just one more crummy thing about this generally crummy situation. I'm feeling great even though I've got one of the world's top ten most hideous diseases. Doesn't seem fair."

"No," I said. "It doesn't."

She didn't say anything for a moment or two. Then she sighed and said, "Well, I don't think we're going to be able to make an appeal from here. I'm going to take a shower, get dressed, and make us some breakfast. Meanwhile, why don't you fill that bird feeder. Those chickadees are about to clean you out."

She made the kind of breakfast that her mother had probably fixed for her when she was growing up in North Carolina. Eggs, country sausage, and grits—she had these "gourmet grits" that a friend sent to her from a place called Bradley's near Tallahassee. Even people who didn't like grits liked these. I made a fresh pot of coffee and we ate at the kitchen table, watching the chickadees.

"This is wonderful," I said.

"Glad you like it," she said, "because you are going to be eating like this for the foreseeable future."

I gave her a look. We usually had yogurt or fruit or a cereal that was supposed to be healthy. I ate short-order breakfasts on the road, and when I'd tell her about them, she'd say I was looking down the barrel of a heart attack with my finger on the trigger.

"You're going to have to get used to some weird ideas coming from me," she said. "You think you can handle it?"

"Try me."

"Okay," she said, and her lively eyes grew even more lively. "For one thing, I plan to outeat this lousy disease. You see these people who have cancer and you can tell that it is just devouring them from the inside. They are all skinny and hollowed out, right? Well, that is not going to be me. I'm in a fight with this thing and if it plans to consume *me* from the inside, then it has got another think coming."

"Makes sense," I said, and meant it. As much sense, I thought, as anything else in my present state of ignorance. More sense than going down to Mexico and getting yourself injected with a fluid distilled from peach pits. I wondered if things would eventually come to that. "Anyway, I like breakfast and I'll clean up. You go back to bed and rest."

"I'm not tired," she said. "And I won't be a patient. Understand?"

"Sure."

"I won't be patronized or nursemaided." Her face was hot.

"I understand."

"Or pitied. I *especially* won't be pitied."

"I get it."

She took a breath and her shoulders rose and fell. The motion flowed into her breasts. Normally this would have been some kind of erotic cue. Saturday mornings had always been good for us, with cartoon shows to distract the kids when they were young.

Not this time.

"But if you want to clean up the kitchen," she said, softening, "I won't stand in your way. I'm not above cashing in on this thing a little bit."

I was just finishing up when she came back into the kitchen. She was wearing khaki shorts and a soft cotton shirt that she had knotted at the waist. She had a flat stomach—"good abs," she liked to say—and could still do that.

So now, I thought, it was time to sit down at the kitchen table and have our talk. That's what we did whenever there was a crisis—sit at the kitchen table and talk. Like we did when we found a bag of pot in our son's jacket pocket. That was something we laughed about now, but it hadn't been funny at the time.

I couldn't imagine ever laughing about this crisis. That happens, I suppose, as you get older. The emergencies in your life no longer turn out to be less serious than they seemed at the time; they stay serious or get even more so. And things certainly no longer have a way of working themselves out, or of turning out for the best.

"Listen," Leslie said. "I wonder if you'd mind if we didn't talk about this thing today. It's Saturday and you just got home. I told you all the big stuff last night. We could talk this thing into the ground, but honestly, Jack, I am sick to death of talking about it."

I nodded. I didn't much like her choice of words, but if she didn't want to talk about it right now, that was okay. Still, I wondered about the kids. I asked her if she'd told them.

She shook her head. It was an ambiguous sort of gesture with her. It could mean either that she hadn't told Brad and Andy, or that she just didn't want to answer my question.

It didn't seem like a good time to press her for an answer.

"Right now, I want to think about this—and talk about it—as little as possible," she said. "The surgery is Monday. You can go down with me, if you want, and we can both talk to the doctor."

"Well, of course."

She held up her hand. "I know you're busy. You just got back from a long trip and you'll be swamped at the office—"

This time I stopped her. "You've got to be kidding. There isn't any such thing as being that busy. I'm going with you."

"I could get somebody to drive me . . ."

"I'm going." Now I was getting a little hot.

"All right. Good. That's good. It means you can ask—we can both ask—the doctors our questions and I won't have to interpret for you. It also means we don't have to talk about it anymore this weekend. We can have some fun."

"Sure," I said. "Sounds good to me. What did you have in mind?"

4

Leslie stood knee deep in the river a few yards downstream from where I had beached the canoe on a sand and gravel bar. She was throwing tight, precise loops across the current, slightly upstream, and following her fly carefully as it drifted back her way. She was a good caster and I always enjoyed watching her. Between casts, I watched a kingfisher perched in a cedar tree on the opposite bank of the river and looking exceedingly alert.

"You know," she said over her shoulder, "we've got the usual people coming tonight."

"Right." I had forgotten.

"So," she said, "what do you think? Do I tell them?"

I didn't know what to say, so I pretended to give the question some thought.

"How do you feel about it?" I said. The oldest evasion in the book. Turn a question into a question. No marriage could work without it. For that matter, nothing in the world could work without it.

"I don't know," she said. "They'll be so *concerned* if I do tell them. But they'll be hurt if I don't and they find out some other way."

"I imagine so," I said.

"I can't stand the thought of being patronized," she said. "I'd keep it all a secret if I had my way."

"You think you could?"

"No way," she said. "But how *do* you tell people?" She put a mend in her line and then picked it cleanly off the water, shot a little line, and dropped the fly at the tail of a long, glassy eddy.

"Nice cast," I said.

"Thanks. You think I should change flies?"

"No," I said. "Nothing's hatching. That Henryville is as good as anything else."

"Maybe I could just get some announcements printed up," she said. "Send them out like wedding invitations. 'Leslie Rockwell regrets to announce that she has breast cancer and, if she is lucky, won't lose anything more than her hair. Please keep expressions of sympathy and concern to yourself. Also prayers. No self-help books, inspirational leaflets, or flowers, please. Mrs. Rockwell desires that this be a private cancer.'"

"Might work."

"It's preposterous and you know it. And I'm changing flies."

"So, how do you tell them . . . and when?"

"I don't know," she said. "And not tonight. I want tonight to be fun."

"Okay," I said. "I can live with that."

"I'll probably tell people after the surgery," she said. "I'm fairly sure I won't be feeling so proud then."

She clipped the fly and replaced it with something I couldn't identify from a distance. It was another dry, though, because after she had tied it on, she smeared some silicone on it to make it float.

I stood up and walked back to the canoe. I took the water bottle from the cooler and poured a cup. The water had been on ice and was so cold that it hurt a little going down. But it was a warm day—for New England, anyway—and it tasted good. I poured the last inch or two in the cup over the back of my neck and shuddered as it ran down my back.

I looked back downstream where Leslie was still casting. She had good form. I looked for the kingfisher, but it had moved on. I pushed the canoe into the river, not quite to the current, then climbed in and started paddling.

"Let's move on," I said when I was close enough for her to hear me, "see if we can't find some better water and a few rising fish somewhere downstream."

"Sounds good to me," she said and reeled up.

The first of our guests arrived just about the time Leslie finished slicing the eggplant and zucchini. I was still arranging the lawn furniture, lighting citronella candles, and getting a charcoal fire started in the grill. The dogs made a big fuss when the first car pulled into the drive.

To look at Leslie, you would never have known anything was troubling her. She looked like a hostess who was enjoying herself. People showed up, couple by couple, and hung around the kitchen, where I filled wineglasses and opened beer bottles and we passed around trays and bowls of smoked fish and cheese. We'd invited four couples, all old friends.

When everyone had arrived, Leslie told us to go outside. We sat in the lawn furniture in the twilight, listening to Lyle Lovett and Nina Simone and Jane Monheit. Leslie had put the CDs on before anyone arrived. She liked to mix things up.

The light faded while we talked and watched the fireflies and the stars come out. I grilled tuna steaks and the vegetables that Leslie had sliced and painted with olive oil. While I watched the grill, one of my friends, a man named Bill Winter, stepped up close and said, quietly, "You doing okay?"

"Me? Yeah, sure. Why?"

"You've got a stare. Looks like your mind is a thousand miles from here."

Bill is one of those men women don't like. They find him insensitive, macho, and crude—all of it probably true. He was on his third marriage and going by the body language when you saw them together, it was no sure thing.

"Comes with being on the road too long, I suppose."

"Yeah," he said. "That'll do it." His tone said he knew it was a line but if I wanted to give it to him, fine with him.

"I have trouble sleeping when I've been traveling. My body got used to a West Coast schedule. You ever have that problem?"

He shook his head. "I solve that one with drugs. Like a lot of other things."

"Why didn't I think of that?"

"You home for a while?"

"Yes."

"Let's get together," he said. "Been too long."

Bill and I went out for a beer now and then and I enjoyed his company. He had a faintly belligerent, independent streak that I liked and even envied. He had a very low tolerance for bullshit and he liked a laugh and I imagined I'd be needing a little of his kind of companionship over the next few months.

"I'll call you."

"Good."

I arranged the food on the platters and tried to do it carefully and with some flair. Leslie is big on what she calls "presentation." I also tried to put on a pleasant, party face. If Bill Winter had picked up on my mood, there was no reason the others couldn't. The party had been Leslie's idea and she wanted it to be fun.

So I drank a few beers, listened to the music, and continued the conversation I'd been having with these same people for what seemed like years now, I guess because it was. Some nights the conversation veered off down self-indulgent, *Big Chill*, dead-end trails and I'd find myself wondering how I wound up in this life, with these people. The old suburban, middle-aged malaise.

Tonight, mercifully, the conversation stayed on track. It was mostly light, fairly humorous, and, for some reason, even a little erotic. Maybe it was just the warm, moist summer night with the fireflies and the stars. It felt like one of those times a million years ago, when you were young and a little music and a little wine gave any night a slightly carnal edge.

By the last hour of the party, there had been enough drinking that people were actually dancing on our little flagstone terrace. The music had drifted back to the time of the Stones and the Band, Otis Redding and Janis Joplin. I'd finally managed to push "it" almost entirely out of my mind and everything felt pretty much the way it had before I'd come home from that trip and Leslie had given me the news. Everything, that is, except an awareness I couldn't shake, a sense that there wouldn't be any more Saturday nights like this one for a long time. In fact, there might not be any Saturday nights like this one ever again.

But the party went on and I did my best to ignore that seed of gloom. That wasn't especially hard to do and by the time the last couple had left, it was fairly late. After one.

I expected the mood to collapse, but Leslie and I kept the music going while we did a superficial cleanup. Before we were done loading the dishwasher we were dancing and then unbuttoning each other's clothes and dropping them on the kitchen floor. Without turning out the lights or turning down the music, we made it to our room, where we lit some candles and turned down the covers and fell into bed. We were soon making love urgently and without restraint, the way we had when we were kids and couldn't get enough of each other and felt, in our blood, that we were indestructible.

5

We spent Sunday morning in bed, with coffee and the papers, the way we almost always did. After reading the papers, we usually made telephone calls to our parents and children.

I'd been brooding on this. Her mother and my father had died of cancer. When we called the survivors, there would be something familiar in the news. It would be a shock, but it wouldn't be something they could never have imagined.

"Andy knows," Leslie said.

I thought about that while I waited for the rest of it. Our daughter—her real name is Andrea but she lisped when she was little and we started calling her Andy to make it easier on her—is a remote, melancholy child who had trouble all through school with dyslexia. For that—or some other—reason, she has a dark streak that has always worried me. When she is cheerful, she is good company, and a couple of trips I have taken with her—just the two of us— remain some of my better memories. But when she is in one of her black spells it is hard to be around her. Not because she is unpleasant—she is more withdrawn than anything—but because it makes me feel helpless and inadequate.

"I went to Boston for tests," Leslie said. A partial explanation. Andy was going to art school in Boston.

"I wasn't going to tell her, Jack. More than anyone else, I wanted to spare her all the worry."

Leslie had the look. Her eyes had the hot sheen that was the first sign her temper was rising. The line of her jaw became very precise and severe.

"I mean, they told me it was only some tests. I thought they meant blood work and x-rays, the usual stuff, so I didn't ask anyone to drive down with me. I hadn't told anyone and I was thinking that maybe I wouldn't have to because it would never amount to anything. Just a scare. A cyst. No big deal.

"But they had to do something called a needle biopsy to find out if the lump was malignant or not. Nobody had bothered to warn me. They just gave me one of those hospital johnny gowns to put on and told me what a needle biopsy is and to get ready.

"And I just freaked. I couldn't do it by myself. I made them reschedule me for the afternoon and that got the nurses and the techs all frosted, but I just said, 'Too bad.' Then I got dressed and I went over to Andy's dorm. God, what a mess. I couldn't imagine living like that. Even at her age . . ."

She took a breath. Her eyes softened a little. Just the thought of her little girl could do that.

"Anyway, she was just getting back from one of her classes. And you know what she said when she saw me?"

I shook my head.

"She said, 'What's wrong, Mom?' "

Leslie's lower lip trembled a little. She cries easily and suddenly and I usually miss the point. But I understood this time. Andy had always been sensitive to the emotional storms and pain around her. She could always sense when Leslie and I were about to start quarreling, before either of us had even raised our voices. When she was very young, she would try to head off the storm. Later, she would just go up to her room and close the door.

"She *knew* I wasn't there just to go shopping and take her out for lunch," Leslie said. "And she was concerned, you know, about *me*. Worried about her mother. *Really* worried . . ."

Leslie stopped for a moment, shook her head, and used a knuckle to dab her eyes.

"Anyway, on the way over to her dorm, I'd been telling myself I'd fudge it with her. Tell her it wasn't anything really serious but I wanted her to be at the hospital just to keep me company. But when she said, 'What's wrong?' and I saw the expression on her face, I just told her the whole thing. Then I started crying, I mean bawling. I just completely lost it.

"She took me into her room and made me sit on the bed. She had to clear a spot first. Then she got me a glass of water and I drank it even though I can't imagine how long it had been since that glass was last washed. Finally I calmed down and washed my face and got myself gathered back up. Then we went to the hospital . . . together."

Leslie drank the last of her coffee. She usually lets it get cold, then makes a face when she realizes it, like it is a big surprise and this has never happened before.

"Want more?" I said.

"No. Thanks."

She put the cup down and folded the "Week in Review" section.

"Andy stayed with me the rest of the day. And I don't mean she sat out in the waiting room, either. She was right there with me. Holding my hand. The tech explained about the needle biopsy, how they put this needle over the lump and then drive it in with compressed air four or five times, so they can get some cells out of the lump and examine them to see if they're malignant. He said not to worry even though the sound of that air gun, firing that needle down into my flesh, might be 'a little startling.'

"'*A little startling.*' Are you kidding me? I knew that it would scare me right out of my skin. I mean, I can handle a little pain. But the idea of listening to that air gun go off just made me come unglued.

"I asked them if they had earplugs, but Andy said, 'No, wait a minute, I'll be right back.' And she got a little Discman with headphones and a selection of CDs out of her backpack. I picked Ray Charles and 'Hit the Road Jack.' Then

I put the headphones on and turned the volume up as loud as I could stand. Ray and the Raylettes did their thing and Andy held my hand while the tech fired that needle. I never felt or heard a thing."

She was smiling, a little ruefully, and her eyes were damp.

"She was great, Jack. My little girl. Holding her mom's hand while she got tested for cancer. She'll be there, at the hospital, on Monday. I told her not to come but you know she'll be there. You should take her to lunch while I'm in recovery."

We were on the road a little after five and my eyes felt grainy. I didn't really want the second cup of coffee that I had poured into my traveling mug, but I drank it anyway. We had the highway—an ancient two-lane—to ourselves.

"There won't be anything on the road from here to the interstate," Leslie said, "except milk trucks and single women who stayed out all night and are hurrying to get home before their kids wake up."

I drove and watched down the high beams for deer.

We had a CD player—a good one—in the car. But Leslie wanted to listen to the BBC news on NPR.

"I love the way they take it all so calmly," she said. "When Dan Rather is hyperventilating over some crisis in the Balkans, it's just another day at the office for the BBC. We could all use a little more of that."

So we listened to a rundown of all the world's troubles, delivered in a near monotone by some woman who sounded like she could not possibly have cared less how many Africans had massacred each other in the last twenty-four hours.

"Isn't she wonderful?" Leslie said.

But when the BBC broadcast was over, she switched channels so we could listen to "Imus," which was another of Leslie's favorite shows. She considered Rob Bartlett the funniest man in America.

"The BBC and Imus," I said. "That covers a lot of waterfront."

"What can I say? Consistency is not my strong suit."

And never has been, I thought. Right from the start, that was a big part of the hold she had on me. I'd been—no other word for it—*enchanted* by the contradictions.

When I asked her, once, about the contradictions, she said, "Oh, well, that's easy. I'm a Gemini and we see both sides of everything."

The startling part of that answer was that she knew or cared about astrology. Another contradiction, all by itself.

"You don't take that stuff seriously?" I'd said.

"Why not? If it was good enough for Yeats, then it is good enough for me."

For some reason, on the way to the hospital, on a morning in late August, I remembered that conversation. I didn't know anything about astrology then and I still don't. When I look up at the sky, it's to find the North Star or Orion or Antares at the heart of the Scorpion—all stuff learned in Boy Scouts, going for the astronomy merit badge.

But maybe I could still learn. Magic, voodoo, astrology . . . why not? Maybe it was a sign of something that Venus was loitering very low and very bright over the eastern horizon, just in front of us, as we dropped off the backside of the Green Mountains and down into the valley of the Connecticut River. The light from the planet had a soft golden quality and there was something almost soothing about it, like candlelight in an otherwise dark room. If I hadn't been driving, I could have stared at it until I fell into a sort of trance. The big, bright celestial objects can do that to you. Instead, I gave it an occasional quick glance and otherwise kept my eyes on the road. By the time we got to the interstate turnoff, the sun was over the horizon, and when I looked over my left shoulder for another glimpse of Venus, it was gone.

"I feel like there should be a sign over the door," Leslie said. We were in the basement garage of Beth Israel hospital, waiting for the elevator.

"Sign?"

"'Abandon Hope All Ye Who Enter Here.' Something like that."

It wasn't hope, actually, that I felt myself giving up. More like control. When you walk into a hospital—especially one that takes up a whole city block, like this one—it feels like your first day of school where the building is overwhelming and you don't know anyone or anything. The people in charge tell you what you need to know or do and you trust them because you don't have much choice.

I'd never been an overnight patient in a hospital. My experience of them came from watching my father die from a cancer that started in his large intestine and then spread everywhere, including, fatally, his pancreas. Then there had been some long, uncertain hours after Andy was born. But I had always been just a spectator.

We changed elevators in the main lobby. Leslie pushed the button for AMBULATORY SURGERY. Before the door closed, a young woman in scrubs pushed a man in a wheelchair into the elevator. I held the DOOR OPEN button and she said "Thank you" very briskly.

The man in the wheelchair had a clear plastic mask over his nose and mouth. A tube went from the mask to a steel cylinder that I assumed held oxygen. The skin on the man's hands was dry as dead leaves and his face was the color of wet putty. The woman studied the elevator panel, pushed the button for ONCOLOGY, then refocused her eyes on something out in front of her, probably beyond the elevator door and even the hospital.

I assumed the man had lung cancer, and I found myself wondering, automatically, how long he had. Then, how ugly the end would be.

When the elevator doors opened, the woman pushed him out. I held the DOOR OPEN button again and she said "Thank you" again.

I followed Leslie. She'd been here before and knew where she was going. We walked down a long corridor and into a waiting room where a couple dozen people were sitting silently and passively in chairs and sofas.

While Leslie went to the desk to check in, I looked around the room for a good place to sit and wait. That's what you did, mostly, at hospitals, I thought. You sat and waited. I'd learned to look for a place that was set off a little so you didn't have to share space with too many sick people.

I was in the middle of that thought when a voice came from over my shoulder.

"Hi, Dad."

It had been almost three months since I'd seen Andy and she had changed so much that it was impossible for me not to notice. She still had Leslie's wide eyes and fine bones, and the mouth that could change from a smile to a pout almost instantly. But there was something different. She had always looked younger than she was, but now she looked older. Almost as though she had skipped all her teenage years and gone straight to her twenties.

Even though she was barely nineteen, she looked like a mature woman with grown-up cares. But then, her mother had cancer.

"You look great, kid," I said, and gave her a hug. "Thanks for being here."

The hug she gave me was brief but affectionate. The one she gave her mother was long and almost fierce, as though they were hugging to give each other strength. When they finished, I could see that Leslie's eyes were wet.

We sat down around a little table to talk. The hugging was easier than talking.

"So," Andy said, "how was the drive?"

"Fine," I said. "We caught a little bit of rush hour at this end. But it was okay. How's school?"

"Fine," she said.

"Are you missing any classes to be here?"

"Just one," she said. "I cleared it with my professor."

"That's good."

"It's summer session," she said. "Everybody is pretty laid-back."

"Sure."

"How's Rufus?" she said. She'd bought a puppy with her baby-sitting money when she was twelve and she asked about the dog whenever we saw her or she called home.

"He's fine," I said.

It went on like this a few minutes longer, then Leslie called the meeting to order.

"The doctor should be here to talk to us any minute," she said.

Andy and I looked at her.

"If you've got any questions," she said, "this will be the time."

"What's his name?" I said.

"*Her* name," Leslie said, "is Sandra."

Somehow that came as a surprise, even though I knew it shouldn't have. I sometimes fall into the old grooves, though, and had imagined myself talking with the surgeon, man to man, while Leslie was still under the anesthesia. It would be straight talk. I'd ask unemotional questions and he'd answer me with the unvarnished truth. It wouldn't work that way, I thought, with a doctor named Sandra.

"Well," I said, "I can't call the doctor 'Sandra' or 'Sandy.' What's her last name?"

"Petofsky."

"Okay."

"I really like her. I feel . . . confident with her."

"Good. That's important."

"Don't you feel that way, Andy?"

"Yeah," Andy said. "I like her. She seems kind of young, though."

"That's *good*," Leslie said. "It means she doesn't think the old way."

"What way was that?" I said.

"That it's all about *cutting*," Leslie said, almost spitting the word. "Cut everything you can cut, because—because it's all nothing but excess flesh. Sandra isn't like that. She's going to cut some—she has to—but she's going to keep as much as she can."

"I see," I said.

Andy looked down at the floor. Her mouth, which always has a melancholy curl, looked even more sorrowful than usual.

"Here she is," Leslie said, and I stood up to meet the doctor.

She was young, like Andy said. She didn't look any older than thirty but she probably was. She was attractive, too, and your mind might even have settled on the word "pretty," except that she was dressed in surgical scrubs, wore no makeup, and had her long, brown hair tied tightly behind her neck. What she looked was efficient.

And she got right down to business.

"The purpose of the procedure we'll be doing today," she said, "is to remove a small tumor, about one and a half centimeters, from the outside upper quadrant of the right breast . . ."

It was the kind of language that normally puts me on the edge of sleep or sends my mind off a thousand miles somewhere. Today I hung on every word. The good news was that the operation (I couldn't think of it as a "procedure") was called a lumpectomy and that it was supposed to do just what it sounded like—cut the lump out of the breast, not the breast off the patient. That had been on my mind, or bubbling just under my consciousness, ever since Leslie had given me the news.

I was relieved without feeling especially good about that.

"In addition to the lump," the doctor went on, "we'll be removing several lymph nodes from the area. We're especially interested in the closest of these. We call it the sentinel node. I can tell a lot just by eyeballing the lymph nodes. But we won't know for sure until the lab tells us."

"Know what?" I said.

"If the cancer has spread."

"How long will that take?" I sounded like an irate customer, even to myself, and I could feel Leslie's impatience.

"About a week."

I nodded. For the next week, I thought, time would hang heavy around our house.

The doctor talked about the "margins" around the incision and the extent of the cut and the unlikelihood, in her opinion, that plastic surgery would be necessary.

More good news, I thought, "good" being a relative thing.

We all nodded and Dr. Petofsky stood up. This session was over. But I had one question and she listened to it impassively.

"What's next?" I said. "After the operation."

"You'll be discussing that," she said, "with the team. After we've gotten the results of the biopsy and the incision has healed. Two, maybe three weeks. Right now we need to get your wife down to nuclear medicine for mapping. You'll have a little while after that's done and before anesthesia if you want to visit again."

"Thank you, Doctor," I said.

The doctor nodded and smiled, just a little, then reached out for Leslie and gave her a hug.

"Don't worry," she said, "everything is going to be fine. I'm very good."

Just then I believed her. For no reason, I suppose, except that I wanted to.

* * *

When the doctor was gone, I said to Leslie, "How did that sound to you?"

She shrugged and said, "Fine. I'd heard it all before."

"You knew about sentinel nodes?"

She smiled. "Are you kidding? That's Breast Cancer One-Oh-One. Freshman survey stuff. I've been cramming for the last three weeks, Jack. I'm up to postgrad level."

"And the doctor . . ."

"What about her?"

"You're all right with her?"

She smiled again and made a *What the hell* gesture with her hand, one I'd seen a million times.

"Trust her with my life," she said, almost gaily. "And a good thing, too."

We took an elevator to the basement and walked to nuclear medicine, where they were ready for Leslie. She signed the paperwork and went behind a large, ominous metal door with a technician, who said it would take an hour or so. When the door closed, Andy and I left, looking for a place to have coffee.

There was a Starbucks on the ground floor of the hospital, right next to the elevator bank, but Andy was boycotting them for some reason. I didn't mind, since I wanted to get outside and breathe some air. Even city air.

We found a place called New World Coffee, where she ordered a tall, skim, decaf latte. It was the sort of thing comics make jokes about—city girls and their coffee. Andy knew the boy at the register, and they did "How's it going" and "Pretty good" and "See you later." She didn't introduce me. I paid for her coffee and my medium black and an oatmeal muffin.

We sat at a table by the window.

I broke the muffin in half and offered her some. She shook her head. I sipped the coffee, which was scalding.

"I'm sorry I wasn't here when this all started," I said.

She shook her head, to say *Don't worry about it.*

"But it sounds like you handled things without me. I really appreciate it. You can't imagine what it meant to your mother."

She shrugged. "No big thing."

"No," I said. "It was important. Very important."

Maybe even vital, I thought. Who knew how much the right gesture lifted the cancer patient's spirits and how much that might count for in the fight? A single kind act could make the difference. But I didn't say that to Andy.

"I just wanted her to feel better," she said. "It wasn't that big of a deal."

Sometime in the last few years, she had found a way to sell herself short, no matter what the situation, and one of her teachers had told Leslie that Andy had "self-esteem issues." I'd hoped that it was just some temporary, adolescent phase; a lack of self-confidence combined with a fondness for self-pity. "Dad," Andy said, raising her eyes from the table to look into mine, "I feel so helpless."

"Me, too," I said.

"I mean . . ." she looked away and bit down on her lower lip. It was something she'd done since she was a baby whenever she felt like things were getting away from her.

"It's okay," I said. I reached across the table and took her hand. It felt larger than I remembered but still small.

"I'm so scared."

"Sure. You'd have to be."

"What if she's dying?"

"We *will not* think that way," I said, sounding like I had when she was ten years old and I could make a point with my tone of voice. "The doctor didn't seem to think that way. And we'll be more positive than the doctors, just to keep *them* pumped."

"Do you trust her? The doctor, I mean?"

A single tear had gathered at the corner of her eye. I expected her to brush it away, like a bug, but she ignored it. Or maybe she wasn't even aware of it. So I reached across the table with a paper napkin and blotted it.

"Trust the doctor?" I said. My notions of trust were so different from hers. I trusted self-interest and incentives.

"Yeah," I said to Andy, "I trust Dr. Petofsky."

"I do, too," Andy said.

"Good."

"I just wish there was something I could do."

"You're doing it, Andy," I said. "And you're doing a great job."

"I guess."

"Trust me."

She nodded and it occurred to me that, when you got down to it, she didn't have any reason to. Parents will lie to you about so many things but especially the big things. You didn't make the team or get invited to the prom or accepted to the college that you had applied to for early admission and your parents had known, or suspected, all along that it would turn out that way but they hadn't told you. They had, in fact, encouraged you to believe that things would go the way you wanted—had lied to you, in short, about something important. Done it out of good motives, perhaps. But they had still done it.

So, would your father tell you that everything was going to be all right when your mother had cancer, even if he knew things might not turn out all right, might go entirely the other way?

Sure he would. Bet your ass.

I wasn't sure, just then, that it was even possible to level with her, but I decided to try.

"Listen, kid. Neither of us knows. Even the doctor may not know. We're all flying partially blind. So we do what we can, you understand, to keep up hope and to make it as easy as we can for your mom. You did a great thing for her with that needle test. It was a gift. The best gift you could give her under the circumstances. You're going to have to let it go with that. Okay?"

"I guess."

I blotted another tear from her eye and we got up to leave. She hadn't finished her coffee. Nothing unusual there, I thought. She'd never once cleaned her plate that I could remember.

But why, I wondered, order the large?

8

Andy and I saw Leslie briefly before she went off through a set of doors to be anesthetized. She wasn't wearing jewelry or makeup but she had good color and she smiled. I asked her how it had gone downstairs.

"Fine," she said in a tone that suggested it couldn't have gone otherwise. "They pumped me full of radioactive stuff that would collect in the sentinel node and show up on their screens. All very high-tech."

"Painful?"

She shrugged. "A little. And it gave me a blue boob. Looks like some drunk tried to give me a tattoo."

We talked a little more and then it was time.

"Why don't you two get out of here and go see a movie or something?" she said. "Waiting around a hospital is such a downer."

"Come on, Mom," Andy said. "What kind of drugs did they give you?"

"Maybe we'll take a walk," I said. There was no chance we'd leave the hospital before we could leave with her. I only said it so she would drop the subject. One of those married-man evasions.

The waiting room, like everything else at this hospital, was clean and bright. They made an effort and you could see it and feel it. All the doctors and nurses and orderlies carried pagers so you didn't hear that constant blaring over speakers, urging Dr. So and So to report to somewhere or other. The place felt calm, if not serene. And even though the furniture in the waiting room was plastic, it was new and the upholstery wasn't cracked or sticky where someone had spilled a soft drink on it. But it was still a waiting room, and like all waiting rooms, while you were there, the time seemed to hang over you like thick, greasy smoke.

I flipped through several magazines, made a couple of calls to the office on the pay phones, and talked aimlessly to Andy. During one of our long silences, I imagined the crew of one of those old square-rigged sailing ships, becalmed at sea, waiting for wind. Then I wished for a pool table, the clean click of the balls and the soothing way they traveled down the green felt.

We took turns going downstairs for something to eat, and eventually I went to sleep. Andy had to shake me awake.

"Dad, the doctor is here."

"Oh. Sorry."

Dr. Petofsky was wearing clean scrubs and carrying a clipboard. She looked calm. Nothing in her face set off any alarms. She could have been a pollster, taking a survey. How did I feel about global warming? The hole in the ozone? Drilling for oil in Alaska?

"Everything went the way I expected," she said, before I had a chance to ask, "and she is doing fine."

Andy, standing next to me, let out a sigh.

"The tumor was the size I expected, and just where the pictures showed it. But I did have to cut it into two pieces. I did that so I wouldn't have to damage any more healthy tissue than absolutely necessary. We'll put the tumor back together in the lab and compare it to the pictures to make sure that we got absolutely everything. I'm certain we did, but that's a necessary precaution."

The old cutters wouldn't have bothered with this kind of refinement, I thought with a gratitude I didn't try to express. I merely nodded. There was more to come.

"In addition to the sentinel node, I took out three lymph nodes that were clustered below it," the doctor continued, "and examined each one visually."

Here it came . . .

"We can't be sure, as I said, until we get the biopsy back from the lab, but the nodes all looked clear to me."

"Yesssssss," Andy said.

The doctor smiled at this.

"She's still out and she will be for another hour. Someone will come for you when she wakes up. We'll need to keep her for another two or three hours after that. She's going to be sore and she'll probably feel pretty low from the anesthesia. If I were king, I'd keep her overnight. But these days people who work for insurance companies make those decisions.

"I'd say bed rest and lots of liquids for a day or two. We'll call you with the lab results in a week. Give it another week after that and then schedule a meeting with the team to discuss where we go from here. She's got—you've all got—some decisions to make on the next phase of her treatment. For now, though, you can relax."

"Thank you, Doctor," I said, hoping that my voice conveyed at least some of my gratitude.

Andy, who was weeping, gave the doctor a hug. The doctor handed me her clipboard so she could return the hug with both arms.

When they broke the clinch, the doctor held her hand out to Andy for a high five. Andy slapped Dr. Petofsky's hand and smiled.

The doctor looked at me and said, "It isn't over. Not by a long way. But what I prescribe is this: Try not to talk about it until we get the lab results back. Pamper her a little. If the results are good, then try to take her someplace and pamper her some more before you have your meeting with the team. Hard as it might be to believe, this is the easy part."

I nodded and said, a little eagerly, "Right. I'll do what you say."

Then Dr. Petofsky looked at Andy and said, "You go back to school. Don't cut any classes for anything. You might need to cut a lot of them later on."

Andy nodded gravely.

"Go out with some friends tonight. Drink some beer, even if it is illegal."

Andy nodded again.

"And both of you get some sleep."

She smiled, said she had another procedure, and left us standing there, relieved and mute.

It was late afternoon and most of the people in the waiting room had gone home. Andy and I were still there, trying to make conversation, when a nurse came through the double doors and asked for me.

"She's awake now," the nurse said. "You can go on back."

Leslie was lying in one of those hospital beds that looks more like construction scaffolding than something you would want to sleep on. She looked a little dazed, like somebody who had been in an accident and was trying to figure out, first, what had happened, and then, if she was hurt. She reached out for Andy, who leaned over the bed and gave her a hug. It was Andy's day for hugs.

"How do you feel?" Andy said.

"Great," Leslie said. "Ready to rock 'n' roll."

"Yeah, right," Andy said.

"No, really. I don't feel any pain at all. Not even like the dentist. But I'll tell you what I do feel." She was looking at me.

"What's that?"

"Thirsty. Like I've been crawling across the desert. Would you get me a Coke? With ice?"

"Sure."

"I'll do it," Andy said.

"No. Stay here with your mother. I'll get it."

I left them there, holding hands, and took the elevator down to the lobby, where I bought a sixteen-ounce bottle of soda and a large cup full of crushed ice. I was glad for the chance to get away from the recovery room, the waiting room, and, I had to admit, from Leslie. I couldn't explain it. Not to myself, anyway. I'd been waiting there for three hours to see her and when I finally got the chance, I took the first opportunity to rabbit.

It was the natural thing, I told myself. Good for Andy and Leslie to have a few minutes alone. But I didn't believe it and I went back upstairs wondering if this was just the first time I would bug out.

Andy and I stayed with Leslie for an hour. We talked, but the conversation was labored and forced and broken up by long, awkward silences. Andy held Leslie's hand and I fed her crushed ice with a spoon. She said it cooled her mouth.

Leslie finally ran us out so she could sleep an hour and then get dressed to go home. I asked her if she wanted me to get us a room somewhere in town for the night.

"It's a long trip," I said.

"No," she said. "I want to sleep in my own bed." She was emphatic, so I didn't argue. An hour later Andy and I followed the orderly who pushed Leslie, sitting in a wheelchair under protest, onto the elevator.

"I'm not crippled, for Christ's sake," she said. "I was in a lot worse shape after I had my wisdom teeth taken out. The Hollywood babes with implants get carved up worse than this."

"Hospital policy, ma'am," the orderly said.

Andy gave her a final hug and kissed her good-bye when we got to the car. They were both wet-eyed. I gave Andy a hundred-dollar bill and told her to take care of herself.

When we were out of town and on the highway headed home, Leslie put her head back and went to sleep. I drove north and west, with the sun going down behind the ridgolines of the Berkshires and then the Green Mountains. It was a restful drive, and for the first time in days, I didn't think about cancer.

9

When we got home, Leslie went straight to bed. I asked if I could fix her something to eat and she said, "Not unless you're interested in cleaning up my vomit."

I went into the study to check the phone messages and e-mail but there was nothing important. So I called Leslie's father, a tough but courtly old country lawyer from North Carolina. He wept when I told him.

"The outlook is actually pretty good, Dan," I said. "The surgeon said the lymph nodes looked clear and that means it hasn't spread. It has to be confirmed by the lab . . . "

"Poor Leslie," he said, as if he hadn't heard me. "My poor little girl."

"I don't want to minimize it, Dan," I said. "But the doctor is optimistic and so is Leslie."

"Listen, Jack," he said, and his tone changed to the one he no doubt used when he had a client who was in real trouble and needed to face facts, "I know it is important for you to be hopeful. We all have to be hopeful. Leslie most of all. But I went through this with Leslie's mother. The doctors know some things. But there are a lot more things they don't know. Make them tell you what they *don't* know."

I wasn't sure I understood. But I said I would do it.

"What can I do to help you out? Do you need some money?"

"No, Dan. But thanks. We're fine."

"You want me to come up and help out?"

God spare me that, I thought.

"No," I said. "Kind of you to offer. And I'll take you up on it if it comes to that. But we're fine now."

"She should be in a hospital," he said. "They send people home these days before they're even out from under the ether. It's outrageous. They just do it to save money."

"She's fine. I think she'd rather be in her own bed."

"Well, you make sure she stays there. You know how she is. She'll be up tomorrow and going to the gym if you let her."

"I know," I said. "Believe me."

"Don't let her."

"I'll do my best," I said. "But you know how she is. Better than anyone, I imagine."

"Yes," he said, his voice going tender. "Yes, I do. I know how she is. You tell her I said to rest and take care of herself."

"I will."

"If you want to hire a nurse," he said, "I'll pay for it."

"We're fine, Dan."

"Tell her to take care of herself, please, and call me when she feels up to it," he said. "Poor little girl."

I said good-bye and hung up. I sat in the chair for a while, looking at the phone and imagining him doing the same and thinking, *First my wife and now my daughter.* I wondered if he had anyone he could call and ask over, to drink some coffee or maybe some whiskey and get what comfort he could from a little companionship. We all live too far away from each other, I thought, and too many of us live alone.

My mother would be home, also alone. It seemed unfair, almost, to unload this on her. She didn't need it and there wasn't anything she could do about it.

But if I didn't call now, then later on she would be hurt that we hadn't told her earlier.

She answered on the third or fourth ring, and from the sound of her voice, she had gone to sleep in front of the television.

She was still sharp, though, and she knew I almost always called on the weekends, usually on Sunday morning. Hardly ever during the week, like this, and never late at night.

"What is it?" she said. "Tell me what's wrong."

I started with the surgery. Which had gone perfectly, I said. I was trying to pacify her, I suppose. Spare her the prelude and all the messy details and just give her the happy-talk stuff at the end.

But she wasn't having any.

"How many lymph nodes did they take out?" she said. "And were they clear?"

She'd always liked medical conversations, and, of course, she'd been through this with friends and the daughters of friends. She had talked with them over the phone and over coffee and at the pool. She had held their hands and comforted them when they cried. She had read the magazine articles and watched the discussions on television. I wasn't getting away with the brush-off. She pinned me down with specific questions and followed up on my answers. It was as if I were a kid all over again, unable to get away with the standard evasions, when saying I'd been "out" only prompted the inevitable, "Out *where?*" Your mother, God knows, is always your mother.

"Do you think Leslie would mind if I called her tomorrow?"

They got along. Which was fine by me.

"She'd love it."

"I'll wait until after lunch. She needs to rest."

"All right."

"You take care of yourself," she said. "I know it's hard on you, too."

"I'm fine," I said.

"Just take care of yourself."

"All right," I said.

Then we said our good-byes and hung up.

There was one more call I needed to make, I thought . . . or maybe not.

Our son Brad was at Quantico, training to be an officer in the marines. I knew him well enough—even though he felt like a stranger at times—to know that this was not something he was doing on impulse or because he was suggestible. It was serious with him as it would be with most anyone. But there was an extra measure of determination with Brad. He treated the service like something he had been called to.

But I knew that if I told him about his mother, he would likely request some kind of compassionate leave. He would feel it was his duty to be here, with us, even though there wasn't a thing he could do to help. And if he left Quantico now, he would have to repeat the training next summer. It would cost him a lot of time. And if he didn't take a leave and knew about his mom, then he would just worry. And he probably did not need to be distracted on the grenade range.

I decided to put off calling him.

I looked in on Leslie. She was sleeping and didn't crack an eye when I opened the door. I hoped she would stay that way through the night. No dreams and no pain.

I went back to the study, but the room felt small and hot, like some kind of cell, so I went outside.

It was one of those nights. The sky was utterly clear and the air was clean. You couldn't help but look up at the stars. Hundreds of them. I found the Dipper and Polaris automatically—I was back to working for merit badges— then moved on to the other big boys I knew. Vega. Arcturus. Altair. I managed to put together enough of Sagittarius, even though I'd never been able to understand how the ancients could make an archer out of those stars. I got the Swan and the Scorpion. But most of the others seemed like a reach.

Inch by Inch

I recalled something while I was looking up at the stars, one of those memories that comes on you spontaneously and with a kind of severe lucidity. I saw myself, at twelve, standing on a sand dune at midnight, looking at the heavens through a cheap pair of 8X40 binoculars that I had bought at a pawnshop with money I saved from a weekend job. I'd been so serious and what they would call today "directed." I'd worked like a beaver for that merit badge and it had seemed vitally important. I found myself wishing I could be that boy again.

But I wasn't going to get anywhere traveling that road. So I went back inside to look for something useful to do.

Back inside, I tried to think of what I should do next. Being alone with nobody to talk to seemed way too hard. I had friends, but none I wanted to call late at night and start the conversation by explaining that my wife had cancer and I was feeling afraid and lonely.

Then I thought of Monk.

Mike Martindale—aka "Monk" for his tight, compact face—was a friend from when we were kids. We'd stayed friends while he went through medical school, a marriage and divorce, and a bitterness so complete that he'd left his practice and his old friends and moved to Alaska. I still talked to him a couple of times a year, and each time he said he had never been happier.

And I believed him.

Six hours earlier where he was, I thought, barely late afternoon.

He answered his own phone.

"Dr. Martindale's office," he said. "Sorry, but we're closed. If it isn't an emergency, call back tomorrow."

"Hello, Monk," I said.

"Well, sonofabitch," he said. "Jack Rockwell. Long time, old man."

We said the things you ordinarily say. But when he asked how the family was, I couldn't just say, "Fine. Everybody is fine."

What I said, instead, was "Actually, Monk, that's why I'm calling."

I could almost hear his mood change. Monk always had an ability to switch, in a heartbeat, from grab-ass to cold serious. I could imagine him going into surgery, laughing at some stupid top-ten list, then changing, as soon as he saw the patient, into the sober professional.

"So tell me," he said. All business.

I told him.

"Ah, *man*," he said. "Goddamnit. I feel like I could puke."

"Well . . . it may not be that bad."

"It's cancer, hoss," he said. "I haven't seen a good one of those yet."

Monk recovered enough to give me a little pep talk about how much "they" had learned about cancer in the last few years and all the wonderful success stories you heard.

"Now tell me about Leslie," he said, and something tender came into his voice. He'd told me, one night after some drinks, that if he'd just married someone like her, there wouldn't have been "any Goddamned divorce."

"She's strong," I said.

"Good," he said. "That's good. But listen to what I'm going to tell you now, because this is one time when I actually know what I'm talking about."

"I'm listening."

"It's cancer, Jack. It's not pneumonia or a heart attack."

"I understand."

"Well," he said, impatiently, "I want to make sure you do. And I especially want to make sure that Leslie does."

"Okay."

"You remember that stiff we found, floating up against the needleweed, a million years ago."

"Sure," I said. Monk and I had been ten or twelve, big boys but still just boys, and we were wading along in some shallow water up against a little island when we saw a shape floating on the tide. We didn't know enough yet to pass some things by, so we walked over to check it out. The shape was a body.

Turned out it was a fisherman who had been working a gill net a couple of nights earlier and fallen out of his boat. He'd pulled the tiller of his outboard all the way over and the boat came around in a circle and ran over him. The prop opened up his head.

Nobody missed him—he had a history of benders—and his boat ran up into the weeds where you couldn't see it until you were right up on it. The body had been in the water for a couple of days.

"Remember how the crabs were eating on that old boy?" Monk said. "How they'd taken enough meat away that you could see some ribs?"

"Not the kind of thing you'd forget, Monk."

"And you know the old thing about cancer and the crab?" he went on. "Allegory or metaphor or one of those damned things."

"Yep."

"Well, let me tell you the part of the metaphor I want you and Leslie to keep in mind. One crab lays about a million eggs and out of all of those eggs, the world gets maybe three full-grown, adult crabs. Each egg is so small you need a microscope to see it."

"All right."

"Now the surgeon got the tumor and told you that the lymph nodes looked clear. That's all good news. But you don't want to start hiring bands and scheduling parades, Jack, because all it takes is for one Goddamned cell to migrate somewhere in her body and find a home, usually in the bones or the liver or the lungs. One little pissant cell.

"She's going to have to make a decision soon. Maybe it's a decision for both of you; I don't know how you two work those things out but you must have figured a way because you're still together.

"Anyway, what you have to decide is what to do next. She could stop right now, especially if the lab doesn't find anything in those lymph nodes, and her odds would be pretty good. Better than eight-to-one, I'd guess."

Those sounded like decent numbers at the track. But not wonderful under these circumstances. I was looking for fifty-to-one. Or better.

"She can get longer odds," Monk said, "by doing two things."

"What are they?" I said, wondering if he was going to give me some kind of testimonial about nutrition. Or prayer.

"Chemo," he said, emphatically, "and radiation."

"Both?"

"Bet your ass."

"Why both?"

"Because it is cancer and you don't want to show it any mercy. It's for damn sure it won't show you any."

We talked some more but Monk wouldn't let up on the business of doing both chemo and radiation.

"She's going to hear from people who'll tell her that she doesn't have to do it, Jack. Especially if the surgery was successful and the lymph nodes were clear."

"Why *wouldn't* you do it?" I said. "If it gives you an edge."

"Because it is a miserable ordeal. You feel sick all the time. You can't eat and you can't sleep. Everything tastes like cold lead and smells like wet paint. And for women, worst of all, it makes your hair fall out. That's hard for any woman. Used to be I didn't understand that. Now I do.

"Leslie is tough. But she's going to be like a teenaged prom queen about losing her hair, I can promise you. And she's right to feel that way. It's *good* that she feels that way. She needs to care about things like that. At some point vanity becomes another life force, if that makes any sense."

"Sure," I said.

"She doesn't want to see herself as this middle-aged woman, all pale and shriveled up and bald, spending the day in bed or puking into the toilet. If she sees herself that way and thinks that nobody could love her or care about her, she'll think that it just isn't worth it, even if it does give her another ten percent chance of staying alive."

"Yeah," I said. "I see."

"You've got some influence with her, Jack. Use it. Tell her you'll love her rich or poor, drunk or sober, with hair or bald as a marble."

There was more he had to tell me, Monk said, but it could wait for another conversation.

"Right now, the important thing is to make sure that she does the whole program. And Jack?"

"Yes."

"Right now is actually a *good* time. The proverbial lull before the storm."

"Oh?"

"If you can possibly do it, take her away somewhere and have some fun."

"All right," I said. I'd heard the same thing from the surgeon. But I'd just come back from that long trip. I had work to do at the office. Also, there were the usual corporate politics and I needed to look after my bureaucratic flanks.

Monk caught my tone.

"I'm serious," he said. "This is the last chance you'll have for a while."

He did not say, "maybe ever." But he didn't have to.

"You're going to need to bank a little sunshine, Jack, to get you through some dark times."

"Okay, Monk, thanks for the advice," I said.

"Call me, will you? Keep me in the loop."

"Sure."

"I'll be your support group. You may not think so now, but you'll be needing one."

"Good-night, Monk."

"Hang in there, Jack. And love to Leslie."

"Right."

* * *

I went to the bedroom to look in on Leslie. Andy's Lab, Rufus, and my short-hair, Silas, followed me into the room, and the clicking of their toenails on the bare wood floor sounded like they were crunching lightbulbs when they walked. I turned on the dogs and said "*Quiet*." They looked down at the floor, guiltily, then seemed to tiptoe to their beanbag beds, keeping their eyes on me to gauge just how much trouble they were in. Through all this, Leslie never opened her eyes. Never even moved.

They had given her something—Tylenol with Codeine, probably—and told her to take it "if she felt any discomfort." Which meant, if she hurt. And not "if," really, but "when." They seemed to have a hard time, around hospitals, I thought, facing up to pain, or even calling it by its right name.

For some reason, that infuriated me, and I felt myself climbing up on the high horse of righteousness that I always seem to ride when I'm dealing with doctors and hospitals and illness.

Damn doctors, anyway. Damn hospitals. Damn insurance companies. Damn them all.

I took a few deep breaths, closed my eyes, and tried to find some sense of calm. To get over the feeling of helpless awe and rage that had been there since I got off the plane and got the news.

What you should be feeling, I told myself, looking down at Leslie, more soundly asleep than I could ever remember seeing her, is . . . gratitude.

I stood there in the bedroom for a little longer, feeling myself growing calmer until I stopped shaking. Then I felt weak and ashamed, the way you do after you have lost control and yelled unfairly at one of your children. I slipped out of the bedroom and closed the door behind me.

In the morning, I made tea and took it into the bedroom. Leslie was awake but still in bed. She looked groggy.

"How do you feel?"

"Like some motorcycle guy with a beard gnawed on my chest all night."

I made a face.

"Sorry," she said and smiled without conviction. "Actually, I feel fine. I think I'm hungover from the anesthesia and the drugs. But I've been hungover before. It isn't terminal."

I didn't like that word but managed not to show it.

"Well, drink this. And I'll fix you something to eat."

"No. You get dressed and go to work. I'll be fine. But thank you for the tea."

"You're sure?"

"Yes. Absolutely. I told you I don't want to be babied. I'll tell you if I need something. I promise."

"All right," I said. "You know the number."

"Yes," she said. "I believe I do."

So I went to the office, where I dealt with the usual accumulation of paper and the calls that I hadn't made from the road. I wrote a couple of memos that summed up what I had learned and accomplished on my trip, and I spent fifteen minutes with my boss. She seemed glad to see me and complimented me on the memos about my trip, which she'd read immediately, and about my work in general. That was her style and it paid off.

When we'd finished with that, she moved on to the bad news and told me what I already knew—what everyone in the company and the whole industry knew—that things were getting very tight out there. It was up to me, and all the other department heads, she said, to hold down costs.

I said I was doing my best and went back to work.

That afternoon I stopped by personnel to check on the health insurance coverage. I was friendly with the head of the department, a middle-aged woman who had been working since her husband, a dentist, took off with his receptionist. She made a point of cheerfulness; a way, I suppose, of refusing to let the rat bastard get to her.

She answered my questions about co-payments and coverage limits and prescription drugs and the rest, which I tried to keep vague. But she couldn't help herself and finally said, "Is something wrong?"

"No," I said. "Not yet. But I've got this knee that is just about worn out. I may have to get it replaced and I wanted to see if that's covered."

"Oh, absolutely," she said. She was proud of the company's insurance; it was her domain.

"Well, I'm glad to know that."

"Amazing the things they can do these days," she said. "To think they can replace actual parts of you that way. Like you were a car or something."

"Pretty amazing."

"You should do the operation soon," she said. "That way you can still go skiing when the snow flies. Call it physical therapy."

"Not a bad idea," I said.

It went like that for the rest of the week. After I'd brought Leslie some tea in the morning, I would leave for work. She had a graphics design and custom publishing business with an office at home. Normally she spent about half her time out on calls, but she stayed at her desk this week, locked up with Quark. I would go straight home from work and find her still there. When I asked how she felt, she would say, "Fine. Honestly, Jack, I'll tell you at the first sign of *any-thing*. Promise."

And when I looked a little stung by that answer, or one like it, she would say, "Really, baby. You don't *feel* anything at this stage of things. The problems are mental . . . and emotional."

"And?"

"I'm doing all right."

"Just 'all right'?"

"That's better than most."

At the hospital, they'd said it would be a week before the lab results came back, and the time seemed to crawl. Leslie and I were young enough to be part of that generation that wants everything right now. Even a biopsy. Or, maybe, especially a biopsy.

When it came, the news would come by telephone. How else? E-mail, maybe? I wondered, pointlessly, if that would be any better.

But it would be a phone call. I carried an image of Leslie sitting at her desk and taking the call, all alone, and sitting very still while one of the doctors delivered what I could not help thinking of as "the verdict."

It seemed pretty cold and I tried to think of a way to get around it. I considered calling the doctor and asking for a heads-up, especially if the news was bad. Asking her for just enough time to get home ahead of the call so I could be there with Leslie and provide whatever comfort I could.

But I didn't have that kind of standing with the doctors. Leslie was the patient and she made the decisions. No chance she would buy into that scheme.

So I was at work when the call finally came, exactly a week after the surgery. When Leslie reached me at work, she said one word.

"Clean."

Odd, how you think of cancer as something almost transcendently dirty. When you are cancer free, then you are clean. It's like the way the people in the Bible talked about leprosy.

"Thank God," I said, and my voice got shaky. I was standing when I took the call and I had to sit down.

"I called you just as soon as I finished crying," she said. "Now go back to work and bring home something interesting for dinner."

I picked up some steaks and a wine that cost about five times what I was used to spending. Then I drove to a grove of tall, mature hemlocks next to a stream and picked some chanterelles. We'd had some rain and there were little bright orange mushrooms sticking up through the duff everywhere I looked. I cut a couple dozen off at the ground with my pocketknife, dusted them lightly with the tail of my shirt, and put them in a baseball cap, which was all I had.

Leslie sautéed the chanterelles in butter and garlic while I cooked the meat over the grill. We ate it very rare, cool in the center, with the wild mushrooms on the side and the thick red wine to drink, and we called it a fine evening. A celebration. We ate by candlelight. While we were finishing the wine, I told her about the plan I'd been working on down at the office.

"And you already got the tickets?"

"Yes."

"First class?"

"I used my frequent-flier points."

"It must have wiped out your account."

"Just about."

"It's very sweet, Jack, but . . ."

"Nope," I said. "I'm not hearing it. I know you have to work. So do I. So do we all. But it's only a week. Seems like you owe it to yourself."

I was thinking—and I almost said—that she might be looking at a long, dismal stretch in medical purgatory and that she deserved a little time and a little fun. But I didn't want to say the words *chemo* and *radiation*. It would spoil the mood and maybe the whole night.

Anyway, she knew.

"What about your office? You've just come back from a long trip."

"I'm okay. And things won't fall apart just because I'm not around."

We went back and forth a little longer, but I think she knew I was right. She had been reading the books about how to get through your cancer and I'd looked at the page where she had left one of them open. It said something about how you had to be sure to be good to yourself.

"When do we leave?" she said, finally.

"Friday," I said.

"Three days," she said. "And you already have the tickets. What if the call from the lab hadn't been good news?"

"I don't know. That might have made this trip an even better idea."

"But what if I hadn't thought so?"

"Then we wouldn't have gone."

"And you'd have lost all your frequent-flier points."

"Easy come . . ."

"No. I'd say you worked hard for those miles. Think of all those triple-six and Super 8 motels."

"I've upgraded," I said. "I do Hampton Inns now. And Doubletree. You get a free continental breakfast and a copy of *USA Today*."

"Listen, baby," she said, looking at me over the rim of her half-full wineglass, "I hate to be the one to tell you this. But in this world, there is no free lunch. No free continental breakfast either."

"What about the *USA Today*?"

"Sorry," she said, "But you pay for that, too."

"Damn. And all this time I thought I was getting over."

She smiled. Drank a little wine. Then said, "Friday?"

"Right," I said. "Not tomorrow. That's Wednesday. And not the day after tomorrow. That's Thursday. But the day after that. Friday."

She nodded. As though, somehow, that made a vast difference. Then she said, "Well, anyway, that gives me time to shop."

We both smiled. It was an old, old joke between us. The kind of joke that I suspect most people who have been married a while have in the inventory somewhere. But even though it was old, and a little silly, it never failed.

By Friday morning, I had taken care of things at the office and Leslie had, in fact, done a little shopping. She likes to have something new to wear when she finds herself in someplace new. That's the joke. I had changed the messages on all the answering machines, boarded the dogs, and called Andy.

We sat in our first-class seats, and when the flight attendant offered us something to drink, we each asked for a Bloody Mary.

"God," Leslie said, "I can't remember the last time I had one of these. It reminds me of New York and Melon's."

Melon's was where we would go for brunch, usually on Saturday morning, when we lived in New York.

"Seems like a long time ago, doesn't it?"

"Another lifetime," she said. "But I don't miss it. I'd rather be drinking my Bloody Mary right here, getting ready to make this trip."

She'd never been much for regrets. She could hate the present but it never seemed to make her long for the past.

We finished our drinks a little after takeoff, and when the plane leveled out we went to sleep and didn't wake up until just before the pilot throttled back for the landing in Salt Lake City.

12

We stopped at a shopping center outside of a town near the Wyoming line. I wanted to pick up a few things at the WalMart. Tent stakes. Stove fuel. Flashlight batteries. I also bought a couple of CDs to listen to on the rest of the drive. There was a grocery store in the shopping center and we bought breakfast stuff and a few basics there.

"How much further?" Leslie said when we were back on the road.

"That's what the kids used to say."

"I know. And I can finally appreciate the way they felt. Why did they put Wyoming all the way out here, anyway?"

"Whose line was that?"

"McGuane's. From *Missouri Breaks.*"

"That's right."

"You still haven't answered my question. How much further?"

"Two hours," I said. "Maybe two and a half. We'll get there before sunset."

"Well, that's something, anyway."

"Here," I said and handed her one of the CDs. "A little music to make the time pass easier."

"Tammy Wynette and George Jones? How droll of you."

The drinking songs, breaking-up songs, and cheating songs carried us to the Salt River valley, south of Jackson, where we were staying in a house that belonged to a friend who had started out as a business acquaintance. He hadn't been sure what an "Internet portal" was when he went with the little start-up that hired him. Now the Wyoming house was one of four places he owned, and at the moment, he wasn't in any of them. He was in a castle in Scotland—for the golf and the salmon fishing.

"If you can't be rich yourself," Leslie said as I opened the door and showed her into the house, "then it certainly is nice to have rich friends."

The house was constructed to look like a log cabin, but it was anything but primitive inside. The downstairs consisted of a kitchen that was all stainless steel and polished glass and bright white tile and a living room furnished with over-stuffed couches and chairs and rough wood tables and bookshelves. The floors were wide, bare boards. There was a big picture window with a view of the valley and then a long, low mountain ridge to the west, in Idaho. The sun was just settling beyond that ridge.

"It's lovely," Leslie said. "I never should have doubted you, Jack. It was a great idea to come here."

"I think we'll have fun," I said.

"I already am. And I am not thinking about cancer. I left all that stuff back east."

"So what are you thinking about?"

"An omelet and a glass of wine. Then bed. Let's get up early in the morning. I don't want to miss any of this."

We took a walk just after dawn. It was cold and there was a heavy coating of dew on the alfalfa in the fields and we got our boots and the bottoms of our pant legs wet. There were sandhill cranes in one of the fields and some ducks that we startled off a wide bend in a slow-moving spring creek. We walked for an hour, then went back up to the house for breakfast.

"I could get used to this," Leslie said when we were sitting outside, drinking coffee with the sun breaking out from behind the Bridger range to the east.

Inch by Inch

"Couldn't you find a job as a cowboy or something?"

"Sure," I said. "And we could live off love in a double-wide."

We drove into Jackson for lunch, and when I complained about how the town was full of tourists, Leslie said, "And what do you call yourself?"

"I come here on business," I said. "Maybe not this time, but often enough. I'm a regular."

"Oh. Well *excuse* me."

It was true that I knew the town. Well enough, anyway, to find a place for lunch. Then we got our fishing licenses and arranged for a guide. We were in luck, the store manager told us. One of the best guides in their stable had a cancellation later in the week. I said we'd take the date and asked for the guide's name.

"Lori Ann Murphy," he said. "Not only is she a great guide, but she is a really wonderful personality. You'll have a great day. Guaranteed."

We left town and drove north, toward Jenny Lake, and stared up at the Grand Teton. Leslie said that one of her regrets was never having tried mountain climbing.

"You could still do it," I said.

"Maybe I will. After I get through with my current project."

We got back to the cabin just before sunset and walked out into the fields to listen to the sand hill cranes flying in to roost and making that strange, otherworldly call as they passed overhead.

"That's one of the wildest sounds in the world," I said. "And one of my favorites."

"What's another?" Leslie said. She was holding my arm and pressing herself against me. It was getting cold again.

"Bugling elk," I said. "We may hear that when we go camping up in the mountains."

"When is that?"

"Tomorrow," I said, "if that's okay with you. We can stay up there two nights, then come down for the float trip on the Snake. That still leaves us with a couple of days. We could drive up into Yellowstone."

"Sounds wonderful," she said. "This trip was such a great idea. I'm glad I thought of it."

I had rented a small sport utility, so we had the vehicle we needed to drive up into the Bridgers. The Oregon Trail had passed through here and there were historical markers at places where you could still see faint impressions of the wagon ruts. In a meadow, under a solitary old ponderosa, there was a headstone marking the grave of a woman who hadn't made it. Her name was Sarah and she had died in childbirth up here in the mountains in 1849 when she was thirty-two years old.

"That is so sad," Leslie said.

We found a campsite on a flat piece of ground, under some pines. It looked down on a sparkling little stream. A couple of hundred yards downhill, the stream took a hard turn against a high bank, making a pool where the water was deep and relatively protected. While I put up the tent and laid out the pads and sleeping bags, Leslie rigged her fly rod and walked down to fish the pool.

"I want to see if I can catch supper," she said. "I like the idea of providing while you do the domestic chores."

"Get after it," I said.

She caught two small trout, a cutthroat and a brookie, and cleaned them in the pool, letting the offal drift downstream just in case we might be in bear country. We cooked the fish and some potatoes in the grease of a couple of bacon strips, using a little one-burner gas stove to do the cooking since the woods were dry and there were fire alerts all over the West. After the potatoes and fish, we boiled some water and cooked noodles in some chicken stock and added some sun-dried tomatoes. I did the dishes down in the pool where Leslie had caught the fish.

We read for a while by the light of a Coleman lantern, then went to sleep. I thought I heard coyotes in the night but couldn't be sure. It seemed like this country was too high. There would be lots more food in the valley. So I probably dreamed the coyotes. Even so, it was a very vivid dream.

13

We stayed up in the mountains for three days, fishing, exploring, and just hanging around the camp. We climbed a mountain which was harder than it looked. The air was thin and neither of us were used to it. And then, Leslie had just had surgery and we couldn't forget about that, even though the point of this trip was to forget about that, for a little while, anyway.

We started out on game trails through some lodgepole and aspen, and after an hour or so we were above the tree line, scrambling over talus rock. It was tough on the knees and the lungs. Still six or seven hundred feet from the top, we were in the middle of a large scree field, like castaways at sea, and we stopped to rest and drink some water. Leslie was breathing very hard. Her face was beaded with sweat and she looked, generally, like someone who was working very hard; maybe even too hard.

"Want to go back?" I said, handing her the water bottle.

"No," she said. "I want to get to the top of this Goddamned mountain." She made it sound very important, like she was Ed Veistures trying to bag another eight-thousand-meter summit.

"You feel okay?"

"I feel fine, Jack. Don't coddle me. I'm going to the top with or without you."

"I'll be right behind you," I said.

So Leslie led and I followed to the top of what I learned by reading the map was an eleven-thousand-foot mountain. We were both panting like winded dogs when we got to the summit and sat on a rock. You could see forever.

"God," Leslie said, between breaths, "it's worth it for the view."

"It sure is."

"Told you I was going to do it, Jack. There's no holding me back. I'm going for the top, just like some Whitney Houston song."

"I believe you."

"I can see why they do it," she said. "You know, the people who climb mountains. And I can see why they keep going, even when they shouldn't. You get keyed on that summit. I mean, it isn't really anything but a piece of ground that is higher than the one you're standing on, but in your mind . . . it's where they keep the keys."

"The keys?"

"The keys to the Kingdom, Jack. The keys that unlock the door."

"Okay, I give up. What door?"

"If you have to ask," she said, shaking her head, "then you'll never understand."

When we got back to camp, I noticed the blood on her shirt. A wet stain about the size of a postcard between the pocket and the armpit.

"What's that?" I said.

"What does it look like? It's blood."

"From what?"

"From the incision, I suppose. I guess I pulled a stitch. I thought I felt something when we were going through that boulder field."

"What can you do?"

She shrugged, like it was the least important thing in her life. "Nothing, I guess. Unless you want to try to stitch it back. You bring your sewing kit?"

She was smiling and it wasn't faked.

"Take off your shirt."

"Well, *Jack,*" she said. "At least let me wash up."

"Maybe I can't sew it," I said, "but I can damn sure bandage it and put some antiseptic on it."

"It's nothing, baby. Really."

"It's a wound," I said, "and it's bleeding."

She took her shirt off and it was the first time I had seen the incision.

It wouldn't have been so bad except for where it was: a place of pure flesh. No bones or organs. Something about blood coming from there . . . it just seemed wrong.

The skin around the wound was blue. Like she had been bruised or had changed her mind about halfway through a jailhouse tattoo.

"That's the dye they used when they mapped me," she said. "You ever seen anything so ugly?"

The cut wasn't more than an inch and a half long. The flaps were held together by four neat sutures. The black thread looked harsh against the ivory flesh. Blood and some kind of clear fluid seeped from the incision where it had pulled apart between two of the sutures.

I got my first-aid kit from my pack. First I poured a little alcohol onto a cotton swab.

"Might sting a little," I said.

"Don't you have a bullet I can bite on?"

I dabbed the cotton over the wound.

"Yikes."

"Hurts?"

"No, damnit. It's *cold.*"

It took three cotton balls to clean the wound; the dried blood was hard to get off and took some pressure.

"Oh God," Leslie said, faking a moan.

"Cut it out," I said. "You're distracting the doctor."

When I had the wound cleaned up, I soaked a swab in Betadine and painted the incision, turning it a yellow color that, for some reason, made me think of tobacco stains.

"Does that sting?"

"Nah."

I had only one of those wrapped butterfly bandages in my kit. There were supposed to be more but it had been a long time since I'd used the kit or checked it. I did have a pair of EMT shears and a roll of adhesive tape. So I used the one butterfly bandage as a pattern and traced its outline on the adhesive tape three times, then cut along the pattern lines with the shears. I was careful and took my time.

"I'm impressed," Leslie said.

I pinched the ridges of the incision together, trying to be firm but not too firm, then put the butterfly bandages I'd made over the cut, the fat parts on either side with the narrow centers across the actual cut. The bandages seemed to hold the cut together.

"That ought to do it," I said.

"Thank you, baby."

"Don't mention it."

The morning after we came back down to the valley, we met our guide Lori Ann just below a dam site on the South Fork of the Snake River. She already had her drift boat in the river and her waders on.

She was a tall woman, blonde and pretty in an unconventional sort of way. Probably it was the smile, which was easy, and the laugh, which was honest. It turned out that she had doubled for Meryl Streep in some movie, and, in fact, you could see the resemblance. But whereas you thought of Streep as icy, Lori Ann Murphy was earthy and spontaneous. After we'd finished with the introductions, I asked her how the fishing had been.

"Sucks," she said. "But we'll have a good time anyway."

And she was right. On both counts.

Leslie and Lori Ann seemed to make some kind of instant connection. Leslie was curious about the life of a guide and Lori Ann was delighted to tell her all about it. So I was left out of the conversation and that was fine with me. I concentrated on my fishing.

There was no hatch of flies to bring the fish up. This meant we had to work the banks with grasshopper imitations, casting over and over. I liked the rhythm of it. There was something soothing about the way the boat moved downstream and the line shot through the rod guides, then unrolled through the air and dropped lightly on the water. Leslie and I each caught one small cutthroat in the morning, before lunch. Slow fishing but I didn't mind.

Lori Ann had a folding table stored in the bottom of the McKenzie boat. Also three folding chairs. She put up the table and covered it with a damask cloth, then laid out cold chicken, fresh tomatoes, and a loaf of freshly baked bread. She opened a bottle of white wine that had been in the cooler. She poured the wine into real glasses and served the food on real china.

"That's the benefit of going with a woman guide," she said. "With one of the guys, you'd have a ham sandwich in Saran wrap, a bag of potato chips, and a can of warm beer."

"I'm sold," I said.

We all lay down on the grass and slept for half an hour after lunch.

"Okay," Lori Ann said, when she had reloaded the boat, "this afternoon, no prisoners."

She was determined that her new friend, Leslie, would catch a trophy fish. So Leslie took the bow and Lori Ann worked the oars hard to keep her in good casting position while we drifted downstream.

Several times during the afternoon, Lori Ann would either beach or anchor the boat and the two of them would get out and wade. Lori Ann would stand on Leslie's left shoulder, very close, and spot the places where she wanted her to cast.

"Just above that cottonwood root," I'd hear her say. "Nice cast. That ought to be a fish."

Then, "Damn. No fish. This isn't fair. Okay, try the head of that little riffle. That looks good . . . nice cast . . . come on, fish."

I fished without much conviction, but that was fine. I felt the way a parent does when a kid has found a new friend and the two of them are playing nicely together. I was happy for Leslie. We'd been together for almost a week and my company went only so far.

I watched a couple of eagles, high overhead, riding a strong thermal. I made some casts, changed my fly, drank a beer, and took a few pictures of Leslie and Lori Ann trying to pound up a trophy trout on a day when nothing much was moving except the water. I had a fine, unproductive afternoon.

They caught a couple of small fish but never raised the big one they were after.

Another guide had driven Lori Ann's truck and trailer to the pull-out. She had the boat on the trailer quickly, then drove us back upstream to where we'd parked. We said our good-byes, promising to stay in touch, and then Leslie and Lori Ann hugged like a couple of old friends.

When we were driving away, Leslie started to cry.

"Oh, Jack," she said.

"What's the matter?"

"Nothing . . . everything."

She had a bandanna knotted around her neck. She loosened it and used it on her eyes.

"It's almost over," she said, "and I hate that. Now I have to go back and deal."

I said something about how it might not be so bad. The surgery had gone fine and maybe that was a good sign.

She nodded and pretended to agree.

"Yes," she said. "You're right. Maybe it is."

Inch by Inch

When we got back to the house, I had to close her wound again. All that casting had opened it up and her shirt was soaked with blood.

We spent the last day of our trip just hanging around the house, reading and resting and packing.

"It was great, Jack," Leslie said. "Everything about it. I'm just sorry you never heard your bugling elk."

"Next time," I said. "Gives me something to live for."

What a dumb thing to say, I thought, and looked off at the sunset. What a monumentally dumb thing to say.

14

The waiting room was nearly full. For some reason, this surprised me. You go from one selfish extreme to the other, I suppose, from thinking cancer is something that happens to other people to thinking you are the only person in the world who has to deal with it. I looked around the room and my eyes picked one woman out of the rest of the waiting patients, the way you will find yourself staring at another passenger when you're waiting at the gate to board an airplane.

The woman appeared to be in her late forties—a little older than Leslie. But then, I thought, cancer almost surely ages you and this woman was clearly further along than Leslie. For one thing, she had no hair.

She was wearing a turban. It hid her baldness but not the fact that she had no hair. The woman's face was puffy and her flesh seemed to have lost something—tone and tension, I guess. The skin around her neck was loose, so she had lost weight. She looked tired, fatigued to the point where no amount of sleep would ever refresh her.

No doubt I stared at her with the unconscious thought that Leslie would soon look like this. Maybe I wanted to get used to the idea.

The woman felt my eyes on her and turned, slightly, to look back at me.

Instead of the glare that I expected and deserved and that you usually get when you're caught staring at someone, she smiled. It was a faint smile, very sweet and oddly compassionate. She had picked up on my nervous unfamiliarity with this whole scene and on the fact that Leslie still had her hair. Her smile was a way of saying *Hang in there; you can do this.*

I tried to smile back and hoped that it didn't come off as a grimace; that I hadn't returned a sweet gesture with something that would be taken as rude. You'd have to be a real bastard, I thought, to bring rudeness into this place.

When the receptionist called Leslie's name, we both stood up. I told her, "I'll be right here."

"No," she said. "I want you to come with me."

I didn't say anything, but I'm sure my expression must have said *What for?*

"I want you to hear all this. I want to be able to talk to you about it."

I wasn't sure I wanted either of those things. But I said "Sure," and followed her through one of those big, heavy doors wide enough to accommodate a stretcher and one of those devices they use to hang IV bottles.

"First office on your right," the receptionist said.

"Thank you," Leslie said.

We waited again. The room was furnished like a cell—only an institutional desk and a couple of chairs and the usual examining table. No window and no pictures or posters on the bare walls. The room had a clean, austere, antiseptic feel.

The doctor didn't keep us waiting long. Less than five minutes. She was short and thin with dark hair that was long and full. She had olive skin and a serious face but a good, sincere smile. She wore one of those cotton jackets that doctors like, a plain khaki skirt, and sensible flat shoes. I liked her as soon as she smiled and introduced herself. Or, probably, I was trying to like her. She was Leslie's new doctor, after all.

"I'm Natalie Charon," she said. "Nice to meet you."

When we'd done the introductions, the doctor took one chair and Leslie took the other. They faced each other from a distance of no more than three feet. I sat on the examining table and tried to be still so I wouldn't rustle the paper covering.

"I've looked at your chart," Dr. Charon began, "and talked with Dr. Petofsky. I think that so far we have a lot to feel good about."

Then she told us about chemotherapy.

It took ten or fifteen minutes and when she'd finished, Dr. Charon got up and left the room. She closed the door behind her. She'd told us that the radiologist—Dr. Riordan—would be along in a few minutes. After a moment or two of silence, I said, "What do you think?"

"I think," Leslie said, "that I like Dr. Charon and trust her. What do you think?"

"Me, too."

"Good."

"What about the things she said?" I was thinking about what Monk had told me. How sometimes a woman will draw the line at chemo.

"I'm considering them."

"Considering?"

"Yes."

"What's to consider?" I said. "Anything that improves the odds . . . I mean, what's the downside? You throw up and you lose your hair."

"No big deal, then, right?"

I didn't say anything. It wasn't my hair and I wouldn't be throwing up everything I tried to eat.

"Of course, it is just *hair*," she said. "And a couple of months of feeling sick to my stomach. I could do that standing on my head . . . right?"

I nodded.

She gave me a different smile.

"But there's more to it than that."

"What more?"

"Later. After we're through here. Once we've heard the whole pitch."

We waited in silence for another five minutes or so. It could have been less, I suppose; time tends to hang heavy for me inside of hospitals. I was relieved when the door opened and Dr. Carolyn Riordan stepped briskly into the room.

She was short and athletic with an oval face, tight curls, and actual dimples. She would have been called "cute" when she was younger. Now the word would be "perky," though I'd read that was going out of fashion. No serious woman wanted to be called "perky," and Carolyn Riordan was a serious woman, working the last line of defense for a lot of desperate people.

Still, she had some attitude.

"This stuff does get old, doesn't it?" she said. "I mean, don't you just get so tired of talking to doctors? I know I do."

I genuinely liked Dr. Carolyn Riordan. She talked like a coach and you could imagine yourself having a couple of beers with her in some bar, talking about the Red Sox. You knew she had to be a fan.

She told Leslie what would happen, exactly, when they "zapped" her, and when Leslie asked her about side effects, Dr. Riordan said, "You'll feel tired. Fatigued. No matter what time you get to bed or how many naps you take, your buns will be constantly dragging. You'll get a little sunburn in the area where we zap you. And that's about it."

She said there wouldn't be any radiation unless there was the chemo first.

"By then, you'll be glad to see me. Tired and sunburned won't seem so bad. Chemo can be a load, no way around it."

When Leslie told her that she still hadn't made up her mind about doing the chemo, Dr. Riordan nodded in a way that said she had been here before and she understood. She stood up to leave—another doctor running behind schedule—

but before she opened the door, she put a hand on Leslie's shoulder and said, "I'll see you in a couple of months—I hope."

It was her way of saying *Do the chemo.*

Leslie went off for more tests and another mammogram. I went back to the waiting room.

My mind kept circling back on hospitals and doctors and Leslie. I had never spent a night in a hospital. Not as a patient, anyway. I had never been anything but a bystander, waiting around for people like my father to die or for my daughter, Andy, to get better.

That was the memory that I couldn't chase. The one about my daughter's first week on earth.

She had been born with a severe Rh blood incompatibility. Before she was even a week old, she was so jaundiced that her skin was the color of an old, rotting peach. She was too sick even to cry but you could look at her and feel her distress. I had never felt so helpless as I did waiting there in that hospital, getting slowly carried away by my own fears until I wanted to grab one of the busy nurses or doctors and scream *Do something!* so we could take our baby home.

A specialist had finally been brought in to perform a transfusion. He was an Indian doctor with a mustache that he kept clipped with the precision of a schematic drawing. He explained that he would use a syringe to do the transfusion and that he would take all of Andy's blood from her navel.

"Not much blood," he said, "only a cup or so."

The child did not have enough blood to make even much of a mess on the floor. That detail got to me more than any other and for a moment I thought I would lose it.

The surgeon had great hands and he did the job as if it were just another day at the office. The next morning I looked through the glass at Andy in her crib. She was kicking and crying, and although I couldn't hear it, I thought it was the most beautiful sound in the world. We took her home the next day.

That memory came to me spontaneously, and I wondered if this time it would turn out that way. If we'd go home and put it all behind us or if it would go the other way and be like it had been with my father, where the news gets a little worse every day and you know it will never get better.

I wished, as I had in that other hospital when my new baby girl was lying behind a glass in yellow distress, that it could be me. My faith was in chemo—in those drugs that Natalie Charon had called the "Red Devil." And I hoped that Leslie would decide to take them and that they would do for her what a cup of untainted blood, donated by one of those busy hospital nurses, had done for Andy. Once again I felt like screaming or crying but couldn't do either. Couldn't do anything; couldn't even read the paper.

"Hello, cowboy," Leslie said from behind me. I hadn't heard her come into the waiting room. "You look like you're a million miles from here."

"I am."

"Well, come on back to earth and let's go get something to eat. I'm starving."

15

We went to a branch of Legal Seafood and ordered chowder. When the waitress left with the order, Leslie said, "So?"

"So, what?"

"You've been thinking about it, right?"

"Sure."

"And what have you decided?"

"Not for me to decide," I said.

"What is it for you to do, then?"

"Hope you'll do the right thing," I said. "And support you."

"Well, that's sweet."

I shrugged.

"I mean it. And I appreciate it. But if I've got to decide, I want to know what you think I should do . . . what you *want* me to do."

"What I want you to do," I said slowly, "is whatever gives you the best odds."

"You want me to stay around, then?" she said, and smiled. It was the *I've got your number* smile.

"Sure. What did you expect?"

"Oh, I'll bet there are husbands out there who would come back 'undecided' if you polled them on that question."

I just shook my head.

"Everybody needs something to live for, Jack. A husband who wants to keep you around is probably a strong incentive for a lot of women who're looking at this thing. So you want me to run the whole circuit? Do the chemo and the radiation?"

The waitress picked that moment to come by and tell us our chowder would be up in "just a minute." When she heard the words *chemo* and *radiation,* she backed off as if she had seen a snake.

"That's what it will be like if I do chemo and lose my hair. I'll be shunned like a leper, even by some of our friends."

"So what?"

"It's something to consider. One of those things to factor in when I'm making this decision. I have to consider that just like I have to consider your feelings."

I wanted to say that she didn't have to consider anything except staying alive. But I didn't. I just nodded and wished that we were having this conversation at the breakfast table back home. Leslie had never minded talking—or even arguing—in public. She had a way of walling off those eyes and ears or of just not caring.

"How are you going to feel about me when I don't have any hair and I'm throwing up all the time?"

"Come on, Les."

"It's a serious question."

"Okay. I probably won't like it. No . . . I *definitely* won't like it. But I think I can tell myself to consider the alternative."

She thought about that for a moment, then said, "Good answer."

The waitress brought the chowder, put the bowls in front of us, and made a hasty getaway. Leslie tasted the soup and carried on about how good it was.

"I don't know why, but hospitals always make me hungry."

"Funny, they kill my appetite."

"That's because you're never the patient. You don't do anything but worry and that shuts down all the normal appetites. You ever notice how worry kills the libido?"

"Sure."

"But if you are the patient in a hospital, you are past worrying. All that just goes away and you go into a passive mode. You aren't anything *except* biology and appetites."

"Really?"

"I don't know about the rest of the world, but it works like that for me. You'll see when we get home."

"Can't wait."

"Neither can I."

We ate for a minute or two, without talking. Then she said, "That's part of it, you know."

"No," I said. "I don't."

"I can get past the throwing up," she said. "I've been there before. Morning sickness, you know. The hair . . . that's harder. I don't expect you'd understand, but that robs you of your femininity. Bad enough that you've got this disease that has attacked a big part of your womanhood. Now you've got to lose one of the outward symbols of it. It's like you're being neutered, somehow. The surgery doesn't do that. Not the kind I had, anyway. That's just a cut. These days, getting cut is usually a way of enhancing your femininity."

"I've noticed."

"Before this happened, I was thinking about a little something around the eyes. But I'm done with surgery for a while."

"Good."

"But do you understand what I'm saying? About the hair?"

The waitress returned, this time to clear. Leslie told her sweetly that the soup was delicious. We asked for coffee. She left in a hurry to get it.

"So do you?" Leslie said to me when the waitress was out of hearing.

"What?"

"Understand about the hair."

"Not really. It's just hair. It grows back."

"That's what I tell myself," she said. "But I don't know . . ."

She looked away. Her lower lip trembled.

This was fear, I thought. And not fear of the discomfort of being sick from chemo or the embarrassment of losing her hair. She was tougher than that. A lot tougher than that. And it wasn't fear of dying, either. This was something else.

"What?" I said.

She looked back at me.

"Right now," she said, talking like she had to force the words from her mouth, "I am just a premenopausal woman who has had some minor surgery to remove a growth. I've got a little scar but I'm just an older version of what I've always been. My body still feels like the same body it has always been. I have to work a little harder at the gym to keep it feeling that way. But the essential thing is still the same. That's going to change—in ways I can't be sure of—if I do chemo and radiation."

I started to say something, but she held up her hand and stopped me.

"I know the hair will grow back. So I might *look* the same . . . or not that different, anyway. They say your hair comes back curly. But that might be fun.

"Still, I'm going to *be* different if I let them pump that stuff into me. It's going to kill a lot more than just the 'fast-growing cells,' and some of the things it kills might not ever come back. I like those things. I'll miss them. Without them, I won't be the same person. And I'm not sure it's worth losing those things just to get another ten percent on the upside. You know what I mean?"

I did and I didn't. I wanted to say that if she took that chance, instead of losing a part of herself that she liked, she might lose the whole thing. But I didn't say it because she knew it. She knew all the arguments.

"Can you understand that? Does it make any sense to you?'

"Yes," I said.

"I'm going to think very hard about it," she said. "I promise. And I know what you want and that's going to be a big factor in the decision. I'm going to think about Andy, too. And Brad. But there's this other thing I've got to think about. I just hope you understand."

I nodded and said I did.

She took the last sip of her coffee. The waitress had brought it so unobtrusively that we'd hardly noticed.

"All right, then," she said, straightening up and smiling. "As long as we've got that settled, why don't you pay up and take me home. I've had enough of this city for today."

16

For three days we talked about everything except chemo. Should we refinish the kitchen floor? Was it time to switch from cable to dish? Eat in or go out? We could pump those conversations up and make them last an hour and never come to any real conclusion. Living with what we could not talk about gave me a case of nerves.

They tell you to throw yourself into your work on the theory that it will get your mind off problems you cannot solve. But things weren't a lot better at the office. The mood there was filled with uncertainty.

I worked for a company that sold outdoor stuff—high-end clothing and equipment for the backpacking and mountaineering set—and two-thirds of our business was mail-order. Palms started getting sweaty in the fall when we were preparing to send out our Christmas catalogs. Those books were responsible for more than half our mail-order volume, and a good October meant a good year. A bad October, on the other hand, meant belt tightening and possibly layoffs. Recessionary clouds were gathering over the economy and everyone was on edge.

I worked on the retail end of things—handling stores and outlets—and my division was up, so far, for the year. I'd done good business and my salespeople had written a lot of orders on the road trip that had ended with my coming home and learning about Leslie's cancer, so I suppose I should have felt confident and secure in my position. But I was still part of the company. If business was bad, I wouldn't be immune no matter how red-hot my division was doing.

So I would leave the house in the morning feeling like I had been dancing on glass in my conversations with Leslie, then go to the office where the air was full of the same kind of apprehension. The most relaxed part of my day was the drive to work, when I would drink coffee and listen to Imus rave on about one thing or another.

The office closed at five, but like most of the company's executives, I would stay a little later. When I got home, Leslie would still be at her desk, crouched over her computer with her fingers dancing over the keyboard. She finished every day by answering all the accumulated e-mails. I would kiss her neck and rub her shoulders while she worked, and when she finished, we would go out and take the dogs for a walk. It was a nice part of the day.

Late in the week, I came home and found her sitting at the breakfast table— crisis central—looking at the door with her face set like stone. She was obviously waiting for me.

"Hello," I said.

"Hello yourself."

I sat down at the table across from her and said, "What's wrong?"

"I can't believe you'd do something like this," she said. "I just can't believe it. How *could* you?"

"Do what?"

"Oh, don't give me that," she said and slapped the table so hard that I flinched. The dogs scurried out of the room.

"You'll have to tell me what I did," I said. "I can't defend myself otherwise."

"You can't defend yourself period," she said. "Not after this."

"Les, please. Tell me what I did."

"You *told.*"

"Told what?"

"You told somebody that I have cancer. *That's* what you told. Who did you tell? Did you just tell everyone at work so that maybe you'd get a little attention and have people feeling sorry for you? 'Poor Jack, his wife has breast cancer.' Is that it? What *could* you have been thinking?"

Her face went rigid. I'd seen her angry before, often enough, but never like this. And, I thought, I didn't blame her.

"It wasn't me," I said.

"Well, it certainly wasn't me. I'm not looking for sympathy. Certainly not from Jo Ann Kempton, who called me today to tell me how 'terribly sorry' she was to hear the news, that she knew what I was going through and would always 'be there' for me and did I want her to come over and talk, that her sister had been through the whole thing and she thought maybe some of the things she had learned would be a help to me and—*God,* she just went on and on until I thought I would scream."

"I haven't talked to Jo Ann since that party."

"Oh, *good.* That's wonderful. It means you talked to someone else who talked to her. So anyone that blabbermouth Jo Ann *doesn't* call up and tell about 'poor Leslie' will hear it from someone else. I can look forward to lots and lots of those calls. Thanks, Jack. Thanks a lot."

"Did you ask her how she found out?"

"No. I didn't ask her how she found out. I was too stunned to say anything. And she was talking too much. She was just gushing with sympathy and loving every minute."

She slapped the table with her hand again. I was ready for it this time and didn't flinch.

She got up from the table and knocked the chair to the floor. Then she spun around and left the room. I could hear each angry step as she made her way back to the bedroom and slammed the door.

I sat at the table for a while. My face was hot. The usual pattern was for me to go after her. The shouting would start, again, and it would last until we were both exhausted.

This time, though, I just sat. Waiting for the heat to pass and trying hard to think. But I couldn't get my brain engaged. It raced like an engine stuck in neutral. No forward motion; just loud, whining noise.

Finally, I got up, called the dogs, and went outside to take them for a walk.

I learned, when I went to work the next morning, who had let the secret out. It had to have been Nell, the woman in personnel I'd spoken to about the medical insurance. I passed her in the hallway and she gave me a look of sympathy or pity or something and asked "How are you *doing?*" in a way that was anything but conversational.

So the insurance claims had come through her office and the news was just too good not to share. I worked for the largest employer in a small town and these things got around.

I thought about confronting Nell and getting her to admit what she had done and then calling Leslie with the news and taking some satisfaction from her apology.

But confessions and apologies seemed beside the point. I couldn't say why I came to that conclusion. There wasn't much logic, these days, in my thinking; I was going mostly on intuition. And my feeling was that blame didn't much matter.

So I finished up the day and stayed the requisite half hour or so at the office, talking shop with a couple of the people in the catalog division. They wanted to know what I thought about some of the copy they had written.

I told them I thought it was dynamite.

On the way home, I stopped at a florist shop where I did some business. The woman who owned the shop always made like she was glad to see me. Her name was Barbara and she called her place Barb's Bouquets.

"What'll it be today?" she said.

"Can you make me a cheer-up arrangement?"

"Sure. I've got just the thing. Somebody sick?"

"No," I said. "Just blue."

"On a day like this? That's terrible."

I hadn't noticed before, but it was, indeed, one of those beautiful, mild early-fall days in New England with the maple leaves just beginning to turn.

"Well, you know how it is."

"I sure do. Sneaks up on you, doesn't it? When you're least expecting it. Sometimes for no reason at all."

"Yes," I said, "it sure does."

She made an arrangement of delphiniums, one of Leslie's favorites. Also asters, irises, and some kind of tender white lilies. I told her it was beautiful, thanked her, and asked her to send me the bill.

"Sure thing," she said. "I hope it works."

When I got to the door at home, I could see Leslie sitting at the kitchen table, waiting for me.

I made a tentative entrance, holding the flowers behind me so she couldn't see them. They could make things worse if she was still upset and angry, and my timing had never been real good in these things.

"Hello," I said.

"You're late," she said. "I was worried."

"I had to make a stop in town."

"I thought maybe you weren't coming home. I wouldn't blame you."

"Come on."

"I was such an ass."

"No, you weren't."

"Yes. I was. And don't argue with me when I'm trying to apologize."

"You don't have to apologize."

"Jack, I promise you. If you keep on arguing with me, I'm going to turn into a screaming shrew again, right before your eyes."

"Okay. I won't argue."

"I feel so awful."

"Then how about some flowers to cheer you up. Some of them are even delphiniums."

"That'll work," she said. "Every time." And then she started crying.

I got her some water to drink and then some for the flowers. She cut the stems and put the flowers carefully into a cut-glass vase that had been a wedding present from someone we'd long since lost touch with. She explained, while she worked, how she'd gotten another one of those calls in the morning.

"This one didn't catch me on the blind side, like yesterday," she said. "I actually managed to keep my head and talk back."

"And?"

"The call was from Gretchen. She's a practical girl, you know, so she wanted to know what hospital I was going to and why I wasn't at Sloan-Kettering and all that. I just started talking to her, about the whole thing. And you know what, Jack?"

"What?"

"It wasn't *that* hard. We could have been talking about the knee scope she had done last year or something ordinary like that. No shame. No mysterious bullshit. Just cancer and you deal with it."

"I see." I'd always liked that side of Gretchen. Her husband, Daniel, was harder to take. He was one of the two or three brokers in town and he tended to come on like Peter Lynch. But they were okay. We saw them fairly often.

"I finally just asked her, 'How did you find out about it?' and she told me that someone in Daniel's office had told him. I asked her to find out who and to track it down. Turned out it started with the personnel woman at your office. She'd seen the insurance claim."

"I'll be damned."

"Yeah. I should have known. Small town. How many times has it happened like that?"

"Enough."

"I don't know why I didn't think of that right away. I really don't. I mean, I'm not that dumb. But this whole thing was making me hysterical."

"Was?"

"Yes," she said. "Was. And I hate it. I hate that part more than anything. I'm really sorry, baby. Can you forgive me?"

"I'm just sorry that Nell ran her mouth," I said.

"Well, I'm not," she said. "Not anymore. Had to happen and I'm glad, now, that it did. It helped me make up my mind about some things. You want to talk to me about it?"

"Sure. Absolutely."

"I'll change shoes, then we can walk the dogs."

17

The house was close by a hundred-acre woodlot that had been tied up in an estate for years. In nice weather we took walks on the trails that spiraled around to the top of the hill, and in the winter we went cross-country skiing on the same trails. Our dogs knew the trails by heart and we went out the back door and followed them.

The leaves were just beginning to turn and the light, once we got into the trees, had the same quality you find in an old church with stained glass windows.

Leslie sighed and said, "I'm going to do it."

I knew what she meant and said, "Good. I'm glad."

"I wasn't going to," she said. "Up until this morning, I thought I had my mind made up."

"What changed it?"

"I guess I decided not to be selfish."

I didn't get it.

"In a way, it's about you . . . and Brad and Andy. But don't worry," she said. "You didn't talk me into doing something I didn't want to do. You didn't even try, and I appreciate that."

"Okay."

"Anyway, I knew what you were thinking but I didn't care. I usually care, even when I think I don't. But on this one, I honestly didn't. I was worried about myself. My cancer, my body, my life. That old song."

We cut off from the main path and followed a smaller one that ran up a steep stretch of the hill. The trees were tighter here and it felt like we were walking down a long yellow tunnel.

"Here's what I was thinking," she said. "Let me try to make it as plain as I can."

"You don't have to do that."

"I want to do that. It's important. I have to know that you understand."

"Okay. I can buy that."

"I don't think this is just any old disease. It isn't chicken pox and it isn't malaria. You don't get it from a mosquito bite. Maybe you get it from smoking or from breathing bad air. But a lot of people who smoke don't get it and people who breathe dirty air every day of their lives don't get it. This disease has something to do with you. In some way, it *is* you. Those are your cells in there, going ballistic and multiplying like crazy."

It was the mystic in her talking. The part I had never really understood, the same part that took astrology semiseriously. But for once I could connect with it.

"All right," I said.

"If I'm going to do this thing, it's going to be me fighting me. You know what I mean?"

"Yes," I said.

"I kept thinking that if I'm going to war with this disease—with part of myself—then I absolutely have to want to win it. And I wasn't sure, really sure, I even wanted to be a cancer survivor. A little surgery is one thing. They cut you for all sorts of reasons. But chemo and radiation . . . they only do that number for one thing."

I nodded and didn't say anything.

"So I was thinking that I'd just see if maybe I could skate on by that part, if that one little cut would be enough. I could take vitamins and eat organic and do it that way. Or just pretend it was like a wisdom tooth and hope for the best.

"But something about that call this morning. Talking to Gretchen made me think. You know, at this point in my life, cancer is just a detail. If it doesn't kill me, something else will. And if that doesn't happen for a long time, then I'll get old and ugly anyway.

"You know how you hear people say that 'so-and-so has a lot to live for'? Well, not everybody does. And some people have less to live for than other people. Maybe having people around who want you to live is all it takes for you to have a lot to live for."

"Yeah, I think so," I said.

"Well, I guess you're going to find out. At first I thought this was going to be easy. But now I think it's going to be hard. It's already been hard on Andy and, God knows, Brad will take it hard. It's going to be hard on you, too."

"Maybe not."

"Yes, it will. What we've been through so far—that's the easy part. The hard part comes now. And I hate putting this on you. This might be the worst part."

We had always been that way. Solitary in our troubles even while we shared a life. We belonged to that generation of people who didn't ever want to have to depend on anyone, and even as a married couple we had trouble sharing the bad stuff.

"I'm going to have to depend on you a lot and I detest that."

"Fine."

"You'll probably hate it, too."

"Maybe."

"I thought about going away, somewhere, and doing it on my own and then coming back if everything worked out. Treat it like I'd gotten a job overseas somewhere and when it was over, come back and start our lives again."

"What made you decide against it?"

She sighed and kicked at a pile of leaves.

"I don't know."

"Well, I'm glad you did."

"Good," she said. "Fine. But tell me if you still feel that way in a couple of months."

18

I got a call from Bill Winter. It was midmorning and I was looking over some reports from vendors who weren't coming through. They were losing business, which meant they were having trouble filling their orders, including ours. You could feel the pressure in those lines of ordinary business prose. I wondered how tight the squeeze would get. Me, I thought, and just about everyone else in the country. Would Mr. Greenspan save us? Could he?

"What's up, Bill?"

"Lunch," he said. "Man's got to eat. You loose?"

I usually skipped lunch and went to the gym. But I said, "Sure. Sounds good."

So we met at Ernie's, a place that tries hard to be one of those big-city sports bars with a half-dozen huge television monitors, most of them tuned to ESPN and SportsCenter. There were framed pictures of athletes on the walls along with blown-up newspaper clippings and headlines from the great games. The beer came in big mugs and the burgers were oversized and served with mounds of fries. Ernie's was a real "guy" place.

I was five minutes late and Bill was waiting for me. He was serious about punctuality.

"You doing okay?" Bill said. He sounded almost grave.

"Fine. You?"

"Sorry to hear about Leslie."

"Thanks. I appreciate that."

"I suspect that's what was on your mind, that night at your house."

"That's right."

"Well, if there's anything . . ." He shrugged.

I nodded.

"You know," he said, "the occasional beer. A night out with the boys. You'll need a break now and then."

"I imagine so."

"How's she doing?"

"Well, she's pretty tough."

He nodded.

I could sense he was curious about the details, but it wasn't his style to ask.

"Most of the news is pretty hopeful," I said, and told him about the biopsy.

"Good," he said. "That's real good. I've had a couple of buddies . . . well, you know, same deal, but the news wasn't so good. They had a tough time."

"We're staying positive," I said.

"That's the most important thing," Bill said. He was an attitude guy. I'd heard him say, more than once, that you made your own luck and that he wasn't interested in problems, only solutions. He'd made a lot of money investing and believed that his attitude was the reason.

"She'll get down and depressed," he said. "Anybody would, even a strong woman like Leslie. You'll have to keep her up. And you'll need to make sure you get some help keeping yourself up."

The waitress arrived and it was a relief. Bill ordered a Guinness and a bacon cheeseburger. I had a tomato juice and one of those salads with strips of chicken. I would have ordered a beer myself, but it violated an unwritten but serious office rule.

Bill drank the first couple of inches off his beer and said, "You mind my bringing it up? I don't want to intrude . . . you understand."

"No. It's okay. There isn't much to talk about. Just medical stuff."

And that was the end of the intimate part of the lunch. We ate and we talked about other things. Bill was a sportsman and he came alive at this time of year. He was planning a trip out west with his two bird dogs. He'd be leaving in a few days and would be gone for two weeks.

"I've got a lease on this one ranch near Lewiston," he said, "where we hunt all day and never cut a road. The place is just thick with sharptails and Huns. We get up early, eat eggs and pancakes, then walk all day long, following the dogs. Come in at sunset, drink a couple of shooters, eat a steak, and go to bed. Get up in the morning and do it all again. Sort of like dying and going to heaven."

I'd learned about bird hunting when Leslie and I moved here from New York, and I liked it. But I didn't get out as much as I once had, so Silas, my short-hair, was getting lazy and fat. I wondered how he would do out west.

"Sounds great," I said. "Wish I were going with you."

"Why don't you?" he said.

"Thanks, Bill . . ."

"It's just two weeks. And you don't have to stay for all of it. Fly out for three days. Hell, bring your dog. I'll meet you at the airport."

"I can't . . ."

"Leslie hasn't started her chemo yet, has she?"

"No."

"I've been through this, man," he said. "Not firsthand. But a buddy of mine, close friend, did the whole course. Even if it all works out, you've got a long slog ahead of you. This is the time to get away for a couple of days. Later on, it won't be an option."

I nodded.

"Think about it. Consider it an open offer. You can decide after I'm out there. I'll send you an e-mail with a number where you can reach me."

"Okay."

We finished our lunch, split the bill, and left together. In the parking lot, Bill put a hand on my shoulder and said, "Hang in there. And don't forget that offer. You can redeem it any time."

"I'll do that, Bill. And thanks."

I probably would have told Leslie about that conversation when I got home that night, but she had a lot of news of her own.

The phone, she said, hadn't stopped ringing.

"I got three different offers," she said, "to go wig shopping."

"Are you going to do it?"

"I don't know," she said. "I don't want to get into one of those deals where everyone is trying so hard to keep it light and I'm expected to do my part. But maybe. If the right moment comes."

"What would that be?"

"I don't know, but I'll recognize it."

Her desk, I noticed, was unusually neat. She was fairly orderly but not compulsive about it. Like most people who keep a lot of balls up in the air, there was an element of chaos in her life. But this afternoon there were many fewer piles than usual and the file folders that were ordinarily stacked on one corner of her desk had been put away. The mound of old mail and bills was gone. There wasn't a stray sheet of paper in sight and hardly any magazines or catalogs where normally there would have been a dozen or more.

"Looks like you spent the day getting squared away."

"Seemed like a good idea," she said. "Before long, I may not have the energy."

"Yeah."

"Which leads me to . . ." She said it in the fake coy fashion she used when she wanted to tell me mildly distressing news. We'd been invited for dinner, say, on a night when I didn't want to go out, or by someone I didn't much like.

"What?" I said.

Inch by Inch

"The yard," she said.

"What about it?"

"We're running out of time. Soon it'll be getting dark before you get home from work, and then it will be snowing. Will you help me put things to bed?"

"All right," I said. "When do you want to start?"

"How about this afternoon?"

"Let me change."

19

Her vegetable garden, her perennial beds, and her hanging plants—these were what Leslie had instead of a grand, or even very nice, house. She had an eye for decorating, but we didn't have the money to give it full rein. So she did the best she could with fabrics and paint and odds and ends of old furniture that she'd refinished. Meanwhile, she put her best energies into the ground, where you could do a lot with some manure and a little imagination, where sunlight and water took the place of money.

During the brief, intense spring planting season, she would work outside from the time she could leave her desk until dark and even a little longer, sometimes setting up her sprinklers by moonlight. Then she would come inside, exhausted and dirty, bitten by blackflies, her fingernails ruined. But she would be glowing with a certain kind of contentment.

If I asked what she had been doing, she would say, "Preparing the beds."

"Seems like they take a lot of preparing."

"The peonies, especially," she'd say, affectionately "They need a lot of love,"

She would still be working when the first of her flowers—crocuses and daffodils—began blooming, and she would work right through the tulip season. When she wasn't turning, weeding, or fertilizing the perennial beds, she would be planting her vegetable gardens. The peas and lettuce had to go in early. Everything else could wait until after the last frost.

That came in late May, and by then the beds had been amply, if not lavishly, prepared. Then, in early June, the payoff came. The peonies would begin to bloom and there was something undeniably voluptuous about them. Leslie liked to call them her "hussies."

By mid-June, she could relax a little, and when we cooked outside, on the grill, she would take me for tours of her gardens while we waited for the coals to burn down. The house may not have been much, but for a couple of months during the summer, the yard was a showplace.

It passed quickly, though. By September, the plants that had been plump and glorious were drying up and dying. This was when she put things to bed. But it didn't go the way it had in the spring and early summer. Now she worked with the kind of urgency that comes with beating an unpleasant deadline, like filing your taxes.

I would offer to help—just like in the spring—but she would generally say no, that I had better things to do, that it was her yard, and anyway, she enjoyed it.

I put on some old Carhartts and a pair of boots, found a pair of work gloves in the garage, and met her in the backyard, where she was already on her knees, scratching the dirt with one of those little clawlike tools.

"What's my job?" I said.

"The irises," she said. "They all need to be cut down to the ground. It's a rotten job. I tell myself, every fall, that I'm just going to dig them up and be done with them. But in the spring, I'm always glad I didn't do it. They bring so much to the party."

I tried a pair of old and very dull hedge clippers on the irises.

"Is this the best you've got for tools?" I said.

"What's wrong with them?"

"They wouldn't cut soup," I said.

Inch by Inch

I took the clippers down to my little basement shop and worked on them with a flat file, then put them on the grinder until they would cut paper like a new pair of scissors. Then I oiled the pivot and put some Armor All on the rubber grips and went back to the job.

It went a lot faster now, and when it was almost dark I asked her what I should do with the irises I had cut and piled.

"Get the cart," she said, "or the tractor, and take them down to the wood line. We'll pile them up for compost. Next spring we'll put it back into the beds."

I took three trips with my small tractor and trailer. I used a pitchfork to load the trailer and make a neat mound just beyond the tree line, where it would be out of view from the house. After the last trip, I admired the mound for a minute or two and thought about the prospect of spring, when the pile of leaves would be a pile of dirt for me to shovel back into the trailer and haul back up and put on the beds.

I watched a ball game that night and tooled around on the Web, checking stock market sites, while Leslie went through her clothes, unpacking woolens and hanging them to air out, then filling the empty boxes with the summer stuff she wanted to keep. She made a pile of the things she would be taking down to the church for the October rummage sale. It was something she did every year but usually much later, just a day or two before the rummage sale, and without this kind of care. There was something very methodical about the way she worked tonight.

From the other room, I could hear her moving boxes and cutting the tape that held them closed. Now and then she would talk to herself about a sweater.

"Oh, I'd forgotten all about you," she would say. Or, "God, I haven't worn you in *years*."

It had been a long time since I'd seen her like this, and back then it had been in the last days of pregnancy when what she'd called her "nesting instinct" was on her.

A thought struck me. Was she listening, again, to signals her body was sending and only she could understand?

Could she be preparing things so carefully because . . . because she expected to die?

I sat up in the chair where I had been slouching. I was now entirely alert. A fragment of a Bible verse came back to me.

Thus saith the Lord: Set thine house in order, for thou shalt die and not live.

I remembered that passage now, with a kind of cold clarity. Of course, you would die and not live. None of us is exempt. Nobody gets out of life alive, and all that. But you don't think about it until something forces you to. Isaiah had spoken to Hezekiah (if I remembered right from Sunday school) and given him the bad news. Had somebody spoken to Leslie? Or was she just listening and understanding, in a way no doctor could, to what her body was telling her?

Now I remembered the tests—more mammograms and other things—that had been done the last time we were at the hospital. She'd never said anything about the results.

I felt cold, but not in the usual way. Instead of starting at the fingertips and toes and then working in, this cold started from the inside and spread out to the rest of my body.

I got up to go into the other room and ask her about those tests, but I couldn't take the first step. If she had wanted me to know, I thought, she would have told me.

"There will be no recreational cancer talk in this house," she had said. The rule was that we were going to treat cancer like the crazy aunt in the upstairs bedroom. We would talk about it only when we had to. Like when the aunt started taking in cats or setting fire to the curtains.

"I'll tell you what you need to know," she'd said.

"And who decides what I need to know?"

"I do."

Inch by Inch

I didn't argue. She was the general in this fight. I'd vowed to be a good soldier.

I sat back down and took a couple of breaths. She'll tell me, I thought, or not. All in her own time.

I shut down the computer and went back to the bedroom where she was working.

"Can I help you with something?" I said.

She was wearing her old Carolina sweatshirt, faded and shapeless, and her hair was in her face so that she had to brush it aside before she answered.

"Aren't you sweet?"

"I wouldn't go that far."

"Don't you have something better to do?"

"Nope."

"All right. Then you can take some of these boxes upstairs and put them in the crawl space."

"I'm all over it."

"What a guy."

I lifted the first box and eased out of the bedroom, being careful not to skin my knuckles on the door molding. On the way up the stairs, I repeated, over and over in my mind, the words *Set thine house in order.*

That would, I decided, be my new mantra.

20

We spent the weekend finishing the yard and the gardens. I raked the cuttings and took them down to the growing mound in the woods. One load consisted almost entirely of the carcasses of Leslie's peonies.

"Such a short life," I said. "Seems kind of sad."

"Short but glorious," she said. "I'd call it a fair trade."

We pulled everything from the vegetable garden except the brussels sprouts and pumpkins. There were a half-dozen big ones—the size of basketballs and larger—and they looked ornamental against the bare gray ground.

When the beds were completely pruned and raked, we covered them with manure and mulch. There was still some daylight, so I took my chain saw down into the woods and dropped an old ash for firewood. I limbed the tree, then cut the trunk into billets. I used a maul to split the billets for firewood. Ash splits cleanly, so it was satisfying work. I felt almost virtuous by the end of the day.

Set thine house in order.

I used the tractor and trailer to bring a couple of loads of firewood up to the house.

We cooked on the grill. The wind had come up and we couldn't see any stars through a thick cover of clouds. It was getting cool at night, so we wore fleece jackets and stood close to the coals and each other, drinking red wine. The yard work had made us hungry, and the smell of the meat, as the fat dripped onto the coals and flamed, made us even hungrier.

"God, I feel so carnivorous," Leslie said. "It's almost indecent."

"All that manual labor."

"I guess."

She took a sip of wine.

"And the wine tastes so good. Do you believe what they say about red wine? That it's healthy?"

"Why not? There has to be at least one thing that's fun and healthy too."

"I wish I'd drunk more of it, then."

"You sound like Brando. In *The Godfather*. How does it go?"

"'I like drinking wine more than I used to,'" she said, doing a bad imitation of Don Corleone talking as if someone had taken a wood rasp to his vocal cords. "'Least I'm drinking more of it than I used to.'"

"We should get that movie. The one where they have both films spliced together. Five hours of DeNiro, Brando, and Pacino. How long has it been since we watched that?"

"About six months," she said. "That's why I've got the dialogue memorized—we've seen it so many times."

"Only six months? You're sure?"

"Yes. But I'd watch it again. We could lie in bed and drink red wine. I wish we had it tonight. Might be my last chance for a while."

"Why?"

"You know."

"Oh," I said. She had made such an effort not to bring it up. I hadn't forgotten, exactly, but it was easy to talk right over it. I wondered if she was saying that she'd never drink wine again or just that it would be a while.

She took another sip from her glass. "Who knows," she said, sounding almost puzzled. "A few people get through it without feeling sick to their stomachs all the time. Maybe I'll get lucky. But tonight I'm going to drink wine like it's my last chance for a while."

Inch by Inch

We ate in front of a fire that I had built from some of the ash I'd cut and split that afternoon. The wood was still green, but ash doesn't need to be aged as much as other wood and it burned all right.

Later we watched the fire, drank more wine, and listened to music. She had made the selections, eclectic as usual. Lyle Lovett, Bonnie Raitt, Ella Fitzgerald, John Coltraine, and Delbert McClinton. She had programmed the discs so the selections were scrambled and the mood of the music seemed to change every few minutes, but the mood in the room was more or less constant. I looked at her face, highlighted in the flickering light, and she looked serene. I wondered if firelight did that no matter what you were thinking or if she could truly go for a while without thinking of the other thing.

The fire burned down and we went into the bedroom, where it was cold.

"I'll turn up the heat," I said.

"No. I like it cold. It makes it nicer under the covers."

She wore a long purple nightgown from Victoria's Secret that I'd bought for her on one of my trips. The nightgown fit tightly, the fabric clinging to her skin, and I could see the shape of the small bandage that she still had to wear over the place where they had made the cut. But it wasn't a turnoff. Just an unimportant disturbance in the smooth symmetry of her body. Like a mole, maybe. Or just a wrinkle in the fabric of the nightgown. Something I did not have to work to ignore because it came naturally.

She slid under the covers and said, "I'm so cold."

"I'll warm you up."

"Please do."

I went very slowly. This was about comfort and not about urgency. We were a long time just languidly touching each other and for a long time after that we were aroused but content and not rushed. One of those times when our moods and our needs meshed like our bodies and we became like one person under the covers in a cold room lit by a single candle.

"I'll remember that," she said. "Let's do it again when I'm back on the red wine."

21

Friday afternoon—three days before Leslie was scheduled to start her treatments—
I left work early to meet Brad at the airport. I had called him at school, where he'd
gone as soon as he finished at Quantico, and told him he needed to come home.
When he asked why, I said I would tell him when I saw him. When he pressed, I
told him not to worry, which was pointless. He would worry and I couldn't help
that. But I wasn't going to tell him that his mother had cancer over the telephone.

Brad had grown more and more distant from us—from me, especially—in
the last four or five years. I knew him as a sensitive boy, which he'd been until
he turned sixteen or seventeen. Then something changed and he seemed to turn
on things, himself included. There had been a brief fling with drugs. Chiefly
grass, I thought . . . or hoped. He had turned solitary, spending hours in his
room reading and listening to music. Then, when it was time to start sending
out college applications, he told me he wanted to go to military school. For some
reason, he settled on VMI. I wasn't sure what the initials stood for until he told
me: Virginia Military Institute.

I'd gone along, expecting him to quit once the realities hit. But he'd stuck it
out and made rank and now he was one of the senior cadet officers.

"A company commander," he'd told me over the phone. "I know it doesn't
mean anything to you, but it's a big responsibility. That's why I needed to come
straight back, to get things organized."

Leslie didn't understand his motives any better than I did, but it didn't seem to bother her. She seemed amused and also proud, in the unequivocal way that mothers are proud of their sons. She told me to be proud of him, too, and I was. But I didn't understand him. I was too young for the draft—Vietnam was over before I turned eighteen—so I didn't know how I would have done. I'd always told myself that I would have gone if I'd been needed, but that bet had never been called. Brad knew a lot more about that world than I ever would, and that just widened the gulf between us.

I picked him out of the crowd without any trouble. His hair was cut so close on the sides that you could see the scalp and wasn't much longer on the top. He'd told me once that this cut was called a "high and tight."

But he was not in uniform this trip. Instead he wore khaki pants and a blue fleece jacket with the letters USMC over the pocket in red.

"You look good," I said. "Thinner."

"Running hills will do it for you," he said. "How are you doing?"

"Fine. You have any luggage?"

"Just this." He held up a small, olive green duffel.

When we were in the car, I asked him about Quantico and he said, "Good training. Well, not training, really. More like a weeding out. About a third of the guys who started didn't make it."

"You did all right?"

"I loved it."

"I'm proud of you," I said. "I probably would have been one of the guys in the other third."

He nodded when I said that. Then, not really trying to recover, he said, "Probably not."

His voice had changed, too. It was huskier now but it sounded like an affectation. But that might have been a memory trick. I remembered a boy with a soft, almost plaintive voice.

"Did you eat on the plane?" I said. "Or do you want to stop somewhere for something?"

He shook his head, as though eating were an unimportant detail that civilians worried about.

"I'm not hungry."

"Okay."

"Listen, Dad," he said, "you're going to have to tell me sometime, so you might as well get on with it. I'm a big boy and I can take it. So what is it? You and Mom are getting a divorce, right?"

Why, I wondered, is that the thing that comes immediately to mind?

"No," I said. "We're fine. Let's stop for a beer and we'll talk."

"Sure," he said. "Works for me."

So we pulled in at the Earl of Kent, where Leslie and I had stopped on the day she gave me the news. I was beginning to date the recent past in that fashion; everything had happened either before or after that day.

It was still midafternoon and the place was empty. We took a table in the corner.

"What'll it be?" the bartender said. He'd come around to wait on us.

"Beer," Brad said. He didn't think much of people who paid attention to labels.

I ordered a Watney.

When our mugs came, we each took a drink. Then I said, "All right. A couple of weeks ago, your mother found a lump." I'd gotten comfortable with this euphemism. *Lump* was much easier for me to say than *cancer*.

Brad nodded. I looked at his face. His eyes were narrow and hard but there was still some youth around his mouth. It was full and made him look, almost, like he was pouting. I could see the strain there and also see that he was working hard to control it.

"She's had surgery," I went on. The words were coming more easily. "A lumpectomy. Very minor. She didn't even spend the night in the hospital. But the lump was malignant."

That word—*malignant*—was a little harder. But I could get it out.

"They got it, though. Right?" he said.

"The surgery was successful," I said. "But that's not the end of it."

But, man, don't I wish, I thought.

"She's going to be doing chemotherapy for the next few months. They use these drugs . . ."

"I know what chemo is, Dad. Cut to the chase, will you. Is she going to make it?"

"Yes. The doctors seem to think her prospects are excellent."

"But?"

"But what?"

"I don't know. You'll have to tell me. But there's more to it, isn't there?"

"No. I've told you what I know."

I could see more of the old Brad, now, in his face. See the familiar expression of a child who had been desolate for days when his dog died.

"Come on," he said. "Level with me."

"I am."

"Well, then," he said, "if everything is all right, why am I home and why aren't you telling me how good the news is? You should be telling me that she was sick but now she's well. But you're not telling me that. And you don't think that, do you?"

"It isn't a disease that works that way," I said. "It's not like you've got pneumonia, where one day the fever goes down and you're well."

"Jesus Christ, Dad," he said. "I *know* that."

"Then you know what I know."

We sat there for a moment in the quiet, empty bar, our mugs on the table between us and Brad giving off suspicion and youthful impatience like heat.

"Do you trust the doctors?"

"Yes."

"Are they telling you everything?"

"Your mother talks to them more than I do."

He thought about that for a minute.

"And she's not telling you everything. That's it, then, isn't it?"

I nodded. "There were more tests," I said. "After the surgery. I still don't know how they turned out."

"You think she might be hiding something from you?"

"Not 'hiding,' exactly."

"Call it what you want."

"All right."

He finished his beer and signaled for another, like he was waving for a trooper in the field to join up with him. He didn't say anything until the bartender had refilled our mugs.

"You know, it would be just like her. I imagine she purely hated telling you in the first place. Almost as much as she hated having the disease. Never wants to be a burden, does she? Doesn't want to depend on anyone. The whole nine yards."

"That's her."

"So what do you really think?"

"I think it's going to be all right."

It occurred to me, as I said it, that this was true. That *was* what I thought. But it wasn't based on any evidence, only the hope that things would go on the way they had been . . . and a fear of what it would be like if they didn't. Still, I wasn't trying to deceive him.

He nodded, and his expression was suddenly grave and looked much too old for his still-fleshy face.

"I do, too. She's so strong . . ."

He didn't finish the thought.

"She's been great," I said. "Very brave. Incredibly brave."

I sounded like I was trying to sell him.

"I can imagine," he said. "I can't remember her ever being sick."

I nodded this time.

We fell into a silence again and I played with the damp napkin under my mug. I needed to do something with my hands. His were on the table and trembling very slightly. He must not have noticed or he wouldn't have let me see it.

"What can I do to help you out?" he said. "I could take a leave from school. Come home for as long as you need me."

"We're not there, yet. If we do get there, I'll call you and take you up on it."

"Is that a promise?"

"Yes."

"There has to be something I can do. I mean, I can't just go back to school and go on like everything is just the same old deal. Not if my mother has cancer."

The word didn't seem to hold the same dread for him. He had no trouble saying it, anyway.

"Call her from school. That makes her day. Send her cards. Flowers."

"You want me to be the morale officer?"

"Sure," I said. "That sounds right."

"Okay, I'm all over it," he said and reached across the table to give me his hand to shake. His hand was larger than mine and his grip was strong and firm. But I couldn't help remembering the tiny hand I'd held so many times when he was little and uncertain and depending on me.

Things had changed. That was before; this was after.

Now holding his hand made *me* feel better.

22

Brad hugged his mother harder than he had in years, until she said, "All right, enough. I'm very glad you're home. You look wonderful, even with that ridiculous haircut, but I want both of you to listen to me. There is something I need to tell you."

We were in the kitchen, where she had been cooking. She always made a production of dinner when one or both of her children came home.

Brad and I looked at each other with "here it comes" expressions.

"I imagine your father has told you about my condition," she said, looking at Brad first and then me.

"Yes."

"Good. I'm glad. Then I don't have to. I have cancer and I'm being treated. I have good doctors. I like them and I trust them. I'm also fighting this wretched disease in my own crackpot ways. I'm being positive and, as your mother, I'm telling you to be positive, too."

She pointed at Brad with a wooden spoon.

"You understand that, don't you?"

"Yes, ma'am," Brad said, sounding like he was six again. In his own mind, probably, he was. He might be a marine but she was still his mother.

"Good. I knew you would. You always were an obedient child—off and on."

She pointed the spoon next at me, where it stayed.

"Now," she said, "here is what I want to say to both of you. I have been looking forward to this weekend like I haven't looked forward to anything since I thought I was getting a pony for Christmas. Andy comes in on the bus in a couple of hours and this will be the first time we've all been together in months. This is my treat and nothing is going to spoil it. I will not have people acting like I'm sick. Do you understand?"

"Yes, ma'am," Brad said.

Leslie had insisted the children call her "ma'am" when they were little. The North Carolina heritage, I suppose. It embarrassed them around their playmates, but she didn't care.

"And you?" she said to me.

"Yes, ma'am," I said.

"All right. Good. And another thing. We are not going to talk about it. Not at all. Not one word."

She paused and we both nodded.

"I may be sick but I feel fine. The only thing that makes me feel bad is talking about cancer. That makes my head hurt. And I won't have that. I'm going to enjoy this little bit of time together with my family and I can't do that if I have a headache."

Brad and I nodded again.

"So we're all straight on that? All on the same page?"

"For sure," Brad said.

"Absolutely," I said.

"Good," Leslie said. "That's good. Now I feel happy. My family is home and we're going to have a wonderful time and . . . that's that."

We had leg of lamb for dinner. It had always been one of the kids' favorite things. Leslie had roasted small red potatoes in garlic and oil and braised carrots and leeks to go with the lamb and we brought out a bottle of wine we'd been saving.

We used the good china and the wedding silver and the wineglasses she saved for dinner parties.

It was all very nice and very adult but the mood, at first, was brittle. We sounded like strangers trying to make small talk and not doing a very good job of it. It was Andy, who had been the imp when she was younger, who brought us all around.

"I wonder what ever happened to Lightning," she said, out of the blue.

"*My* turtle, you mean," Brad said.

And that got us started. We were quickly back to another time, more than ten years ago, searching the house for the box turtle Brad had found somewhere. The turtle had lived in a cage he'd fixed up in his room. Andy had taken the turtle out to play with it and gone on to something else. Then, when Brad had come home and asked about the turtle, she'd confessed. But the turtle wasn't where she'd left it in her room, and for the next several days it was one of those family crises with a lot of tears from Brad and Andy and a lot of impatient yelling from me. I remembered that part and still regretted it.

We went through the house, again and again, including the crawl spaces and all the closets. We looked under everything and behind everything and in every little hiding place we could think of. But we never found Lightning.

"You took him outside and let him go," Brad said. "I said so then, and I say so now."

He was smiling now, but he hadn't been back then.

"You just had the only turtle in the world that could walk downstairs and open a door," Andy said defiantly. "And you shouldn't have been keeping him in a cage, anyway. Animals need to be free."

She raised her arm over her head and made a fist. "Free Lightning," she said. "Power to the turtles. The man has been putting the turtles down for too long."

"What *do* you suppose happened to that turtle?" Leslie said. She was laughing now. In the light of the candles, holding her wineglass in one hand and gesturing with her other, she looked utterly untroubled.

* * *

After dinner, I made a fire and we played hearts in front of it. Brad concentrated on the game and won. Andy, who couldn't keep track of what had been played, was the big loser.

"Picking on me. You are all picking on me," she said. "All my life, I've been picked on. I suffer from SCS."

"What's that?" Brad said.

"Second child syndrome," she said smugly.

"You want victim points for that, I guess?" Brad said.

"It's only fair."

When we lost interest in the cards, we sat in the room where we had spent so much time together and watched the fire as it burned down. Leslie and Andy sat close together on a small sofa, and when I looked at them I was struck, as always, by the resemblance, and also by the fragility of it all. We weren't much more than shared genes and shared memories and it could all disappear without a trace.

Just like Lightning.

23

In the morning, before it was fully light, I heard Brad coming down the stairs, trying to be silent about it, the way he had when he was a little boy, sneaking food. But the stairs still creaked, the way they had back then. I heard the door open when he went outside, and I made it to the window in time to see him, in his running clothes, heading down the driveway. I went back to sleep, fitfully, until I heard the door open again.

He was in the kitchen, drying off with a towel. His clothes were soaked with sweat.

"Good run?"

"Sorry," he said. "I didn't mean to wake you up."

"No problem."

"What about Mom?"

"She's still sleeping."

"Good,"

"You want coffee? I'll make some."

"Sure," he said. "You know, Dad, Mom looks good."

"Yeah," I said. "She does."

"I mean, she doesn't look like someone who just had surgery."

"The surgery was pretty minor. Like I told you, she was home that night."

"Yeah. Still . . ."

"She says she's never felt better."

The beeper on the coffeemaker went off and I poured two cups.

"Milk or sugar?"

"Black," he said.

We sat at the kitchen table.

"I can't believe the way she's handling it."

"She's strong," I said.

"It's almost like . . ." He struggled with the thought for a minute and took a sip of his coffee while he tried to find the words. "Like, I'm more worried, you know, than she is. I mean, this is some scary stuff. I know I don't have to tell you that. But I couldn't get to sleep last night."

I nodded.

"Last night was fun, you know. All of us laughing and remembering those things. It was like nothing's changed. But Andy is in Boston, being a hippie artist, and I'm in Virginia trying to be a stud marine. And Mom's still here, just like always, but she's got cancer."

His voice had lost all its authority and seemed to tremble just a little.

"I know what you mean," I said.

"Look, Dad," he said. "Make me a promise, will you?"

"Sure. I'll try."

"Just keep me in the loop. Tell me everything. Good or bad."

"All right."

"It's just such a really bad deal. I mean, why her?"

"That's what everyone says."

"Yeah, I guess."

We'd just finished breakfast when Leslie came into the kitchen.

"You two are going to be on your own for most of the day," she said. "I know you won't mind. Just do some boy things. Change the oil. Watch a football game. Drink beer and bond."

"What are you and Andy doing?" I said.

"We have errands to run. It's a girl thing. You wouldn't understand."

So Brad and I changed the oil in my truck. We also flushed the radiator, changed the plugs and the air filter, and hit all the lube points. Brad slid under the truck, without my asking, and I handed him the filter wrench and the grease gun. In the old days it had been the other way around.

We made sandwiches for lunch and sat in the backyard while we ate. Then we took the tractor and the chain saw down to the tree line to finish splitting and bucking the fallen ash. Brad did the sawing. He was wearing a T-shirt and his arms glistened with sweat. They were thick and supple from hours in the weight room and the weeks at Quantico. He would not let me take over after he'd run through the first tank of gas.

"Give me a break, will you?" I said. "I'm not so old I can't run a chain saw."

"I know. But I don't get the chance and it's fun."

We had the tools cleaned up and put away and were drinking beer in the back-yard when Leslie and Andy drove in.

"Well, well. Did you boys have fun?" Leslie said.

"Yes, ma'am," Brad said. "We do everything you tell us to."

"Good. Now I want you to go up to your room and bring down all those old baseball hats that are sitting on your closet shelf."

He gave her a puzzled look. "Are you going to throw them away? Like you did all my old Power Ranger toys?"

"Just be a good boy and do what I tell you."

"Yes, ma'am."

"And you go get one of the bar stools from the kitchen counter," she said to Andy, who simply nodded with an expression that said she knew why her mother wanted the bar stool and did not necessarily like it.

"What's up?" I said.

"You'll see. Meanwhile, you can get me a long extension cord. Plug it in somewhere inside and run it out here."

When we were all back outside with the bar stool, the hats, and the extension cord, Leslie said, "All right, the only thing we need now is some music."

She went inside, and when she came back out the sound of Delbert McClinton was coming loudly through the open window.

She carried a small shopping bag in one hand and an old beach towel in the other. She tied the corners of the towel behind her neck and knotted them so she looked like a kid wearing an absurdly long bib. Then she reached into the bag, pulled out a pair of barber's clippers, and plugged them into the extension cord.

She handed the clippers to Andy and said, "All right. Everybody get a good look. This is the last time you'll see me with hair for a long time."

"Wait a second," I said.

"Hey, *Mom*," Brad said.

She held up her hands like a speaker at a podium, calling for silence.

"Hush. Andy and I spent the morning shopping for wigs and turbans and we did a very good job. I have two wigs that are just divinely trashy and a turban that makes me look like a nun. I'll give you a fashion show, lucky boys, but not until I get rid of this hair. So just shut up and watch."

"I don't think . . ."

But she didn't let me finish. She gave me the look that said she had thought it over and made up her mind and there was no point in discussing it further.

"This hair," she said firmly, "is going. One way or the other. It can be the slow way, where you pull a handful out every time you shampoo, or wake up and find a clump on the pillow and cry. Or, it can be fast and clean. Hair one minute and gone the next."

None of us laughed. Or even tried to.

"All right," she said, and her eyes began to glitter, "you can stand here and sulk, if you want, or you can go off somewhere and do it in private. I don't care.

I'm going to get rid of this hair, right now, even if I have to shave my head myself. But I'd appreciate it if you'd stay around and try not to act like it's a funeral or something. It's just hair. Isn't that what you've always said?"

She looked at me when she said it and she wanted an answer.

"Just hair," I said. "Absolutely."

I caught a glimpse of Andy from the corner of my eye. She was trying to smile but her lip was quivering. She held the clippers like they had scales.

"Hair grows back," Leslie said. "Next year we'll all be back here and Andy can give me a wave."

"Right," I said. "A wave. Whatever that is."

"And you?" She looked at Brad.

He looked back at her with a frozen stare.

"Well?"

He tried to say something, but couldn't form the words.

"Come on. Speak up or go somewhere and come back when it's over."

I could see the muscle below his ear working. Wood chips were stuck to his neck and they were moving as he swallowed.

He looked up. His eyes glistened but he forced a smile.

"Just hair," he said. "Expendable civilian baggage. Bald is beautiful. Bald is bad. Go for it, Mom."

So Leslie sat down on the bar stool and said, almost gaily, "Okay, Andy, let's do it."

24

Andy ran the clippers through Leslie's hair, right down close to the scalp, taking away a clean two-inch-wide row like a mower going through a field of hay. She started right in the middle of Leslie's head, so the cut was like a part, only wider. Seeing the white of Leslie's scalp was a shock and felt faintly embarrassing, like walking into a room without knocking and surprising someone who's naked.

Each pass of the clippers left another exposed trail of pale, white scalp, and as I watched, my memory dredged up old images from pictures I'd seen in some magazine of the French women who had taken German soldiers for lovers during the occupation and were marched, after the liberation, into the town square, where patriots ceremoniously shaved their heads as some kind of punishment and example. It seemed simultaneously petty and cruel.

I also thought, as the hair from Leslie's head dropped from the beach towel to the ground, of all the hours of attention and concern she had lavished on it. All the photographs she had studied in all the magazines, wondering if she could make her hair do what Farrah Fawcett's did. Or, lately, what Ashley Judd's did. All those hours sitting in other chairs while another woman worked on that hair and talked with Leslie about how to get the look she wanted. I'd seen the hair in different lengths and different colors, straight and curled, coiffed and casual. I could tell from the faint burned-rope smell when I came home after work that she was fooling with some new dye. I'd listened to her talk on the phone with her friends about some new look or other and whether it worked or not. It was, I suppose, like watching someone who had spent years in a gym—lifting weights, building muscle, and sculpting his body—now wasting away in a few seconds right before your eyes.

Leslie's face was set. Hard, like she was trying not to flinch. It was a look I'd seen when I worked on her with a needle and tweezers, trying to get a splinter out.

"Talk about your new look," I said, trying for a mood.

She made an attempt at a smile but it came off as a grimace.

Andy was biting down on her lower lip, trying not to cry. She kept her eyes on her hands, probably so she wouldn't be able to take in the whole picture.

Brad stood next to me, not saying anything and trying not to show anything and revealing everything in the effort.

The first shearing took less than ten minutes.

"Now change to the other shears and get rid of the burr," Leslie said when Andy was finished. Her head looked like it was covered with a layer of soot.

Andy's fingers trembled and she had trouble making them work. Brad took the clippers from her and changed the comb deftly, like he was at the range, swapping magazines in his M-16.

"Here," he said tenderly, handing the clippers back to Andy. "You're doing great."

"Thanks," she said. Her voice sounded thin and very young.

"Once more, into the breach, dear friends," Brad said, and put his hand on her shoulder.

"What?"

"Nothing. Never mind. Just press on; you're doing fine."

Andy ran the clippers over Leslie's head again. The burr disappeared, leaving skin that wasn't exactly white but not dirty gray anymore, either. It was the color of the keys on a well-used piano.

There was a jagged three-inch scar, slightly down from the centerline of Leslie's head, above her right ear.

"What's that?" I said.

"What?"

"The scar."

"Just a kid thing," she said. "I fell out of a tree. Fractured my skull and cut my scalp. Bled like crazy and scared my poor mother to death."

"How old were you?" Andy said. She had her voice back, now that she was curious about some detail from her mother's life.

"Seven. I remember they had to shave a big patch of my head then, too. So this isn't anything new. I'm an old hand at it. Pass me that mirror."

Andy gave her a little makeup mirror that had been in the bag with the clippers.

Leslie took it and, without hesitating, held it up to examine herself. She studied the mirror with a kind of detached expression and said, "Not bad. Helps to have a nice, symmetrical head."

And, in fact, it *wasn't* that bad. A little strange, maybe, but not bad. Not something that made you want to cut your eyes away and look at the ground. Or maybe you just get used to things you didn't think you'd ever be able to accommodate, and much more quickly than you ever thought you could.

"Should I shave it? Like Michael Jordan and them?"

"Why not? Then you can wax and buff it. I've got a can of Simonize."

"No. That's too much. We don't want to go over the top."

But I did go inside and get a new disposable razor and a can of shaving cream. Andy lathered Leslie's head, then worked the razor through the creamy white soap. Her hands were no longer shaking and her strokes were clean and precise.

"Nice job," Leslie said when Andy finished. "Never nicked me. Not even once."

"I'll get a garbage bag," Brad said, "for all this old hair."

We all looked down at the mound of hair at Leslie's feet, piled like wool on the ground after a sheep has been sheared.

"No," Leslie said. "No garbage bag."

She bent over and collected the hair with both hands.

"This goes on the compost," she said. "And next spring it goes on my peonies."

We all picked up a scrap or two of the hair that she had missed and followed her to the wood line where I'd piled the plant cuttings.

We'd buried a dog, once, not far from this spot. The kids had been young and had cried over the dog and brought little clumps of wildflowers to decorate the grave for the first few days before grass grew back over the bare ground and they lost interest. I wondered if they remembered now and decided probably not and good for them.

25

Leslie tried on all of Brad's old baseball hats and settled on one in The University of North Carolina's color.

"If God is not a Tarheel," she said, "then explain to me why the sky is Carolina blue. Come on; anyone?"

Nobody had an answer.

"All right, then, this will be my main hat. As a backup, I'm going with this cute little red number from Ford with the slogan, 'This is Ford country. At night we sit around and listen to the Chevys rust.'"

Brad promised to send her one in blue with red letters that spelled out USMC.

The turbans, which she modeled, weren't much of a hit. There was something formal and austere about them and they didn't suit the mood. The wigs, though, went over big.

Especially the one she wore to dinner. It was short, brushed back, and curled up sort of dramatically at the ends. It brought back to my mind images of miniskirts and knee-high vinyl boots.

"I mean," Leslie said when she modeled it for us, "do I look like a tart, or what?"

"Way bad, Mom," Brad said. "Way, way bad."

* * *

Later, when we played cards in the living room, she said, "This thing is so hot. I don't see how Dolly Parton can stand it. Does anyone mind if I take it off and switch to a baseball hat?"

"No," we said, almost in unison.

And, actually, it was easier getting used to the hat than the fake hair. Even though I couldn't remember having ever seen Leslie in a baseball hat before. For some reason, it looked right for her to be wearing the one from Carolina with the bill bent just so and the crown crimped perfectly.

"Styling, Mom," Brad said. "You do know how to wear that hat."

"Well, thank you," Leslie said. "That's sweet of you to say."

Brad left Sunday afternoon. He got a ride to the airport from one of his old high-school friends who had dropped out of college and come back home to live with his parents. Brad and Leslie hugged in the kitchen.

"Listen, Mom," Brad said, standing at the open door, "there is one thing I gotta ask you before I go."

She seemed to flinch a little. It had all gone so well up until now.

"All right," she said, warily.

"It's been bothering me all weekend and I have to know."

"What?"

"Well, I can't go back to school until I find out . . ."

"Fine, *fine*. But what is it?"

Brad took a deep breath and said, "Okay. What I want to know is . . . did you get the pony?"

"Of course," Leslie said, smiling broadly. "I always get what I want."

Andy went to the movies with a friend. It was the first time Leslie and I had been alone all weekend.

"I'd almost forgotten what it was like to have them around," she said.

"Amazing how much quieter things are."

"I miss it, though," Leslie said.

"Me, too . . . I guess."

"You do," she said. "Go on and admit it."

"All right. I miss them. I also like it when it is just us."

"Just you, the dogs, and your bald, sick wife."

"You look good bald," I said.

"Kind of you to say so."

"And you don't act sick."

"I don't feel sick."

"That might change tomorrow."

"Why should it?"

"Well, you know . . . the chemo."

I couldn't imagine that she'd forgotten.

"There's no chemo tomorrow," she said. There was something behind the matter-of-fact words and tone that chilled me.

"Why not? I thought we were going to the hospital tomorrow so you could start the treatments."

"Something came up," she said. "I didn't want to tell you and spoil the weekend."

"What?" I said.

"That last mammogram?" she said, making it sound like a question.

"Yes."

"They found another lump."

I felt my insides go cold and then liquid and I wanted to sit down.

"So we'll do more tests tomorrow. This one isn't cancer, but we still have to do the tests."

"How do they know it isn't cancer?" The word came out, almost without my realizing it.

"They don't. That's why they're doing the tests."

"I don't get it."

"They might not know it isn't cancer. But I know."

"How?"

"I'm not sure. I just do."

"Okay," I said.

She put a hand on my cheek. "I know how it sounds," she said. "But trust me. I found the first lump and I knew it was cancer even when I was telling myself it wasn't. They found this one and when I felt it, I knew it wasn't cancer."

"And the tests?"

"Same as before. A needle biopsy. We'll know the results before lunch."

"So what time do we leave in the morning?"

"You don't need to go. Andy and I will drive down."

"I'm going. What time?"

"Aren't you worried about missing too much time at the office? We'll be fine. Really."

"What time?"

"Same as before."

I couldn't think of anything to say, so I just said, "We'd better get to bed early."

Which was a great help to everyone, I'm sure.

26

Leslie was right. It wasn't cancer; just some kind of cyst.

After the hospital, we went to the Legal and ordered chowder for lunch again. And I asked her, again, how she'd known.

"I just knew what the first one felt like," she shrugged, "and this one felt different."

"How sure were you?"

"Close enough. There aren't any sure things."

"So why cut your hair? What's the hurry? Why not wait another week?"

"I wanted to do it while Brad and Andy were home," she said, as though it should be obvious. "That was the whole point. I didn't want Brad coming home for Christmas and finding some bald-headed old woman living in his mother's house."

She was wearing her Carolina baseball hat. It made her look younger.

"So, now that the doctors agree with me on this new thing they found, I'll still do chemo. I'll just start a week later. I was never in that big of a hurry anyway.

"So what I'm going to do right now is enjoy this chowder. I may even order some cherrystones. I don't imagine I'll have much of an appetite for them once the chemo starts."

* * *

There were several messages on the machine when we got home but only one for me, from my assistant. They wanted me to be in a little early. Around seven-thirty, say. And would I please call if I couldn't make it.

"What's that about?" Leslie said.

"I dunno."

"Take a guess," she said.

"Something about the way business is going south, I'd guess. Not just us. The whole industry. So we're probably in a stage-one panic. At this meeting, they'll tell all department heads to freeze hiring, make sure that you book a Saturday overnight when you travel, cut back on FedEx if you can use the USPS, write on both sides of the paper and reuse paper clips. That sort of thing."

"Are you worried?"

"Nope."

"What if you're in trouble?"

"You mean the company?"

"No, *you*."

"My department is ahead of projections," I said. "It's showing the highest net profit of any department in the company. When the whole company goes down, then I'll worry."

"What about all this time you've been taking off?"

"Three or four days?" I said. "In ten years I've never taken a sick day. Anyway, they don't keep track of my hours. They look at the P&L."

"You're sure?"

"Yes. Not something for you to worry about."

But I worried. I lay awake, watching the glowing digital numbers roll over on the alarm clock, feeling like there was something in the air and that maybe this meeting would be about a lot more than holding down on the FedEx bills.

I'd find out soon enough. That, anyway, is what I kept telling myself, and sometime around three o'clock I made my point and went to sleep.

Inch by Inch

The meeting started right on time. The CEO—and majority shareholder in a family that held them all—looked good. Thin and tanned. He traveled a lot and had just come back from trekking in the Himalayas. When he learned his company was struggling, he called this meeting and told his assistant to order in fruit, rolls, bagels, coffee, tea, and juice.

"I was hoping for an Egg McMuffin," I heard somebody say under his breath.

"Hi, I'm Ron," the CEO said to start the meeting. "Most of you know me and I know most of you. The two or three of you who are new should stick around after this meeting is over so I can meet you and we can get acquainted."

This was followed by a little homily about the great company he owned and we all worked for. The tradition. The success. The reputation for excellence. *Excellence* was one of Ron's favorite words.

Then came the bad news. Because of "general economic conditions," the company was "experiencing a shrinking revenue stream." Furthermore, "forecasts were not promising."

I heard someone whisper, "Hey, Ron, tell us something we don't already know."

Which Ron proceeded to do.

To "meet the coming challenges," Ron said, the company was going to have to "accommodate and innovate." We would have to "move inside the cycle."

Whatever that meant.

He had hired some outside consultants, Ron went on, and they would be "studying the company, taking it down to the last nuts and bolts, over the next several weeks."

They would be looking for ways to "reshape and reorganize" to make the company "leaner and more effective."

Looking for people to fire, in other words.

When the consultants dropped by our offices to talk, Ron went on, he hoped we would cooperate enthusiastically, since we were "all in this together" and a successful reorganization meant a "brighter future for all of us."

As we were all standing up to leave, the man who had been sitting next to me—he was in accounting and I never could remember his name—said, "And I got up early for *that*?"

On the way out of the meeting room, my boss stopped me and said, "We have things to talk about. Come by my office, please."

"Sure."

"In an hour," she said.

"See you then."

Elena LeFevre had been with the company for one year. That gave me nine years on her. I was one of the old-timers from the days before we had voice mail or even interoffice mail. Back then we would just shout down the hall if we needed to talk to someone about something.

But it wasn't necessarily a good thing to be one of the old hands. Among the new breed of MBAs, like Elena, we were considered dinosaurs and obstructionists who couldn't—or wouldn't—adjust to the new ways of thinking. A lot of those people I had once shouted to down the hall were gone. Not all of them by choice.

I'd worked hard adjusting, though. I liked to tell myself that I was actually valued by the new wave as a voice of experience, but not one who was always talking about how we'd done things in the old days.

Like a lot of the new blood, Elena was smart about business in the abstract but didn't know much about the actual business we were in. We sold outdoor gear and she was fond of saying that her idea of roughing it was a night at the Holiday Inn. She had learned how to fly-fish by going to a glossy lodge for three days where they taught you on stocked ponds before letting you get out on a river for a couple of hours on your last afternoon.

"I've *been* fishing," she said a couple of weeks later when someone invited her to go out to a local stream. As far as I knew she had never been again.

But she was a demon for work and one of the stars in the company. She liked the idea of business as conflict and she was always talking about "burying" our competition. One of her favorite expressions was "Take no prisoners."

Still, we got along. She had energy and she didn't mind passing the credit around when things went well. She could laugh about herself and the way that she was completely unlike the people we tried to sell things to. She was divorced and had a daughter who was barely school-age and she would occasionally ask me about some little thing having to do with the kid, like how to get her riding a bike. Her child was what we talked about other than work.

She listened when I made suggestions, as long as I stayed within what she considered my area of expertise. She thought I was knowledgeable about tents, sleeping bags, and parkas. When I got into the new areas where the company was expanding—"broadening the brand"—her eyes would glaze over and you could feel her impatience.

"You'd better shut the door, Jack," she said when I was inside her office. "And sit down."

I did.

"So," she said, "what do you think?"

"It sounds serious," I said.

She nodded. "Have you ever been through a downsizing?"

"No."

"It can get very ugly."

"Since I've been here, this company has done nothing but grow."

"That's one of the problems."

"Really? Seems like we're always trying to 'grow the company,'" I said, trying to mimic Ron. That was one of his trademark expressions.

She frowned. Which I took as a sign that she thought I was being flip and that it was inappropriate. She was a good-looking woman but she seldom smiled.

She had full hair that framed her face and she was always made up carefully in a way that was not quite austere. She had perfect white teeth and when she did smile, it lit up her whole face. But she was more than just "attractive," and now and then you would hear people around the office speculating on her love life. The gossips thought she didn't have one, that she would consider it a distraction, unless the man could help her on the corporate ladder. I'd always considered that unfair. When I thought about it at all, I thought she might be lonely.

When she frowned, I waited. No point in trying to rush in and cover my tracks. If she didn't like my little joke, it wouldn't be the first time. One of the knocks on us old guys was that we weren't serious enough.

"When flowers grow," she said, "that's good. When weeds grow, that's bad. When they both grow . . . well, the weeds can kill the flowers. Unless you pull them, or poison them."

It occurred to me that she hadn't used cancer for her growth metaphor. I wondered if that was from sensitivity.

"You're saying that's where the company is? That it's time to pull weeds?"

"Isn't it obvious?"

I didn't say anything.

"Even Ron realizes it," she said. "That's got to be hard on him. You know how he's always saying about how this company is "family"? Well, I think he's finally looked around and seen that he's going to have to cut off some of the deadbeat in-laws or lose the whole estate. He likes going to Nepal and he likes sitting on boards and going to conferences. But he needs a healthy company to keep that going."

I didn't have anything to add to that. I nodded so she would know I got it.

"Since we're all 'family,' Ron can't bear to do what's necessary and he's hired an outplacement specialist to do it for him. I've seen it before. Those guys are like undertakers who love their work."

"So what do we do?"

"Start pulling weeds," she said, emphatically. "I want ten names by the end of the week."

"What if we don't have that many weeds?"

"Pick out the flowers that are stunted. And put it in a memo, on paper. No e-mail."

"Ten?"

"We're going to be proactive on this. I'm the one running this division. Not the consultants."

"All right," I said, feeling a sense of dismay. I'd never fired anyone.

I stood up and was leaving when she said, "By the way . . ."

I turned back around and she was looking at me with an expression I couldn't quite read. Concern? Curiosity? Compassion?

"Yes?"

"Is everything all right with you, Jack?"

"Sure," I said. "This is just unexpected news. Takes a while."

"No," she said, "I mean with you. Personally."

"Sure," I said. "I'm fine."

I was saying that more and more, it seemed.

"Okay," she said. "But you've been out a lot lately, so I thought I should ask. In case, you know, there might be something I could do."

"No. Nothing. But thanks for thinking of it."

"Certainly," she said, and gave me one of her rare smiles.

I nodded and turned again to go back to my own work.

"Leave it open," she said behind me when I got to the door.

27

It was still a shock, seeing Leslie with no hair when I came home at night. I felt something else, too. Pity, maybe, but I tried not to let it show.

"Takes some getting used to, doesn't it?" she would say.

"No. I'm just surprised at how good you look without hair."

"You're a liar, Jack. A sweet one, but a liar just the same."

"It just takes some getting used to."

"Tell me about it. Just imagine *my* surprise when I reach up to fluff my hair."

"It'll grow back."

"I know. Anyway, I'm over it. Don't worry about me."

When she asked, ritually, about my day, I would say it was just another boring day at the office and wonder if I shouldn't be leveling with her.

Trust your instincts, I thought. And my instinct was that she didn't need to hear it. She had enough to worry about and my woes were no big deal. I was just feeling the pressure of having to decide which ten people out of forty who worked for me were going to be fired. Those were the people who would have a reason to feel sorry for themselves. Not me.

Still, I'd always considered myself a fairly open sort. It wasn't a virtue and might have been laziness more than anything else. I'd always found it hard to keep secrets, but I was learning to conceal things and trying to get good at it. One more thing in my life that had changed, I thought, and surely not the last.

By the end of the week I had the ten names. I put them on paper and put the paper in an envelope, which I sealed and left on Elena's desk. I went home feeling a kind of guilty relief and did not think about it again all weekend long. Early Monday morning Leslie and I left for Boston and the first of her treatments.

Leslie called it "Chemoville," and that made it sound sinister. I'm not sure just what I expected. But something worse than what it turned out to be.

There was the usual counter where you identified yourself to someone who looked your name up on a computer and gave you some forms to fill out. There was a jar of hard candy on the counter. Also a flower arrangement.

Once the paperwork was done, the receptionist told Leslie to have a seat, that the nurse would be along in a minute. And, for once, it wasn't much longer than that.

"Hi," she said, "I'm Patty. I know you're nervous, but try not to be."

She was short and very fair, with a wide smile and green eyes that just screamed Irish. Right away you imagined her as the adored daughter of a cop or a fireman whose sons caught unshirted hell any time they teased their sister.

"Nice to meet you," Leslie said.

We followed her around a partition. There were a lot of them. They'd been put up to make semiprivate little spaces where patients sat in easy chairs with needles in their arms and tubes running from the needles to IV bags full of red fluid. We walked by a half-dozen of those little partitioned spaces, all of them occupied. None of the patients seemed to notice. They looked right past you. Or right through you.

When we came to an unoccupied space with an empty chair, Patty said, "Go ahead and sit down. I'll be right back."

With her hands on her hips, Leslie surveyed the little space like it was a Manhattan apartment and she was considering a sublease.

"Well, well," she said. "Isn't this nice. Very cozy."

"If you say so."

"I do," Leslie said. She took off her jacket, hung it on a hook, and sat in the chair.

"And the furniture is nice, too. Very plush."

Her voice sounded a little thin. I tried to think of something to say.

"You need a cushion or something? I could run out and get one."

She smiled. Wanly. "No. But you're sweet to ask. There's nothing wrong with the chair, or the room. I just wish it didn't have to be a needle. I hate needles. I never did get the junkie thing. How could anyone *like* needles?"

"Just don't look," I said. Helpful as always.

"You can be sure of that," she said. "I am going to close my eyes and keep them closed until I feel that thing come out of my arm. I don't care if I have to keep them closed all day."

"It won't be that long, will it?"

"More like an hour," Patty said, "maybe an hour and a half." She had come back around the partition, wheeling one of those rigs they use to hang the IVs. A bag of red fluid was swinging from the arm.

Patty's smile was kind and reassuring. She talked while she arranged things, going on about how far we'd had to drive and was the traffic bad and were the leaves turning where we lived and wasn't it just beautiful there. The talk was as diverting as it was probably meant to be. The mood was more school-mixer than cancer ward.

When everything was in place and Patty was about to wrap the rubber strap to make a vein pop, Leslie said, "Wait a minute. I need to get ready."

She had a disc player and headphones in her bag. Also four double-A batteries that were still in the blister pack. She unwrapped them and put them in the disc player, handing me the old batteries and the plastic wrapping.

"I want to make sure the music lasts all the way through this thing," she said.

"What are you listening to?" Patty said.

"I've got Lou Rawls and Vladimir Horowitz. I figure one of them ought to work."

She plugged the headphones into the CD player. Before she put them on, she looked up at me. "You don't have to stick around, Jack. Go out and find something to do for an hour. I'm going to turn on the music and close my eyes and I'm not going to open them again until I feel that thing come out of my arm."

"Then you won't know whether I'm here or not. So don't worry about it."

"I see your point."

She put the headphones on and closed her eyes.

28

Patty wrapped the rubber strap around Leslie's arm, made a quick swipe with the alcohol swab, and then stuck the needle into her vein. It went in so deftly that Leslie didn't even flinch.

She laid a small strip of tape over the needle and pressed the edges down to make them stick. With the needle held in place, she checked the tube running to the bottle of red fluid and then fine-tuned the flow.

"That should do it," she said.

Leslie had the headphones on and couldn't hear.

"Thank you," I said.

"Not a problem," Patty said. "She's a good patient."

She had other patients to set up—I wondered how many arms she stabbed every day—and said she would be back in a little while to see how things were going.

I stood next to Leslie, looking at her and thinking *Well, it has started now,* and even though the room all around us was full of other cancer patients with poison dripping into their veins, too, it felt like it was just the two of us. For her, I imagine, it was worse. She had to feel like she was entirely alone. I reached for her free hand and held it. Without opening her eyes, she squeezed my hand and I squeezed back. We sat like that for fifteen or twenty minutes, until Patty returned to check on Leslie. A few minutes later Andy came by after her morning classes.

I gave Andy a hug and she gave me a sad, limpid smile. I stayed around another minute or two, then left to find a bathroom. I didn't know where to look, so I wandered for a while and felt, almost, like I had gotten myself into a maze. The entire floor, a full city block, seemed to be divided by partitions that created dozens of small spaces like the one where Leslie was sitting. In every one of these spaces, there was someone sitting in a chair with drugs dripping into a vein. There was a lot of hope riding on all that red fluid, some of it the quiet, firm kind that Leslie seemed to have found. But a lot of it, judging by the bleak and ashen faces I found myself staring into when I came around some of those partitions, was desperate and almost forlorn, like the hope of someone who has put his last chip on the table in Atlantic City and doesn't have enough left in his pocket for a bus ticket back to Queens.

I felt guilty for being healthy while they were ill. Like a young guy in civilian clothes, standing on a dock somewhere, watching while the casualties are being loaded off a troopship on stretchers.

I finally asked an orderly how to find the men's room and then how to get back to the admitting desk, where I'd get directions to Patty's station.

When I got there, Leslie had taken her headphones off. She was holding Andy's hand and the two of them were talking. They looked cheerful, like a couple of women who were glad to have run into each other accidentally because they had a lot to catch up on. Leslie was sitting in her chair, looking away from the arm with the needle stuck in it. Andy was sitting on the arm of the chair.

She sensed my presence before her mother did.

"Hey, Dad, I got you some coffee. Here."

She handed me a cup—a large one—of coffee that was not Starbucks.

"You went out for this?"

"Nah. I didn't want to wait around in line, so I got a friend to bring it up for me. I keep her cat every now and then, so she owes me."

"Well, thanks."

"No prob."

"Patty says I should be ready to leave in a little bit," Leslie said.

"Good. What else did she tell you?"

"Like what?"

"You know. Medical stuff. Special diet. Reaction to the drugs. Stuff like that."

"She said the same thing everyone says. I'm probably going to have trouble eating just about everything and I'm going to feel like hell."

"So what should you do?"

"Get through it. I've *been* knowing that, Jack."

"Right."

So we dropped the subject and talked about other things. Andy's schoolwork, mostly, and when she thought she could come home again for the weekend. Then Patty came back around. The IV bag was nearly empty and the red fluid was now inside of Leslie, killing off the fast-growing cells.

"Looks like you've drained this one," Patty said. "How do you feel?"

"Okay," Leslie said. "A little light-headed, so maybe I won't have another."

Patty smiled; I wondered how many times she'd heard that one. Then she peeled the bandage from around the needle and pulled it from Leslie's arm.

"Feeling light-headed, that's normal," she said, swabbing the tiny hole where the needle had been and a small bead of blood had formed.

She put another bandage over the wound and smiled.

"You won't know how you're going to react to these drugs until you do. Everyone reacts differently. You might just lose your hair—but you've already taken care of that—and feel a little queasy. That's if you're lucky. But it might be worse. You might have a lot of nausea and disorientation. I'll be honest with you; it's very hard for some people. So hard, they want to quit the treatments."

"I won't do that," Leslie said. "I promise."

"I wouldn't let you, anyway," Patty said, and flashed a luminous smile. "I've seen your family, some of it anyway. I know you can do this, even if it does make you sick."

"Thanks, Patty."

"Sure. See you in three weeks. Be careful driving home."

We said good-bye to Andy and did the hugs in the parking lot.

When we were driving past Fenway Park, Leslie said, "Doesn't seem like such a big deal, does it?"

"No," I said. I didn't tell her about the faces I kept seeing every time I went around another partition.

"Just one more crappy thing about cancer," she said. "No drama. If you have a heart attack or a stroke, get in a car wreck or shot with a gun or something, then you get to ride to the hospital in an ambulance with the siren and the flashers going. They wheel you in on a gurney with all kinds of people clustered around you, yelling things and giving orders. They make a big fuss, you know what I mean? They make you feel like you're somebody and your condition isn't merely life threatening, it is also important.

"Cancer? Humph. You drive yourself to the hospital. Don't even get to park free. You ride the elevator, standing up, and you get to sit in a little space that looks like it was decorated by the guy who got fired from the Holiday Inn account. Everybody is very nice but nobody is alarmed. There is nothing very urgent about your case. You're just another cancer patient, don't you know. One of millions. Strictly routine. 'Fill her up with a bottle of the red stuff that looks like Kool-Aid and make another appointment for her, three weeks from today.'

"Cripes, Jack, they made a lot bigger fuss over me when I was pregnant."

"I remember."

"I mean, this is mundane. It's like cancer is common or something."

"Seems like," I said. I hadn't seen this side of her for a while, but she'd always been one for long, spontaneous riffs.

"I can't stand common. It just seems so *unfair*. Here I have this dreaded, loathsome disease and instead of being treated like some romantic, consumptive heroine in a Victorian sanatorium in the Alps, I get the downtown hospital, a partitioned space with an easy chair, and a bag full of red stuff they drain into me in an hour before they tell me to go home and try not to puke too much. It is so banal."

I drove and she kept talking until we were almost to the prison—MCI Concord—and the last roundabout. There was heavy traffic and I had to keep my eyes on the road. I just said what I was expected to say whenever she paused for breath. When she stopped talking and had been quiet for five minutes or so, I glanced over to see if I could tell anything about her mood.

She was asleep.

29

"God, I'm thirsty," Leslie said. "Where are we?"

"Just about to the state line. You slept a long time."

"I guess."

"How do you feel?"

"Fine. And please don't ask again."

"Okay."

"Except I am so *thirsty*."

"We'll stop. Next exit."

It came up in another couple of miles. I pulled off and filled the tank. When I started inside, Leslie rolled down the window and said, "Plain Coke with *lots* of ice."

That was what she drank when she was feeling sick. Cold, flu, headache—she would always drink Coca Cola with lots of crushed ice.

She sipped the Coke and chewed the ice and didn't say much the rest of the way home.

"I'm going to bed," she said when we got there. "And I don't feel so great. You might want to use the guest room."

She looked tired, and when she took off her sky blue Carolina baseball hat, she also looked vulnerable. It was not a word I'd ever associated with her.

"You want me to check on you?"

"No. I'll be all right."

"Then bang on the floor if you want something."

"Okay. I'll be fine. I'm just tired."

And for the rest of the week, that seemed to cover it. She went to bed early and she would be just getting up when I left the house for work. She napped, she told me, every afternoon.

"No energy, Jack. I feel like I did when I had mono in college."

She had lost a lot of color so her face was pale, with a kind of translucence that I could remember seeing only once, when she was still in the hospital after Andy had been born and we didn't know, for sure, if the baby was going to make it. But she didn't have that ashen look. Not yet, anyway. And she was using cosmetics to give herself some color so that when she went out or one of her friends came by to see her, she didn't look pale and sick.

There were visits, it seemed, every day. I'd find the cups and plates where she'd had tea and something to eat. Also the flowers that people had sent or brought along with them when they came calling.

"I've never had so many people come by to see me. It's kind of strange," she said. "I almost wish they wouldn't. I mean, I know they're trying and I appreciate it, God knows. But I'd like to pretend it isn't happening and people coming by with flowers . . . that doesn't help."

"No."

"But people will always be kind, isn't that right?"

It was a line of poetry that she liked and used a lot.

"They're just trying. What else can they do?"

"I know."

I was trying, too. And I didn't have any better ideas than the people who came by to drink tea and leave flowers. Most nights she said she didn't feel like eating, but since she knew she had to, she would let me make something. I would roast a chicken and make some rice to go with it and steam some broccoli or some other green thing. We would sit at the breakfast table and she would force herself to eat. Each bite looked like a struggle and the fork would sometimes tremble on the way from the plate to her mouth.

While I was cleaning up, she would leave the room and I guessed that she was in the bathroom, vomiting. Later, there would be sweat beading on her face and the makeup she had put on so carefully would be streaked in places. She was trying hard and I wondered how long she could keep it up. The chemo was supposed to last three months.

Things were bad at the office, too. When I thought about it, I told myself that it wasn't as bad as it was at home. This, after all, was just work. Whatever happened on the job, it was still just a job. Worst possible case, you were out of work, on the street and looking for another job. At home . . . well, I didn't like thinking about those possibilities.

So when I got home and Leslie asked how things were at the office, I would say something like "Okay" or "The usual."

She didn't have the interest or the energy to press it, so I didn't offer to elaborate. But in truth, things were uncertain at best and grim at worst. A memo had already been sent around announcing a hiring freeze. That one was followed, almost immediately, by another memo that stopped all promotions and raises. By the time we got the one telling us not to count on the usual Christmas bonus, it was no surprise.

"This is just the first phase," Elena said to me one day in her office. "They're talking baby steps right now. Wait until they get their legs and start really moving. There aren't enough mops in this place to clean up all the blood that's going to be on these floors."

She had never said anything about the list of names I had given her. When I dealt with the people whose names were on that list—which was almost every day—I felt a kind of wariness and found myself acting with almost formal correctness.

Everyone at the office knew that there were going to be firings. That would be the next thing and there was no chance that the economy would turn around or the company would suddenly start doing better before the ax fell, though I'm sure a lot of people hoped, or prayed, for that kind of deliverance.

The consultants brought in to help with the reorganization had set up in a conference room on the floor where the CEO and other senior executives had their offices. They came in early and they stayed late and there were a lot of meetings in that conference room that everyone started calling "the chamber." The rest of us heard about the meetings through the office grapevine and people tried to read their own fates by interpreting the evidence of those meetings.

There wasn't much to go on, though. All the paper that came out of the chamber had been shredded and the people who attended the meetings—generally department heads or higher—seemed to have been warned against saying anything. Elena had been called in for three meetings that I knew about but she never discussed them with me.

A distinct whiff of paranoia hung in the air. Conversations would stop abruptly when you walked into an office where two or three people had been talking. If you went to use the copy machine, people who were already there would furtively cover the sheets they had been copying and you'd know they were working up a résumé and sending it out as a precaution. There was a lot of whispering into telephones.

I told myself that it was pointless to try to divine any meaning or predict any results from all of this, but it was like a lot of the advice I gave myself—sound in the abstract but impossible to follow.

The consultants—they were called the "Doctors of Doom" or "the Ghouls" around the office—were a couple of men who looked to be in their thirties. They wore good, expensive suits which set them off from the rest of the company. We'd been casual, especially the men, for years, and if you showed up in the morning wearing a tie, people inevitably asked if you were going to a funeral or to testify. The Doctors of Doom not only wore suits, they never seemed to take off their jackets or loosen their ties. And, of course, they did not smile or say anything more than "Hello" when you ran into them in the hall.

While they spent most of their time in the chamber, they would come out now and then and walk the corridors, looking over the cubicles where people were trying to work and pretending they were not under observation. The Doctors would stand off in a corner and survey the scene like architects who had been hired to gut and remodel the building and were checking to see which walls could go and which were weight bearing. Now and then one of them would write something down in a small notebook.

It was like that at work every day. And at the end of the day, I would go home and ask how things had gone for Leslie.

30

"I hear it's pretty bad at work," Leslie said one day when I came home.

"Who says?"

"It's a small town, Jack, and you work for the biggest company in it. Word gets around."

"I guess."

"So?"

"So what?"

"Is it bad?"

"Pretty ugly."

"'Doctors of Doom,' huh? That's pretty good."

"Yeah. And lately people have started calling them 'the Ghouls.'"

"Want to drink a bottle of wine and talk about it?" she said. "Would that make it better?"

"Is that a good idea?" I said.

"I think it's a great idea."

"What about . . ."

"What? Me? What's the worst that can happen? The wine will hit my stomach like a bomb and I'll throw up. Big deal."

"You're sure?"

"Absolutely. I'm getting pretty good at throwing up. Lots of practice."

"I didn't know."

"Yes, you did. I just didn't tell you. But you knew. Same as I knew things were crummy at work for you even though you didn't tell me. So what will it be? Red or white?"

"Seems like that should be your decision."

"Why? Because of my touchy stomach? Red or white doesn't make any difference to me; it's all the same coming up. Find a bottle you like and open it."

She didn't drink much. Not even half a glass. And we didn't finish the bottle. But for an hour or so it was like old times. I told her about the situation at the office and tried to make it funny. She smiled and said things like "Oh, get out" and "That's absurd."

When I felt like I'd said all I could say, we sat on the sofa and looked into the fire with her head resting on my shoulder. I tried not to react to her baldness, but I wasn't good enough and she said, "Takes some getting used to, doesn't it?"

"No, it's fine."

"Ha. You are such a bad liar. I hope you do better at the office when you have to."

"Really. I hardly even notice anymore." Which was almost true. I suppose you get used to anything. But when my cheek touched her bald head, that was still a surprise.

"You know," she said, "I can go for a whole hour, sometimes, without thinking about it. Then something will remind me. Usually, I'll reach up to fuss with my hair and I'll touch this bare skin and it always comes as this great big shock. Like you suddenly remember you were supposed to be somewhere and have completely forgotten. You know, an appointment with the dentist. Or the hairdresser . . . but I guess I won't be missing any of those for a while."

"No."

"Funny how everything seems to go like that with this crummy disease."

Her cancer was always that "crummy disease." Almost like it was a nuisance that could have been avoided somehow, like a bad case of poison ivy.

"You remember how it was when we were out in the mountains? What was it, two months ago? Seems like a lifetime."

"Two months," I said.

"I mean, there we were all alone in that place and I don't think I've ever felt so good. A little bleeding from the cut, but that was just a detail. Everything else was so perfect I really didn't notice. Hard to believe you could be so high one day and then, two months later, it's all different. I felt so—I don't know, so strong then. And now I feel so weak. Sometimes I can feel myself getting weaker by the minute. Like your vitality is just sand in an hourglass. That's just one more thing about this crummy disease. The way it just whipsaws you."

"A lot of that is you," I said, "the way you bounce back." My voice sounded husky, even to me. Some of that was the wine, no doubt. Also the fire. But I meant what I said. When you are married to someone for more than twenty years, your feelings for that person are going to cover pretty much the whole spectrum. But I'd never felt so much admiration for her.

"Phooey," she said. "You make me sound like I'm something special."

"You are."

"No," she said. "Not hardly."

"I'm serious," I said, and I was.

"Jack, old sweetie, if there is one thing this crummy disease has taught me, it is that I am definitely not something special. If cancer doesn't make you believe in anything else, it convinces you entirely of the democracy of biology. We are all flesh. It may be all we are and it is pretty thin stuff."

"Okay. But . . ."

"No. I don't need to hear what a hero I am. I just want to sit here with my ugly bald head on your shoulder while the fire burns down."

"All right."

"And then, I guess I'll need to eat something. I don't have much appetite. Don't have any, in fact. But I'm still going to outeat this crummy disease. So if you want to do something nice for me, instead of making speeches, fix me something I can eat for dinner."

"Sure. Name it."

"You always ask the hard ones," she said and thought for a moment. "I don't think I can do dinner, after the wine. But I have to eat something."

She paused and thought about it again.

"You know what I have a craving for?" she said. "It's silly, but it's the only thing I can imagine eating."

"What's that?"

"Rice pudding. Could you make me some rice pudding, maybe with raisins and a little extra brown sugar?"

"I'm all over it."

"No. Wait a little longer. Just till the fire burns down."

I found the recipe in a battered copy of *The Joy of Cooking* that we'd owned as long as we'd been married. Leslie could improvise in the kitchen, but I had to follow a script. So I started with the rice—boiling water, butter and salt, cover and let simmer. Done it a thousand times.

While the rice was cooking I made the pudding part: milk, eggs, butter, and so forth. Then I buttered a cooking dish. I took a dozen vanilla wafers from a half-full box and broke them until they were fine crumbs and spread the crumbs on the bottom of the cooking dish.

You know, I said to myself, *you could get good at this.*

When the rice was done and fluffy, I stirred it into the pudding, then poured the whole mixture into the cooking dish and covered it with the rest of the vanilla wafer crumbs. Then I put the dish into the oven and let it bake. The whole process lasted almost two hours.

Inch by Inch

I made up a tray with a bowl of the rice pudding along with a napkin, a spoon, and a glass full of crushed ice and Coca Cola. It looked like the kind of thing a mother would take to a child who was sick in bed and staying home from school.

I took the tray into the bedroom, where Leslie was lying down on top of the covers. She was pale and her face was damp.

"Thank you," she said when I gave her the tray. Part of me wanted to stay around and wait for her to take the first bite and tell me how good it tasted and what a great cook I was and so forth.

"I'll come back for the tray," I said.

"Don't bother," she said. "I'm going to eat and go to sleep. I'll leave it outside the door."

"Okay."

"It was fun," she said. "Drinking wine and talking. Sorry I couldn't hold up my end."

I said something about how she'd done fine and went back to the kitchen to clean up. After I'd finished, I sat in front of the computer for a while, surfing pointlessly around the Web. When I got tired of that, I went back to pick up the tray. She hadn't eaten more than a bite or two of the rice pudding.

I tasted it and it was awful. It did not taste sweet, or even bland, like it is supposed to. The stuff was so salty it would have gagged a starving dog. I went back to *The Joy of Cooking* and wrote a note in the margin, next to the recipe for rice pudding. *No salt when you cook the rice, Dumbass.*

I went to bed feeling a peculiar, and entirely new, sense of failure.

31

Bill Winter and I had lunch again at the same place. He looked good. He'd gotten a lot of sun and lost a few pounds.

"Walking the Montana hills all day will do it for you every time," he said. "I'm sorry you missed it."

"Me, too."

"You don't look like you've been getting out much."

"No," I said. "Not at all."

"So how are things going? Leslie started the treatments?"

"Couple of weeks ago."

"And?"

I shrugged.

"If you don't want to talk about it . . ."

"No . . ."

"I understand."

Which, of course, he didn't. But somehow he'd managed to put me on the spot. Bill might not have been the one person in the world I would choose to talk to about it, but that person didn't seem to exist. There wasn't anyone I talked to about it. In one sense, I didn't even talk to Leslie about it. When we talked, it was according to her rules.

So I suppose I must have wanted to talk about it according to other rules, because I found myself telling Bill Winter how things were going. I didn't go into intimate detail but I said a lot more than I would have guessed I would. And he listened or did a good job of faking it, anyway. And I appreciated it. I didn't see Bill as one of those cancer voyeurs. Wasn't sure, in fact, why he was interested, but didn't really care. I just wanted to talk.

I was still talking when the waitress brought his mug of Guinness and my glass of sparkling water, dressed with a wedge of lime.

"Got to be tough," he said, raising the mug in my direction. He sounded sincere. "For both of you."

"Something to get through," I said, sorry now for having talked so much about it. For having talked at all.

"And you will. Just don't put too much on yourself."

I nodded.

Neither of us said anything for a moment. A sign that we'd pretty much covered that territory.

"I've been hearing rumors about your shop," Bill said.

"We're calling it a recession," I said. "No matter what anyone else says."

"How bad is it?"

"About as bad as you've heard, I imagine."

"I hear they brought in the outside guys for cover?"

"I guess that's it."

"Well, that's typical. That way, whatever happens, they can say the consultants made them do it."

He had a lot to say about that and I listened. When the food came, he switched lanes and started talking about his trip to Montana. I listened to that, too, and said the appropriate things.

When we'd finished and Bill had ordered another Guinness, he said, "I don't know if it'll make you feel any better, but things are bad all over. My business sucks. Market went down almost every day while I was gone. But I didn't know about it, so I didn't care.

"When I got home, my wife had her war paint on. She wanted to know how I could just take off for Montana for two weeks with everything going to hell. I asked her what she thought I should do. Go down to Washington and ask for a meeting with Greenspan or something? She liked that a lot.

"So much, she took off for New York to see some old friends and spend some money. One of those *I'll show you, you sonofabitch* shopping trips. I expect she'll be calling a lawyer when she gets back."

"You're joking, right?"

"I've been through two divorces," he said. "Haven't laughed yet."

"I'm sorry to hear that, Bill."

He shrugged. "It happens. This one has been getting ready to happen for a while now. If the market had been going great while I was gone, she would have wanted to know why I went to Montana when I could have taken her to London. Like I say, I've been through it before. I'll survive."

"Still . . ."

He waved it away with the hand that wasn't on his mug. "Beth has been gearing up for this. She's one of those modern women, you know, and a divorce is just one of those rites of passage. You need to get an abortion, divorce a husband, and have your face lifted before you can call yourself a real veteran of the gender wars."

I nodded.

"I've got a good pre-nup. It'll be a pain in the ass, but I'll come out okay. And, like they say, at least there are no children. I did that the first time around and that *is* tough. This one will be clean. Or as clean as these things can be, anyway."

"Small favors."

"And a man should be grateful for all of them."

I didn't figure Bill was looking to me for comfort and a shoulder to cry on, so I waited for him to say something.

"If things got real shaky at your shop," he said carefully, "would you consider making a move?"

"I don't know. Maybe."

"I've been talking to some people," he said, "putting some things together. I can't get into the specifics—hell, I can't even get into generalities—but there might be a place for you."

"Appreciate your thinking of me."

"It's not a favor," he said. "If it happens, we'll need someone like you."

"Sounds interesting," I said. "Let me know."

We split the check and went back to our jobs.

32

On the way home that night, I stopped at the bookstore in town. I found what I was looking for—a cookbook for people with cancer—and went to the front to pay. The owner was standing behind the counter. He was a friend of Leslie's. She'd done some brochures for him and I'd talked to him at parties but didn't really know him.

"Jack," he said, and I was impressed he remembered my name. "How've you been?"

"Good," I said, not remembering his. "Real good. How about you?"

"Fine," he said. "Busy."

"Beats the alternative," I said. If I wasn't good with names, I was terrible with small talk.

"Absolutely," he said. "What can I help you with?"

I handed him the book, reluctantly. I had imagined myself dealing with a clerk I didn't know. He looked inside the cover of the book for the price. I got the credit card out of my wallet. The silence was thick and awkward.

"I heard about Leslie," he said somberly. "I'm so sorry."

"I appreciate that."

"How is she?"

"Strong," I said.

He ran the card through the scanner and said, "My sister-in-law went through it two years ago," while we waited for the authorization.

"Uh-huh," I said.

"No recurrence since the chemo," he said.

"That's good."

"Yes. We're all very hopeful."

The approval came up on the card, and he pushed the receipt across the counter for me to sign.

"There is so much they can do these days. It's amazing," he said.

"Yes," I said. "It is."

"If there is anything I can do . . ." He nodded, almost shyly.

"Thanks," I said. "I appreciate that."

"Just call. Or tell Leslie to call. And tell her I'm thinking about her and praying for her."

"Thanks," I said. "I will."

I left the store recalling the line of poetry that Leslie liked and used so often: *People will always be kind.*

I put together a plan for dinner out of the new cookbook. I was going to make chicken breasts meunière that I would serve over a bed of spinach with some lemon-butter sauce. I'd call it Chicken Florentine qua Jack and I would serve it with garlic-roasted potatoes and a small watercress salad. Also a wine that I had picked up on sale at the grocery. A Napa Valley pinot noir of some sort. I didn't know the label but I liked the price.

I'd learned a lot by helping out in the kitchen when the cooking fever was on Leslie. I was good with a knife and a whisk and fair with the blender and the Cuisinart. I couldn't keep a lot of balls in the air, though, the way good cooks can. Leslie had the touch and could juggle three or four dishes and have them all finished and ready to serve simultaneously. It was fun to watch and way beyond me.

But this, I thought, should be a cinch. I was fully in the grip of the "man in the kitchen" bullshit.

I had some music playing; the spinach beds were on the plates and I was just turning the floured chicken breasts when Leslie came into the kitchen.

"Stand back," I said, "and behold an artist at work."

"What are you *doing*?"

"Making dinner," I said. "Chicken Florentine qua Jack. Be ready in five minutes. Want some wine?"

"God, Jack. The house smells like garlic and spinach. I feel so nauseous . . . no way I could eat."

"Oh," I said stupidly. "Oh, I'm sorry. I don't know what I was thinking."

Which is a way of saying that I wasn't thinking.

"Just turn the oven off and open the windows, will you?" She turned away and left the room like she was seasick and needed the rail.

I cut the heat off under the chicken breasts, opened all the windows in the kitchen, and hit the switch for the exhaust fan. I dumped all the food into a black plastic garbage bag, tied a knot in the top, and took it out to the garage and put it into a big can.

I went back inside and cleaned the kitchen. When I'd finished wiping the counters and sweeping the floor, I poured a glass of the bargain pinot noir. It tasted a little like chalk, but I sat down at the kitchen table anyway and drank a glass.

33

I knocked and heard Leslie say, weakly, "It's open."

She was lying on her back with her forearm over her eyes. A small, weak light on her desk illuminated the room.

"Can I come in?"

"Sure. But keep the dogs out."

"Okay."

"How about a hot towel for your forehead?"

"That sounds wonderful," she said. Her voice was soft, like she was afraid of how a loud noise would make her feel. She remained very still, virtually motionless.

I'd brought a tray with me. It held a couple of hot towels, some ice, water, and Coca Cola.

"Move your arm," I said, almost whispering.

When she pulled her arm away from her forehead, I laid the towel there.

"That feels good," she said. "Real good."

"I've got another one right here," I said. "And I can keep bringing them."

"Good."

"I've got a glass of ice water, too, if you're thirsty."

"I don't want to sit up."

"Not necessary. I've got one of those flexible straws. Just turn your head to this side of the bed."

I put the straw between her lips and held it while she took a few sips of water.

"Nice," she said.

"Want to upgrade to Coca Cola?"

"Not yet. Maybe in a little while."

"Okay. Just say the word. How about a candy?"

"I'll pass," she said.

"Okay. I'll leave them here."

"I'm awfully sorry about your dinner, Jack."

"Don't be ridiculous."

"Really. It was a sweet thing for you to do and . . . well, who knew?"

"You must have had some kind of rough day."

"I've had better. I've got anti-nausea pills that I didn't take. I kept thinking I could hold my ground. I hate taking pills. By the time I was ready, it was too late. Next time I'll be quicker."

She stopped talking and I stayed next to her, changing the towels, refilling the water glass, and holding her hand. She didn't go to sleep exactly, but the tension did seem to ease slowly and she began breathing softly and rhythmically.

"Want to be a hero?" she said, without opening her eyes. I'd been with her almost an hour.

"Sure."

"Fill up the bathtub for me. Make it as hot as you think I can stand it."

"Bubbles?"

"But of course."

"I'm all over it."

We'd put in a large tub with some of those circulating jets so that you get the effect of a whirlpool. It was a minor extravagance but Leslie liked to soak in it and sometimes I'd get in with her. In the winter we liked to sit in there and drink wine after we'd been skiing.

I cranked up the faucets and dropped a couple of gelatin balls full of bubble-soap under the flowing hot water. The bathroom filled with steam. When the tub was full, I went back into the bedroom.

"You need an arm?"

"Just a hand, please. To help me up."

Once she had her feet on the floor, she walked to the bathroom on her own. A little slowly and a little unsteady.

"You're okay?"

"I'm fine. And I'll be even better once I've had my bath."

"Call if you want me to do your back," I said as the door to the bathroom closed behind her.

I sat on the bed and flipped through a magazine. There was nothing I wanted to read; nothing but celebrity stuff. Nothing on any of the three or four hundred television channels, either. Just more celebrity stuff. So I lay on my back with my hands locked behind my head, looking at the ceiling and thinking pointless things. I was hoping Leslie would summon me. Feeling useful was getting to be like a narcotic.

"Jack," she called, finally. I had just about given up.

I went to the bathroom door.

"You want something?"

"Yes. I want you to scrub my back."

"I thought you'd never ask."

34

"So," Patty said, "how's it been going?"

She was smiling and cheerful and you might have thought she was talking to a friend who had been away on vacation.

"Oh, you know," Leslie said. "Some good days and some not-so-good days."

"Tell me about the not-so-good days."

Leslie told her about the day of the cooking smells—that's how we referred to it—and said that was just about the worst.

"Do you remember what day that was?"

Leslie considered it a moment, then told her.

Patty nodded and said, "Right in the middle of the cycle."

"That's typical?"

"Yes. The chemicals go to work sort of gradually and the effects are the strongest halfway between treatments. After that you start to feel a little better each day. Is that what happened?"

"I guess so. But I sure don't feel like I did before I got the first treatment."

"No. Unfortunately, it doesn't work that way. You're going downhill all the way through the treatments. But there are these little cycles along the way. Do you ski?"

"Some," Leslie said. Her tone made it clear she didn't get the connection.

"Well, it's like going down a long ski run that has bumps on it."

"Oh."

"You've already skied down twenty-five percent of the mountain. And next time I see you, it'll be half."

An outlook, I thought, that was pure Patty.

Leslie grabbed on to it. "Absolutely," she said. "I hadn't thought of it that way. Where's my jar of Red Devil? I'm ready for it."

"First we have to do some blood work," Patty said.

She drew the blood and left us. We waited and talked in hushed voices. You didn't want to intrude on the privacy of the people behind the screens, walls, and partitions of this place. More than just about anyone, they needed their space.

Andy arrived a few minutes after Patty had gone. She looked thin and pale and troubled. I felt a tug and the absurd sort of hope that it was her mother's condition that was bothering her and not something else. A boyfriend who was treating her badly, say, or worse. Andy hugged me and said "Hi, Dad." She had a way of saying those words. No special inflection or anything like that. But it always got to me just the same.

Andy hugged Leslie, then sat on the edge of her chair. They held hands, and Leslie immediately started telling Andy that she looked pale and needed to get more sleep and start exercising.

"I know, Mom."

"Really, sweetie. You'll feel so much better."

"Okay," Andy said, without conviction.

"I worry about you."

Andy smiled mournfully. "You worry about *me?*"

Leslie smiled happily. "Well, yes, I see your point."

It was as though we'd all taken a deep breath and started over. We talked about other things until Patty returned with the bad news.

"Your white count is too low for you to get a treatment today," she said.

"What does that mean?" Leslie said, sounding a little desperate.

"Don't worry," Patty said, and put her hand over Leslie's. "It happens. Not all of the time, but a lot. I think your doctor wanted to start you on a very strong dose because you're so healthy and she thought you were up to it. After today, she'll cut back just a little."

"What do I do?"

"Go home. Rest and eat right. Come back next week."

"You can't change the dosage today?" Leslie said, pleading a little, as though she'd had her heart set on getting her veins filled with poison. She had spent the weekend getting herself mentally ready for this. She had taken long, solitary walks with the dogs and she had gone to the house of a friend who had offered to show her some meditation techniques. She'd spent the last hour before we left for the hospital sitting cross-legged on the living room floor, her eyes closed, absolutely motionless and silent.

Now she was like an athlete, keyed and ready before a vital game that had been called for some arbitrary, unforeseen, chickenshit reason. She was flattened.

"I'm so sorry," Patty said. And you could tell she was.

"Well, damn," Leslie said and touched her face tentatively. Her eyes were damp but she was not crying. Her lip trembled, very slightly, and that may have been why she needed to put a hand to her face.

The mood seemed to teeter, for a moment, on some kind of brink.

"Damn," she said again. "Here I am with a whole day to spend in the big city and I don't even have my hair. I left my slutty wig at home."

"Wear your baseball hat," I said. "You look fine. Hip, almost."

The look she shot me was only about half mocking.

"Baseball hat? In Filene's? Lord and Taylor?"

"Sorry," I said. "I don't know what I was thinking."

"I guess not," she said.

"There's a shop out by the elevators," Patty said. "You could buy a wig there."

"Buy another wig?" Leslie said. "That seems like an extravagance."

"Insurance usually pays for the first one," Patty said.

"I'll pay for this one," I said. "Call it an anniversary present."

"Fine, I accept," Leslie said, rising from the chair. "Andy, come on. Let's you and me go shopping."

Andy shrugged and said, "Whatever."

"Patty, I'll see you next week," Leslie said. "And I promise you, my white count will blow those lab guys away."

"All right," Patty said and pumped the air with her small fist.

Leslie and Andy started for the door and I followed, carrying their coats.

35

Leslie spent the week in a campaign to "get my blood into shape." She'd been given some supplements at the hospital and had picked up other pills and powders at the health food store. I offered to cook things that would help.

"No way," she said. "I mean, it's a nice offer and you aren't that bad. But you don't even like to cook."

"So what?"

"Well, I do. So I should do the cooking. Anyway, I'm better at it than you."

"But you can't stand the smells."

"One time."

"How do you know it won't happen again?"

"I don't. But you know what?"

"What?"

"I wasn't even cooking that time. You were. So there."

She stuck her tongue out at me. She did that when the argument wasn't serious and she'd made a point.

"Okay," I said. "Have it your way."

"Hey," she said, "come on. Don't be like that."

"If you want to cook," I said, "that's up to you. I just don't want you to get sick again."

I sounded self-righteous, even to myself.

"I mean it," I said. "You should do what you want to do and what you think works for you."

"I know. And you're sweet. But if I get sick from the smells, no matter who does the cooking, then what difference does it make?"

"I thought I'd do the cooking some other place. Bring the plates here once they're done. That way, the house won't fill up with smells."

She raised an eyebrow.

"Where?"

"Bill Winter's," I said. "His kitchen is available."

She thought about it for a few seconds.

"You know, that makes sense. Maybe we should try it."

I realized then, when I caught her tone, that this was actually a serious concession for her. She was trying hard to keep her grip on all the parts of what she thought of as her normal life. And the cancer was straining to pry her fingers loose. She hated to lose any fight, no matter how small.

"It's just for the next couple of months," I said. "Strictly temporary. We'll handle it like they do in football. You don't lose your job to injury."

"Deal."

"Hell, yes," Bill Winter said when I asked about using his kitchen. "Goddamned place is state-of-the-art. Garmen range, the whole nine yards, and since Beth hit the road, it just sits there. Be my guest. I'll give you a key."

Which he did, even though it turned out not to be necessary. He generally left his office shortly after the market closed every day and was home before five. When I came through his kitchen door, carrying a bag of groceries, he would be sitting on a stool at the long, gleaming cherry-wood counter, drinking a glass of what I assumed was expensive wine, reading the papers, and listening to soft music.

"You mind a little company?"

"I'd appreciate it."

"Some of this wine? It's pretty good."

"No, thanks."

"Supposed to be good for you," Bill said. "This week, anyway."

"I know. But I need all my concentration."

"For a pork loin?"

"Never done one before," I said.

The recipe came from the book I'd bought. It would never have occurred to me to cook pork for a cancer patient.

"Well, it looks like you're doing a fine, professional job."

"Maybe I've found my next career."

"You looking for one?"

"No," I said. "Not really."

He studied his wineglass, took a delicate sip from it, and said, "Lots of people at your shop will be, I imagine." He said it in a way that implied he knew even more than he was saying, which was something people in his line seemed to have in common. The ones I knew, anyway. They always wanted you to think they knew more than the next guy about, say, the price of North Sea crude or the success of the anchovy harvest in the waters off Peru and how it would affect the price of live cattle. No matter what it was, they wanted you to think they had better and more recent information about it than you did.

"So how is the mood around the office these days?"

"Nervous," I said. "Very nervous."

"I can imagine. But you're all right?"

"I'm fine," I said without elaborating. If he knew so much, I thought, then he should know the answer. Otherwise, let him find out.

"Being all right personally at a company that isn't," he said, "can still be a lot of no fun."

"I'm sure," I said, and checked my sweet potatoes and stirred the brown rice. Five to ten minutes, I thought. Then I'd put everything on a warming platter and into an insulated bag like the pizza delivery guys used and hustle it on home.

* * *

"Those conversations I was telling you about?" Bill said. "With the people who are starting up that new company?"

"Yes."

"They're picking up speed. Things are going to start happening real soon."

"I see."

"You could get in early. There would be an equity position in it for you. If the thing does grow wings, when it flies, it could mean some real money for you. Get you out of the wage-slave ditch and up onto the fast lane."

"I could stand that."

"Seriously?"

"Sure," I said, thinking medical bills and, who knew, possibly a new house for Leslie. Her dream house at last.

"You might have to move fast. Make the jump before this thing with Leslie is over."

"Let's talk about it," I said. "When I can concentrate."

"Fine."

I packed everything into the insulated case, quickly rinsed the utensils and dishes I'd used, and put them in the dishwasher.

"Thanks again, Bill."

"Don't mention it."

36

It was like that for the rest of the week. Leslie swallowed supplements and pills. She told one of her friends that she was doing it to make sure "my white count makes the cut."

It was plainly hard on her, though. She couldn't stop thinking of that one missed chemo session as a setback. I could see it in her face when I left for work in the morning. Her eyes were haunted and hollow and her mouth was tight with anxiety.

The office was a distraction but not an especially pleasant one. The Ghouls were still appraising things and the rumor was that the ax would fall any day now. Elena and I were meeting more often than ever, going over plans she had developed for reorganizing the department. Most of them needed work and we were constantly revising.

"Look," she said near the end of one of our meetings, "we keep going around and around on this and we never get anywhere. Next week, you come in here with your plan. I want something new, top to bottom—and I'll do the same. We'll take the best of both plans, put it together, and make it happen."

I added that to my list of things to worry about, and at night, after Leslie had gone to bed, I worked at the computer trying to come up with a plan that would work without the ten people I'd already recommended for termination.

In the evenings, while I cooked in his kitchen, Bill Winter sat at the counter drinking wine and telling me about this new opportunity that might be perfect for me. I was getting more and more interested.

"Who are these people, Bill?"

"Couple of young guys who got rich in the tech boom. They got out ahead of the posse and started climbing mountains. Now they want to get back into business."

"In outdoor gear?"

"Sure."

"Pretty crowded field. L.L.Bean, North Face, Patagonia, Columbia . . ."

"These guys think they can find a niche. They aren't stupid and they sure aren't going to be undercapitalized."

"You've seen the plan?"

"Absolutely."

"Would you invest?"

"I already have."

When I didn't say anything, he took another sip of wine and said, "Look, it's a risk. No getting around that. And I know risk isn't especially appealing to you right now, given Leslie's situation."

I nodded.

"There is no denying the downside. But where there is risk, there is also opportunity. On the upside, you get something you'll never see if you stay where you are—tall money. Probably some equity."

I nodded.

"Get you off the old, endless paycheck cycle."

Like everyone, I'd been drowning in money talk and money images over the last ten years. The idea of actually getting my hands on some money was tempting. Seductive, even.

"I've told these guys about you," Bill said. "They're interested. You should meet with them."

"How soon?"

"Pretty soon."

"Days?"

He thought about that.

"Maybe not days. But not months, either. Weeks, for sure. Just a few weeks. You should think about it."

"I will. I'll think about it seriously and I'll let you know."

"Good."

The week finally ended and Leslie and I drove to Boston again early Monday morning. It was a familiar, silent drive and we parked on the same level of the hospital garage, rode the same elevator, and went into the same partitioned space where Patty met us and greeted us with her usual bright smile.

She took some blood from Leslie's arm and we waited for the word from the lab. It was a strange feeling of suspense. Good news for Leslie would be that she could get a pint of poison drained into her bloodstream. Bad news would be that she couldn't.

The news was good.

Andy came by and held her mother's hand while the red fluid dripped from the bottle into her arm.

Leslie kept her eyes resolutely on Andy's face.

"I swear it feels hot," she said.

"Sure. Why shouldn't it?" Andy said.

"They say it's just my imagination."

"Yeah?" Andy said in full adolescent righteousness. "Well, what do they know? You think they've stuck needles in their arms and tried it themselves?"

"No," Leslie said mildly. "I don't suppose they have."

"Well, then? Maybe you should tell them what it feels like."

"Maybe I should."

They kept holding hands until the bottle was drained and Patty had pulled the needle from Leslie's arm, wiped away a bead of blood, and put a Band-Aid over the wound.

"Good-bye, sweetie," Leslie said to Andy when we reached the hospital lobby. "Thanks for coming."

"Are you kidding?"

Leslie hugged her.

"Take care of yourself."

"You take care of *yourself*, Mom. I mean it."

"I will. I love you."

"Love you, too."

I hugged Andy and found myself wishing she were coming home with us. We needed a kid around the house, I thought, even one who was grown up.

We didn't talk on the way home. There was nothing sullen or testy about the silence. She was just tired, I thought. If she wanted to talk, she would. If she didn't want to talk, then I wouldn't be doing her any favors by trying to get her started.

Somewhere around Greenfield, she nodded off.

We were at a slightly higher altitude now. The last leaves were down and the hills were a barren and monochromatic gray. Normally I liked the way this country looked before the first snow; there was something austere about it that appealed to me, like an empty beach in the winter. But not today.

I kept thinking about what Andy had said, back in the hospital, about the hot medicine—Adriamycin by name—that was going into Leslie's body by the pint.

Of course they didn't know how it felt. How could they?

And, of course, neither did I. How could I? But I wanted to know. I wanted to know as much as I could. For some reason, I believed it would help.

Like a lot of cancer patients, Leslie had been reading books and articles about the disease, making clip files, downloading and bookmarking things on the Net. I tried to keep up with all that she was reading, but there was so much I felt overloaded. When I read the clip about how some German researchers had come up with the theory that riding a bike regularly could prevent breast cancer, I'd had enough.

I would, I decided, stay with what I could actually know and what would help me to help Leslie. The rest was theory. As useful to me as the latest refinement of the Big Bang. I wanted something I could use.

I remembered what the doctor had said when she discussed chemo with Leslie and me. Nausea, fatigue, and blah, blah, blah. She could have been talking about the flu. And I knew what Leslie had told me, which was even less.

"I'm a little tired, Jack, and my stomach is a little upset."

Not exactly a great help, but as much as I was likely to get.

I brooded on that the rest of the way home.

37

Leslie went to bed as soon as we were home.

"I took the pills," she said bleakly. "For the nausea. I didn't want to be sick in the car."

"Nothing wrong with that," I said.

"I just want to sleep now."

"Want me to wake you up for dinner?"

"No."

I took the dogs for a walk, checked the phone messages, and then caught up on my e-mail. I made some calls, ate cold chicken for supper, and, when it was finally late enough, I called Monk.

"Martindale," he said, answering his own phone.

"Can't you afford a receptionist?" I said.

"She's having a baby," he said. "How's Leslie? And give me all the details."

I did.

"She holding up all right?" he said.

"Yes."

"And you?"

"I'm fine."

Once we'd talked a little about other things, I asked him if he could tell me—specifically—what Leslie was experiencing. It had been on my mind since Boston.

"You mean the nausea and all that?"

"Yeah," I said. "All that."

"Doctors aren't very good at that stuff," he said. "When we say 'discomfort' it means you're feeling bite-on-a-bullet pain. We cut; we sew; we send out a bill. Sorry."

"Who is good at it?"

"Somebody who has been there, I guess. If you don't know someone, try one of those support groups. They have them for men, too."

"Okay," I said, without much conviction.

"Listen, Jack," Monk said, "don't get too hung up on this. The point is not exactly what she's feeling. I mean, you know she feels like hell and that's enough. Just do what you can to make it easier for her. Try to make her laugh a little and take her mind off things. With any luck, in a while it will be over. It won't help to empathize with every little symptom. Might even hurt."

"You're probably right," I said.

But as soon as I hung up, I picked up the phone book and started looking for cancer support groups.

In the morning, I called the first one in the book and found myself speaking to Janet Cartright, which was a surprise. She was a friend of ours. More a friend of Leslie's, actually.

I tried to get off the line.

"Listen, Jack," she said, "don't be embarrassed. I know all about it. Leslie and I have talked."

"You have?" I said. Stupidly.

"Yes. That's why I'm here, to talk to women in treatment. I'm a survivor."

The word did something to me. I don't know why. Maybe it was just kind of confusion. For a long time, I'd associated the word with the people who'd made it out of concentration camps alive. Then you heard show business people who'd gone down with drugs and were trying to make a comeback, talking on the late night shows about how "I'm a survivor." And now there was that television show where people ate worms. Maybe, I thought, cancer needed its own word.

And, anyway, I knew Janet as a good-looking woman with a tart mouth who liked to laugh at parties. This seemed way too intimate.

"Meet me for lunch," she said. "I don't know what you're after but I'll try to help."

We ate at a place the young, professional women in town liked and that Bill Winter wouldn't have set foot inside. The tables were small, the specials were written on a blackboard, and the menu was heavy on salads. Janet ordered a glass of chardonnay and cold salmon with caper sauce. I had the chicken Caesar and plain water to drink.

"You on the wagon?" Janet said.

"No. It's just a lunch thing."

"Good."

"Why?"

"We see it all the time. Spouses stop drinking—stop doing all the things they used to do for pleasure—because it makes them feel guilty to have fun, I guess. They feel like they have to suffer, too. Understandable but counterproductive."

"Well, I still drink a beer or two at night," I said. "Maybe a glass of wine."

"Good. You need some relief even if you don't think you do. It's hard on everyone, including you."

I'd heard that before.

Janet drank a little of her wine, and I noticed that she had a way of holding the glass and putting it to her lips that was faintly erotic. She was thin and had very dark hair, very green eyes, and an olive complexion that made her look vaguely Mediterranean. Greek, maybe. She had a wide mouth, brilliantly white teeth, and a sort of skeptical smile. She looked like someone who had secrets.

We made a little small talk, and then she said, abruptly, "Why did you want to talk to me, Jack?"

"Leslie doesn't tell me much."

"No. I'd be surprised if she did."

"Why?"

"You're asking me, Jack? You married her."

"Okay. She's not into pity. Hers. Mine. Anyone's."

Janet nodded.

"And I can understand that," I said.

Janet nodded again, but in a way that said my understanding didn't count for much one way or the other.

"But I'd like to know what she's going through."

"Why?"

"Might help me somehow."

"You're doing fine," she said, like a teacher with a slow learner.

"News to me."

"Leslie told me you're very considerate and supportive."

I didn't say anything.

"That ought to be enough, Jack."

"All right," I said. My tone was abrupt. I kept running into this same soft stone wall, this same condescending attitude that said *Oh, you couldn't possibly understand.* My job was to give money, wear a pink ribbon on my lapel, run in the 5K Race for the Cure, and otherwise shut up. I would take it from Leslie. But I didn't have to take it from anyone else, including Janet Cartright.

"Now, don't be that way."

"How's Richard?" I said. "I haven't seem him for a while."

She gave me a look. The same one Richard got, I imagined, when he'd said the wrong thing at the dinner table. Richard could be loud about his opinions. Bringing up Richard's name was sort of a mild dig and I felt a little ashamed of myself for doing it. But just a little.

"Richard is fine," Janet said with some frost on the edge of her voice.

"Good. The kids? Dick Junior must be away by now, right?"

She took another sip of wine, very deliberately. And she put the glass back on the table with the sort of care you'd use with crystal.

"Listen, Jack, I understand you are under a lot of stress."

"No," I interrupted. "That's not it. I can deal with my stress. What I'm asking for is a little advice on how to help my wife deal with her situation. She won't tell me because she's proud and I can handle that. I'm looking for another source. If you can't talk to me—well, no hard feelings—I'll keep looking. Something will turn up."

She stared at me and her face softened a little. She took a deep breath.

"What do you want me to tell you, Jack?"

"I don't know. I'm looking for . . . tips, I guess."

"Tips?"

"You know, little ways to make things better."

I paused, but she didn't say anything.

"I went through an IRS audit a while ago," I said. "The woman who was doing it was a young trainee—they didn't need to send the heavy hitters after me—and we got along really well, given the circumstances. We'd drink coffee and talk for a few minutes before she started going through all the old receipts and canceled checks. Turned out she and her husband were dog breeders who specialized in Labs."

Janet took another sip of wine and gave me a look that said she wondered where on earth this was going.

"Well, I told her we had a Lab puppy at home and that I loved him to death except for one thing.

"And without my telling her, she said, 'Chewing, right?'

"'Whatever he can get his mouth around,' I said. 'Furniture, shoes, kids' toys, the vacuum cleaner—you name it.'

"So she told me to go to the hardware store and buy a couple of hardwood dowels and saw them into six-inch lengths. Leave a couple of those in every room of the house and as long as the puppy was teething, encourage him to chew on those dowels instead of the chair leg.

"And it worked," I said. "Made a big difference in things around our house. So that's what I'm looking for. Just a tip or two that might help me make things a little easier for Leslie. The kind of thing that you don't find in the magazine articles that tell you, over and over, to 'be supportive.'

"And I don't see why that should be so hard."

38

It was a long speech for me, and I felt like a fool when I'd finished. But Janet's eyes had stayed on mine through the whole thing.

"Showers," she said.

"Showers?"

"You know, hot water, soap, shampoo. That kind of shower. Not the kind for some woman who's pregnant."

"Oh. *Showers.* What about them?"

"No matter how many you usually take, Jack, take more. Lots more. I don't know the medical reasons for it, but when you are on chemo, your sense of smell is so sensitive you just can't believe it. Or stand it. You smell every little thing. And the littlest thing can make you nauseous. I would open a can of tuna and that would be the end of it.

"Richard would walk into the house at the end of the day, and I'd swear he smelled like the boys' locker room in high school. Before I started chemo, I'd never thought he smelled one way or the other, unless he changed deodorant or was fooling around with one of those horrible men's colognes. But during chemo, the smell that came off him made me gag. Literally."

"Oh, man."

"It's silly, I know, but I didn't want to tell him. I knew he'd be insulted. But I finally couldn't stand it any longer and I asked him to take a shower."

"What happened?"

"He was insulted," she said. "But I didn't care and he got over it. I don't know if that's any help to you . . ."

"It is," I said. "Absolutely."

The food came and without saying so, we agreed not to talk about cancer and chemo while we ate. She asked about my work and wanted to know if things were as bad as she'd heard. I said they were pretty bad but it looked like a business cycle deal to me. She said that was good and she hoped it would turn around soon.

We finished our lunch and both asked for coffee. Janet stirred cream into hers and said, "There's more to the scent thing than taking showers and wearing freshly washed clothes. You know about cooking smells, Leslie told me that, but you might want to pick up some scented candles. Nothing too sweet. I liked pine, myself. And clove. Stay away from lilacs and anything like that."

"Okay," I said. "I believe I can handle that."

"Change the sheets and towels—every day, if you can."

"Okay."

"Open some windows and air things out."

"Right."

"Buy some music . . ."

"For the smell?"

"No." She smiled. "Music for her mood. Your body is being jacked around all over the place by the chemicals and you just feel like you could fly apart. The right kind of music gives you a sense of . . . oh, I don't know. Tranquility, maybe."

"What kind of music?"

"I liked Bach, myself. Hilary Hahn. There is a clarity to the way she plays."

I nodded. I didn't even know what Hilary Hahn played but I didn't want to give myself away with Janet on a roll.

"I'll e-mail you a list of the CDs that worked for me," she said.

"I'd appreciate that," I said.

"And there's something else," she said. "It's a little weird . . ."

"I can take it."

"Well, if you could find some special slippers."

"Slippers?"

"Like bedroom slippers," she said. "Only with more cushioning than you could ever imagine."

I must have looked baffled.

"When you are on chemo, you shed all that tough skin on the bottoms of your feet. There is nothing down there but tender, sensitive, pink stuff, and when you go to the bathroom to get a drink of water, it feels like you're walking on ground glass. Any kind of slippers are a help. But the kind with deep cushioning are better."

"Sure," I said. "I know somebody in the office—a buyer for the women's catalog—who might be able to help me out."

"Good."

"Soft things to wear, too. Especially to wear to bed. You shed a lot of cells and you're sensitive all over, like when you have a sunburn and just moving a little across the sheets feels like you are sandpapering your body. Even when you are dead tired, you can have trouble sleeping."

"So what do I do for that?'

"Cotton flannel. The expensive stuff. Pajamas more than nightgowns. It isn't real sexy but that's for later, after she's finished the radiation and you take her to Paris."

She smiled.

"Anyway, nice cotton flannel and . . . what else?"

She thought for a moment.

"I can't think of any other 'tips,' as you call them, Jack. If I do, I'll call you."

"You've been a great help, Janet," I said. "I really appreciate it."

"Do you mind," she said a little stiffly, "if I give you some general advice to go along with the 'tips'?"

"No," I said, "of course not. I'd appreciate it. And I apologize for earlier."

She shook her head, just a little, to show it was both unnecessary and appreciated.

"You know what the worst thing is about where Leslie is right now?"

I shook my head.

"Well, maybe not the worst. It's all bad. But one of the hardest things I had to deal with—and I hear it all the time from other women—is the loneliness."

I nodded.

"Leslie is a gregarious girl. I don't have to tell you that."

"No."

"But everyone who has this disease feels cut off and alone. When you're well, and you feel lonely, what do you do? If you're like Leslie or like me, you pick up the phone and call somebody for lunch. But when you're in deep chemo depression, you can't imagine that anyone would want to talk to you on the phone, much less meet you for lunch. You feel so—ugly. And the more time you spend alone, the worse it gets. So even when people call you on the phone, you find ways not to talk for very long and you turn down invitations to lunch and you spend more and more time alone—just you and your cancer—feeling hopeless."

"Doesn't sound like Leslie," I said.

"Maybe not. But she's not immune. Cancer is a pretty serious equalizer."

I nodded.

"Do all those other things for her, Jack. Take a lot of showers and buy her soft flannel pajamas. But spend time with her, too, even when you think she might want to be alone. And make her get out of the house and spend time with other people. It's important. Really important."

"Okay," I said. "I will."

"I'll call her. I should have before now."

"Don't tell her we talked."

Janet smiled her faintly wicked, bad-girl smile.

"I will," she said, "if I want to."

39

Leslie liked the slippers I had sent to the house by FedEx. She also liked the soft flannel pajamas that I found in the same catalog and ordered in pink and yellow. And the new thick terry cloth robe to replace the one from some distant hotel. She didn't say anything about the extra showers I took every day but I assumed she appreciated them, too.

But those were trivial fixes. Band-Aids on a cut that went all the way to the bone. She was on the downslope of the second chemo treatment and there was no way to get off or slow things down. She felt weaker, and got sicker, every day. She didn't tell me this but she didn't have to. I could see the effort it took for her to get out of bed in the morning.

So I took my showers and laundered the sheets and towels so they would always be fresh. But these were feeble gestures and wouldn't alter the outcome any more than painting your house would if you lived in a city under siege.

Some days were better than others, but there were fewer and fewer good days, especially as she got closer to the trough between treatments.

I never knew until I got home what kind of shape Leslie would be in, so I tried to get home as early as I could after stopping at Bill Winter's to make something for dinner.

But when Elena asked me, one afternoon, if I could stay late, I didn't have a lot of choice.

"Sure," I said. "What's up?"

"I'll explain then," she said.

I called Leslie. When I started to apologize, she cut me off.

"Don't be silly," she said. "If you have to work late, you have to work late. I'll see you when I see you."

So I spent the rest of the day doing my work and wondering what was happening at the company. The Ghouls were still holding their meetings in the chamber, but so far nothing had happened. No early retirement packages had been offered; no departments had been eliminated; no corporate reorganization had been proposed.

"I figure the ax will fall about Christmas," I heard one of the people in my department say. "That's the kind of modern, caring company we work for."

I suspected the man was right and hoped he wasn't. He was one of the people I'd recommended for termination.

Elena LeFevre had told me to come up with a plan and I'd worked nights, at home, until I had something on paper. I'd left it on her desk and I'd been in suspense, every day since, waiting for her to say something about it. I'd never been exactly eaten up with ambition in the office or desperate for corporate approval. I'd thought, kind of smugly, that I was hip to all that and understood, unlike a lot of people, that it was all a delusion. But it seemed like that had changed and cancer, of course, was the reason.

We had moved here—to "the country," as we called it—so we wouldn't have to give up our lives to our work. That's the way we had talked, and thought, back then. We'd probably even used the word *lifestyle*. I know we had gotten serious about things like organic gardening and woodstoves. Back then, my job had been merely a job. No nights or weekends at the office. No agonizing over promotions and bigger offices.

Now, I wanted to lash myself to my job and the company and anything else that promised to keep me afloat. I'd worked hard on my reorganization plan hoping, like junior executives everywhere, that my boss would be impressed. I wanted a promotion, a raise, a bigger office and the illusion, anyway, of security. I'd settle happily for illusion.

"Okay," Elena said, when we met in her office to discuss my plan, "it's a good start. Let's see where we can go from there."

There was something that was almost conspiratorial in the way she said it, and my hopes rose.

40

We started out by doing new job titles and descriptions as part of a revised mission statement for our department.

I sat in front of Elena's computer and typed out notes on the things that we'd agreed needed to be done. She had a leather-covered notebook open on her lap and was jotting things on one of its pages in pencil. I got caught up in the work, and noticed it with a twinge of guilt. I'd rather be here, I realized, dealing with these problems, than home trying to handle what couldn't be fixed.

Around seven she closed the notebook and said, "Let's go someplace nice for dinner."

She called for a reservation and we took our separate vehicles—her Audi and my Ford 150—to one of the more expensive places in town. It was called the Post Road, and it did most of its business with skiers and other condo owners up from the city. Leslie and I ate there on special occasions.

We got a table in the back, next to a window that looked out on a little mountain stream that sparkled under floodlights, flowing around large boulders and dropping off a rock ledge into a small waterfall.

We ordered drinks and, when they came, tipped our glasses in each other's direction.

"To opportunities," Elena said, and I nodded with conviction.

The waiter arrived to hand us our menus. Before he could begin his discussion of the specials, Elena said, "Let me just say, the veal here is wonderful."

I nodded again.

I listened while the waiter described the specials, but only with about half my brain. I was thinking about veal. Or, to be precise, how it had been thirteen years since I'd eaten any.

Back then, we had gone in with some friends on a calf each year. We would split the cost—including slaughter and butchering—and since we had a freezer, we kept all the meat at our house. We worked out an alternating deal where we got the sweetbreads one year, the liver the next. Leslie had a way of doing the sweetbreads that beat anything I had ever eaten in a restaurant. I'd always considered the odd-numbered years lucky since it meant our turn for the sweetbreads.

Then Andy found out about veal. When she was in the first grade, some kid whose parents were vegetarians told her the whole thing and even showed her a picture of one of those calves chained to a metal stake that had been augured into the ground outside one of those ugly plastic shelters where veal calves live their short, unhappy lives.

I explained to Andy that our calf was never chained—which was true—and that it wasn't even purely milk fed; that it got to spend a couple of weeks on grass. But that didn't make any difference. Not only would she not eat veal, she would not sit at the table with the rest of us when we did. And she wouldn't leave it alone. She talked about the cruelty of raising calves for veal so much and with such conviction that Leslie and I finally gave in and promised never to eat veal again. We both believed that kids needed some victories—something we'd picked up, probably, from a book about raising kids or from one of those "experts" who appear on the morning news shows—and we thought Andy had earned this one.

The hardest part had been explaining to our friends, not merely why we couldn't go in with them on the calf any longer, but also why we couldn't store their veal in our freezer, not even for a price.

* * *

I looked down the menu and, inevitably, one of the featured entrees was sautéed sweetbreads.

"The striped bass, please," I said to the waiter. "That sounds good."

After the waiter left, Elena looked out at the little waterfall glittering under the spotlights.

"Nice view, don't you think?" she said.

"Beats the office."

"I've had enough of that place for today," she said. "Let's talk about something else."

"All right."

I didn't ask her what she did want to talk about. I figured I'd find out.

"It's beautiful here, where we live," she said. "But you can get so busy you don't even notice it anymore. It's all just a blur. You have to remind yourself to slow down so you can see it and appreciate it."

I said something about how that was for sure.

"I wonder if anyone would stay here if it weren't so beautiful—the mountain views and the leaves in the fall and all that. Once you get past that, life here can be pretty boring."

I agreed with that, too.

"You've been here a long time, though," she said.

"Yes."

"Do you stay because you like it? Or is it because of the job?"

"I have a life here."

"You can have a life anywhere," she said, "if you're willing to risk starting over."

I told her I could buy that.

"I love change," she said. "No, actually, I need it. If something new doesn't come into my life, after a while I start feeling like I'm drying up and dying inside."

She paused for a moment and I wondered if she thought she might have said the wrong thing. If she did, she got over it quickly.

"Life is all about risk and change and trying something new. That's what's wrong with living in a place like this. Yes, it's very beautiful and the air is clean and the people are nice. But when you get down to it, that's not enough."

"You need action?" I said.

"Right."

"Doesn't sound like you'll be staying here long."

"I came here for the job," she said. "Right now—*especially* right now—it's a challenge."

I asked her what she'd done before. They say most people are happiest talking about themselves. I believed it, even though I sure didn't want to talk about myself just then.

She told me about working for Fields and living in Chicago, where she had a floor-through walk-up on Lincoln Park. She'd met her husband there. He worked at the Board of Trade.

"Those were wild times," she said. "Some days we were filthy rich and then sometimes we were just dead broke and needed everything I made just to stay alive. Champagne today and beer tomorrow. I loved it."

"Why did you leave?" I felt like I was supposed to ask.

"He burned out. Couldn't take it anymore. He didn't come home for two days and when he finally showed up, he was wasted and talking about how we had to move to Michigan—the Upper Peninsula, for God's sake—and buy a farm and start over living a simpler life."

"It didn't take?"

"No. Because I never tried it. I never even considered it."

"What did you do?"

"Something new. Like I say, change is good. I got a job with Filene's and moved to Boston. And after a couple of years, I got this job and moved here. I don't believe in letting a lot of grass grow."

* * *

It was late, almost midnight, when I got home. Leslie had left the lights on for me and I turned them out behind me as I made my way to the bedroom, where she was asleep and breathing deeply. She had probably taken one of the pills they gave her for nausea, I thought. She wasn't normally a very sound sleeper but those things put her under.

Still, I went into the bathroom so I could undress quietly. I didn't want to wake her.

One of the scented candles was burning in the bathroom and I knew what that meant. Before I undressed, I took the clothes out of the hamper and down to the basement, where I started them in the washing machine. Then I showered.

When I slipped under the covers a few minutes later, she said "Hi" in a voice that sounded like she was talking into a bucket.

"Sorry," I said. "I tried to be quiet."

"Not a problem," she said. "What time is it?"

I told her.

"God. Poor baby. You must be exhausted."

"I'm fine," I said. "How are you?"

"Me?" she said. "I'm just peachy."

"Peachy?"

"Yeah," she said. "Peachy. Want to make something of it?"

I put my arms around her, and after a couple of minutes she went back to sleep.

I was awake for another hour or so with my eyes wide open, staring at the ceiling, or at nothing.

When I left in the morning, Leslie was still sleeping. I left a note on the kitchen table, then tried calling in the middle of the morning. I got the machine and left a message.

Sometime after lunch, Elena said she thought we should stay late again.

"Till seven or so. Maybe eight. I know you like to get home."

"Sure," I said. I didn't know what the last part meant. Like I'd told myself before, it was a small town and an incestuous company. I assumed Elena had heard about Leslie and her situation.

I called home again in the afternoon.

Leslie sounded like she'd been asleep.

"I'm sorry," I said.

"Not a problem. I was out fifteen minutes and that's all you need."

"Oh?"

"Yeah," she said, yawning. "There was a study in one of those medical magazines. *JAMA* or one of those. Said naps were good but you only needed fifteen minutes. Anything more was not just wasted, but counterproductive."

"I didn't know you read the medical journals," I said. Then I thought, why not? What else would really grab your interest if you had cancer?

"I'm impressed," I said.

"I was reading *Allure*," she said. "The title of the article was 'Power Naps.'"

"I see."

"So what's up? You working late again?"

"Yes," I said. "Sorry."

"Listen," she said firmly. "Don't worry about it. I'm fine and when I'm not, and you can't come help me, I'll call someone who can. Do your work."

"There's some of that chicken left . . ."

"Jack," she said. "Give it a rest. If you have time to take care of dinner for me, that's fine. But if you don't, I'll get by. I promise."

"Okay."

"I'll see you later," she said. "And good luck. Sounds like things are a real mess down there."

"They are."

"Well, why don't you fix them? Be a hero."

Elena and I worked in her office until almost nine that night, and when we finished we had a plan for totally reorganizing our sales force—chiefly by getting rid of the people we kept on payroll and using independent contractors during the two heavy buying seasons. I would be taking up a lot of the slack the rest of the year as part of my new, still vague responsibilities. We also came up with a scheme for getting rid of all the agencies we used and producing our advertising in-house. There was good stuff on our own Web site and we planned to cannibalize from it. Elena especially liked this part of the plan, since it gave her a toehold in Internet sales, which is where she thought the growth would be in the next few years.

"You know," she said, almost defiantly, "if I got the chance, I could do such a great job running this company."

"I'm sure."

"The business part—the marketing, positioning, financials, personnel—I could handle that, no sweat. Better than the present management," she said a little contemptuously. "Of course, that isn't saying much."

"They haven't been too shiny," I said.

"I'd need someone who really understands the core business and loves what the company sells."

I nodded again.

"Someone like you," she said, then added, "No, not someone like you. It should *be* you."

I nodded once more and tried to make the motion both thoughtful and noncommittal. I didn't know how serious she was with this or how far it might go, but I recognized a little thrill of possibility.

"We'd be such a great team," she said. "Don't you think so?"

"Absolutely," I said.

We were sitting with our knees almost touching, behind the large cherry-wood table that she used as a desk. She had folded up the spreadsheets and other papers we'd been working with and put them on a shelf, so her desk was clean—no papers, no file folders, no books, no magazines. Nothing but a phone and a lamp, her leather-bound notebook, and a stainless steel mechanical pencil.

Her desk was always clean that way and I suppose it made some kind of statement about how, at her level, business was done. It was not about clutter and grubby little memos, reports, and columns of figures. It was clean, abstract, and conceptual.

She looked at me and I saw the same thing in her expression. It was austere and purposeful.

"It could happen, Jack."

"I wouldn't be surprised," I said, to fill space.

"It could happen sooner than you think."

I raised my eyebrows and even that wasn't necessary. She wanted to explain it and didn't need to be asked.

"All the other department heads are playing defense. They're all afraid. They want everything to be the way it has always been.

"But that's not going to cut it. You don't need x-ray vision to know what's going on around here; a blind idiot could see it. Either this place does a major restructuring, or it dies. It may die slowly but it's going to die, for sure."

I nodded, one more time. She could take it however she wanted. My mind went one place when the subject was slow death.

"My plan—our plan—recognizes that and takes the necessary, logical steps."

She was still and tense. Like she was expecting to be attacked. Or challenged, anyway.

"When they see my plan—*our* plan—they'll have to decide. Change or die. If they decide to change—well, there is only one person inside this company they can go to."

She considered that for a moment or two. "Of course, they could agree with me and still go outside. If they do, I'm outta here."

"High stakes," I said.

"I know." She sounded grim. "But I think we've got a shot. I need to have everything finished by Friday. I really do need your help but it means more late nights. Can you handle that?"

"Sure," I said.

"I mean, it could actually pay off for you, too," she said. "Who knows?"

Leslie was still awake, lying in bed reading, when I got home. She was pale and she looked tired.

"Home early," she said.

"Home late," I said. "It's almost nine."

"Early," she said. Insisting, almost.

"Okay," I said. "Early."

"Too early, anyway, for you to have already eaten dinner at the Post Road," she said.

I felt a little cold spasm pass down my body. We didn't do this, I thought. We'd fought, for sure, but we'd never done this.

"Somebody cared enough to call and tell me about it," she said. "She felt 'just terrible' doing it but she thought I should know."

"Who?" I said.

"Doesn't matter."

"Why not?"

"Because the whole thing doesn't matter. My 'friend'—that's what she called herself, can you believe that?" Leslie had a way of laughing that expressed the purest contempt, and that's the way she laughed now.

"My 'friend,'" she went on, "thinks it should matter. But you didn't have a chance to tell me, did you? When you came home last night, I was asleep. And when you got up this morning, I was still asleep. I'm sick from the drugs and you knew that, so you didn't wake me up to tell me you'd gone out to dinner with your boss."

I nodded and she said, "Right?" at exactly the same time.

"You would have told me. I know that."

I sat down on the edge of the bed and held her hand. It was cold. She was either feverish or cold most of the time. I felt the familiar, mingled feelings of helplessness and compassion.

"You would have told me. Probably tonight."

"I imagine," I said, but I wasn't sure I would have.

"You would have," she said. "I know it for a fact. You know why?"

I shook my head.

"No," she said, smiling thinly, "you wouldn't. That's part of it."

"You lost me."

"You're not very mysterious, Jack," she said.

"Maybe I'll work on it," I said.

"Don't bother," she said, "and that's not my point."

"What is your point?"

"I don't know . . . I guess I was just trying to make sense out of that phone call."

"Any luck?"

She shrugged. "I know one thing, for sure. The woman who called me?"

"Yes?"

"She made it sound like she was so sorry. That she would have given anything in the world for it not to be true but she just felt like she owed it to me to call and tell me. But you know what?"

"What?"

"She *loved* it. She's married to a man who will sleep with anything in a skirt. So she wanted me to know that, in spite of what I might think, we're in the same shape—only she doesn't have cancer and she lives in a bigger house than mine."

"Sounds like a certified creep."

"Not necessarily. Just a woman who's getting older and more bitter. Not that different from the rest of us.

"I was mad, at first, after that call. Then I spent some time feeling sorry for myself. Your boss is younger than I am and she has big, beautiful hair. So it didn't take much to work up a real good case of self-pity. But after a while I got bored with that, so I turned magnanimous and spent some time feeling sorry for the woman who called.

"You know how that goes—you have to be really unhappy to do something like that. That old song.

"But I got over that, too. Then I started trying to imagine how things would be if you were more mysterious and out at the Post Road late at night having what my mother used to call 'an assignation.' Leaving your bald wife to throw up at home alone."

She paused for a moment and gave me a kind of rueful smile.

"You know what I came up with?"

I shook my head.

"I decided I'm okay with that, too. If it happened, I'd kick you out and give you two hours to get your stuff out before the garbage man came to haul it away.

And I'd still have enough left over, when I was done with that, to beat this rotten cancer and get on with my life."

I nodded because I believed her.

"And I'll tell you something else," she said, looking at me with her eyes level.

"What's that?"

"Realizing that has made me feel better than anything that's happened since the day I found that miserable lump."

42

Leslie passed through the low point between treatments and was climbing up the other side. She started spending a little time at her desk, saw some friends, and took the dogs for walks. But she was still deeply fatigued and taking naps in the afternoon.

I was working late every night and if I tried to apologize, she would hold up her hand, palm facing me, and say, "Jack, you don't have any choice. It is your job. And anyway, baby, we need that health insurance."

Elena had stopped asking if I could stay late. It was just assumed that I could. It seemed to me that we were no longer working up anything new or even fine-tuning what we already had. But that was in character for Elena. When she submitted her plan to the Ghouls and Ron, she would be certain there were no loose ends for them to pull at. It would be perfect and they would have two choices—reject it or accept it.

We did not go out to the Post Road again. We did not, in fact, go out at all. We ordered pizza or Chinese and kept working.

Thursday, when we were finishing, she said, "You feel like going somewhere for a drink?"

It had been five hours of close company and I could smell her perfume. Sitting next to each other in front of the computer, studying columns of figures on the monitor, our knees and shoulders touched. Now and then she put her hand over mine to guide the mouse and click on something that caught her attention. Her fingers were long and delicate and her skin was cool and soft.

She wore a black sweater made from some kind of soft, clinging material—mohair, maybe—and she'd left it unbuttoned at the throat, exposing just a little of the swell of her breasts where they weren't covered by a black bra. Neither of us were kids and we knew what was going on.

I should have said no when she asked about the drink. I knew that, too.

"Sounds good," I said.

It was a ten-minute drive to the place she suggested. She drove her car and I followed, telling myself that I had said yes simply because she was the boss and when the boss asked you for a drink, that's what you did. You said yes.

But that was pure futility.

"Okay, then," I said, out loud. "Are you ready for this?"

Since there was no one actually riding shotgun, I answered my own question out loud.

"No."

But that didn't stop me from pulling up in an empty space next to her Audi. Just about the time I cut the engine, I had a vague, unprompted thought: *Sooner or later in this life, you'll run up against your sorry, inadequate self.*

She drank vodka and I had a beer. The table was very small . . . that, or I was just acutely aware of her and it felt like we were sitting very close. We raised our glasses to each other.

"To good work," she said. "And I couldn't have done it without you. As long as we've worked together, I didn't know how much you understood about things."

I nodded and felt . . . what? Flattered, sure. But also needed in a way. That, and a dismal sense of guilt. I fought the one back and rode with the others.

"When this is over," she said, "I'm going to the Islands."

I asked where and she talked dreamily about Martinique, going on about the diving, the food, the beaches, and the sun. I said something about how it sounded wonderful.

"Oh, it's better than that. You need to try it yourself. You've been working just as hard as I have. You should get away, too."

"I just might do that," I said.

We finished our drinks and I offered to get the check and she didn't fight me.

When I held her car door open, before she got in, she said, "That was nice, Jack. Thank you."

"Good-night," I said.

"Only a few more of these nights."

43

The next morning, when I brought her some tea and orange juice in bed, Leslie said, "I meant to tell you; I'm going to New York this weekend. Betsy invited me down. Her husband is at some conference and she wants to take me shopping."

"Should be fun for you," I said, even though a part of me didn't like the idea of her being away. I had started thinking of myself as her protector even though I couldn't say what I was protecting her from. And then there was the other thing . . .

"I told Betsy it wasn't really my season for shopping and she said, 'Why? Because you've got cancer? Don't be silly, that's exactly why you need to shop. We'll look for things that will cheer you up, just like if you were getting divorced from Jake, or whatever his name is.'"

Betsy had never bothered to remember my name. The way she saw it, she'd been there with Leslie a long time before I came on the scene and would probably still be there long after I was gone.

"New clothes might be good for your morale," I said.

"My morale is fine, thank you very much. And I'm not sure I'm up for Bloomingdale's. I mean, I'm feeling stronger than I did a week ago. But I'm not sure I feel *that* strong."

"Pace yourself," I said. "You'll do fine."

"I guess," she said. "What about you? Will you be all right?"

"What do you mean?" I said, trying to sound offhand and wondering if she had picked up some signal. Or heard something on the gossip line.

"You know, by yourself."

"Sure," I said, now trying hard not to come off too casual. "Why not?"

"I don't know. I thought maybe you'd miss me and be lonesome."

"I will. But I'll also be all right."

"And you've got that work thing—the reorganization—to keep you busy."

"Yes," I said, "there's always that."

"But you know what, Jack. You've been working awfully hard. You ought to do something for yourself this weekend. Go up in the woods like you used to. It's been years and you used to love it."

"Maybe I will."

"Do it, please. It'll make me feel happy, when I'm trying on clothes at Sak's, if I know you're doing something that makes you feel good."

"Okay," I said. "You got it."

I could feel that other person—my very own Mr. Hyde—leering and saying, *Right. Whatever makes me feel good.*

At dawn on Saturday morning I was standing on a ledge on a soft, round mountain a mile or so from the house, holding the old Fred Bear bow I hadn't used in years. It had taken me almost an hour to get there, walking an old, overgrown logging trace with lots of switchbacks. I was sweating and panting when I finally reached the ledge.

This had been my best place to hunt. I was here when I drew down on my first deer and watched the flight of the arrow until it struck just behind the animal's shoulder with a hard thump that sounded like something you'd hear on a football field. I waited for half an hour before I went out to find the blood trail and start tracking. I was shaking the whole time.

I found the deer, stone dead, less than fifty yards from where he'd been standing when the arrow went through his heart, and I sat down on the ground next to him. I was still shaking and thought I might actually cry.

Inch by Inch

It was almost dark by the time I started out of the woods. The leaves and dirt made for resistance and it was hard work dragging the deer. But there was a fat October moon, so I could see my way. The blood on my hands and wrists seemed to shine like bronze in the moonlight.

That had been more than ten years ago and it should have felt good, being back. But I felt like I was hiding out, not hunting.

The woods seemed to gather light slowly for an hour or so, and the sun felt good when it did finally climb over the ridge. I stopped shuddering and took off the sweater I'd been wearing. I ate one of the local apples I'd picked off a wind-seeded tree on the walk in. It was hard and tart.

I moved around the ledge as the breeze and the light changed. I walked a couple of trails. There was a pile of fairly fresh bear scat on one of them. The bear had been eating apples, too; tearing up one of the old, abandoned orchards in the area.

By midday, it was warm and I was sleepy. I found a level place with no rocks, rolled up my sweater for a pillow, and lay down on the ground for a nap. I slept for an hour or so.

When I woke up, I moved to another part of the ledge and found a place to stand where I could survey the clearing with the wind in my face. The few remaining leaves, mostly on the birch trees, had turned a rich golden color and seemed to gleam in the otherwise monochromatic woods.

The sun dropped behind the mountain and I put my sweater back on. There was barely ten or fifteen minutes of light left when I saw the deer.

I saw the antlers first. That happens a lot, and my theory is that the antlers are as much for masculine display—a version of a peacock's feathers—as they are tools for combat.

This was a handsome rack, with the thickness and the spread that trophy hunters like. The deer's body was heavy and muscled like a linebacker's. It was easily the best buck I'd ever seen.

With the light dying, he had come out to feed on acorns and beechnuts, and I suspected he would move around the ledge, trying to quarter the wind, and it would be dark before he came in range.

He moved carefully, raising his head and testing the wind every few steps. But he also moved quickly. Unless something spooked him, I thought, he'd be in range while there was still enough light to shoot.

I felt my heart beating heavier and faster than normal and my breathing sounded loud enough to alert the deer, though I knew it wasn't. My legs trembled slightly and my mouth felt dry. The old, eternal signals.

The buck came closer, not quite in range, and when he went behind a heavy oak, I raised the bow. It seemed to take a long time for him to cross those last few yards before he was in range. My shoulders ached, then burned, and I wanted to lower the bow to rest. But the movement would spook the deer.

I could see his lips move, hear the crunch when he bit down on an acorn. He looked straight at me and I could not blink until he looked away. Twenty steps—no more—from where I stood, the buck turned, giving me a heart-lung shot.

I drew back on the bowstring, careful but steady. The deer stiffened slightly, aware of the movement but not yet alarmed.

I had taught myself to shoot instinctively, and when my knuckle touched my cheek, the deer was still broadside to me, framed against the background of a light gray space in the woods. It was perfect.

44

There was a moon, but this time my hands weren't shining with blood and I was not dragging something I'd killed.

I hadn't missed. I hadn't even shot. When the knuckle of my thumb touched my cheekbone, my fingers had stayed firm on the knock of the arrow. I'd held at full draw for a second or two, then released the tension on the string and lowered the bow. The buck crashed off through the woods, and I saw his flag moving through the trees and heard the sound of branches breaking as he strained for the safety of the conifers.

It was a minute or two before I settled down. Then I put the arrow back in the quiver and started for home on the logging road.

When I got back to the house, I fed the dogs and made eggs and bacon for myself. Four eggs, four strips of bacon, and four pieces of toast. I'd had a bowl of oatmeal before I left the house and since then only a couple of sour, wormy apples. I ate standing up in the kitchen.

When I finished eating, I left the dishes in the sink and went to my study, where the message light was blinking on the answering machine. One call.

I pressed the button. The tape hissed, then began to play out the message:

"Hello. This is Elena LeFevre calling. Jack, I'm sorry to bother you and your family at home on the weekend, but I really need to talk to you. It will take more than a quick phone conversation, I'm afraid, so could you call me and we'll set something up."

She rattled off her home phone number and I wrote it down. Then the tape hissed again before rewinding.

I looked at the number; studied it so hard I could have been trying to break some kind of code that was buried inside it.

I picked up the phone. Hesitated. Put it back down without dialing the number or feeling especially virtuous about that.

Maybe it was just my day for not pulling the trigger.

I felt like drinking some bourbon, which is what I'd usually done in the past when I came back from hunting trips. But the night wasn't over and I figured that it wouldn't take more than a hit or two of Beam before I'd start looking at the number I'd written down and think about picking up the phone.

So I took a hot shower and put on an old cotton sweat suit and sat at my desk. I took care of some e-mail, then looked at a shelf of books I'd read and loved twenty years ago. There was some comfort, I supposed, in the familiar.

This night I read *The Bear.* It was touch and go with the dense language, but it had the right feel after a day in the woods and after a while I was transported back to the Mississippi wilderness. Two hours passed and I would have said it had been fifteen minutes.

Sam Fathers, Lion, Ike, Boone Hoggenbeck . . . I was with them until a sudden noise shocked me out of my trance.

It was, of course, the telephone. I let it ring and when the machine kicked in, whoever was calling hung up.

45

I was in early on Monday and left a voice mail for Elena, apologizing for not calling her back over the weekend. But I did not explain.

And she never mentioned it.

We worked late Monday and Tuesday but there was no casual touching and nothing said about drinks after. On Wednesday, when we were finishing up, I said, "I won't be in Monday. Personal business."

She looked up from the chart she had been studying. Her eyes were level and cold. I'd used the wrong phrase. Personal business was what some woman in the shipping department would say when she was going down to swear out a restraining order against a boyfriend. Or when a forklift driver told you he had to be in court on a DUI or was going up to Maine for a little early deer hunting.

Executives like us didn't have personal business. Not, anyway, the kind that caused us to miss work during a critical time like this.

"You can't reschedule?" Elena said so that it did not sound much like a question.

"No."

She kept her eyes on me, waiting for a fuller explanation or some sign that I knew I was letting her down and was at least aware of it and remorseful about it. But I didn't say anything.

"I see," she said, cutting her eyes away and going for her hair.

"That's unfortunate," she said. "Really inconvenient, as a matter of fact. I'm planning on putting this"—she picked up the thick folder that held our plan for reorganizing our division and, if you read between the lines, the whole company—"in the hands of Ron and the Ghouls on Friday. It will give them something to read and think about over the weekend. I was counting on your help Monday if they want to talk to me about it."

She dropped the file and it landed with a heavy thud on the top of the polished cherry-wood table.

"I'll be here Tuesday," I said. "But Monday is out of the question."

"You can't really expect me to tell them that their questions will just have to wait for a day or two until it's convenient for me to meet with them."

"Tell them whatever you want," I said. "I can't make it Monday."

She kept staring at me and I suppose it was meant to rattle me.

"If we are going to be a team," she said, "then I have to know I can depend on you."

"You can depend on my being here on Tuesday."

Another long, still silence.

Then she said, simply, "Fine."

Leslie and I drove to Boston Monday morning. It was getting to be a routine sort of deal. We'd make small talk with Patty for a few minutes before she got down to business and hooked Leslie up to her bag of hot red fluid. Leslie would sit in her chair with her eyes closed and I would hold her hand. Andy would come by after class and relieve me. When the IV bag was empty, Patty would put the customary Band-Aid over the hole in Leslie's arm. Then we would ride down on the elevator, get our parking ticket validated, and hug Andy and say good-bye.

* * *

Inch by Inch

On the way out of town, Leslie said, "You remember how I couldn't get that second treatment when I was supposed to, because my white blood count was too low? How I had to wait an extra week?"

"Sure."

"Remember how upset I was at the time?"

"No more than anyone would have been."

"Maybe. But I was pretty bent out of shape. And you know what?"

"What?"

"Turns out that it was a great piece of luck."

"How do you figure?"

"Well, I've been studying the calendar and the way I see it, I just had my third treatment. I'll be in the low point between treatments in two weeks, right?"

"Right."

"And two weeks after that, I'll have climbed out of the hole, right?"

"Right."

"Well, that is exactly Thanksgiving weekend."

"Really?"

"Yes. Really. And it means the kids can come home for the long weekend. Andy and I will cook a big dinner. We were working on the menu today. It's going to be an absolutely traditional Thanksgiving. Turkey, cranberry sauce, acorn squash, wild rice, pumpkin pie. The whole deal."

"Sounds great," I said, wondering as the words came out of my mouth if I would have been able to talk about roast turkey and candied yams with poison running through my veins

"And you want some more good news?"

"Absolutely."

"I come back here for my next—and last—treatment on the Monday after Thanksgiving. That means that I'll have climbed back out of the hole in time for Christmas."

From the tone of her voice, she couldn't have been happier.

"That is good news," I said.

"It will be a wonderful Christmas," she said, "with a lot to celebrate."

Then she put her head back on the seat and went to sleep. She didn't wake up until we were almost home. She was so sick, she almost didn't make it inside when I parked. But she went to bed happy, still talking about Thanksgiving and Christmas.

46

Bill Winter sat at his kitchen table and we talked while I cooked.

"Those people I mentioned" he said, "the ones who were thinking about starting up a new business in your line?"

"I remember."

"Well," he said, "they're ready to start making some serious moves. Including hiring some key people."

"I see."

"Listen, Jack," he said, "it's none of my business and if you don't want to talk about it . . ."

"No. I'm interested, but it's going to have to wait till tomorrow. I need to get dinner home to Leslie."

A week or so later, Bill and I met with the men he'd been telling me about. They were in town to discuss with Bill the financing for their new company. And, according to Bill, because they wanted to talk to me.

We met at the local steak house, a place called On the Hoof. Bill already had a table when I got there. Back corner.

"They should be here any minute," he said. "What are you drinking?"

I ordered a beer. I'd taken my first sip when the two men arrived and there were handshakes all around. Steve and Jay were both in their thirties. The skiing and the climbing showed. They had very white teeth, good tans, and most of their hair. They radiated a kind of easy vitality.

We followed the usual protocols—small talk over drinks, a little general business conversation during dinner—and then we got down to cases. Bill had a brandy. The rest of us finished up the wine that we'd ordered with dinner—a cabernet that Steve liked. We all had coffee.

They were serious about the company they wanted to start. Their mission statement, which they read to me, made it sound like they were going to liberate Tibet or at least save the redwoods. But they were sincere about it. Their inspiration, I thought, was probably Chouinard and that was understandable, since his sincerity had a lot to do with the making of Patagonia.

Anyway, I didn't mind it that they took themselves seriously. I was at a pretty serious point myself.

They asked questions and I answered them. I had a feeling that I was doing all right. I wasn't trying too hard and the words seemed to come naturally.

Nobody made any offers. That wasn't part of the protocol. But I felt sure one would be coming.

I thought about it over the next few days, but not much. There were other things on my mind.

Leslie was in bad shape, barely able to make it out of bed. She looked worse than tired and beyond fatigue. It was a look I remembered seeing in New York on the face of addicts who had been running a long high without food or sleep and looked like they were being devoured from the inside out.

"I'm sorry, Jack," she said one night. "I'm trying but I just can't rally."

"I think you're doing great," I said.

"You are such a bad liar."

"I mean it."

"I know I'm a drag right now," she said. "And I apologize. But wait till you see me at Thanksgiving. This little girl is going to shine, shine, shine."

* * *

"Will you take it?" Bill Winter said. He was sitting at his kitchen counter, sipping a Côte du Rhone that he'd said was "not too shabby."

"That's assuming," I said, "that they make an offer."

"They will, and I can promise you'll make two, maybe three times what you're pulling down now. Bigger office, better title . . . fatter package all the way around."

"I could live with that," I said.

"So what's the downside?"

I thought for a second or two while I checked the chicken that was roasting in the oven.

"Two things I can think of," I said.

"Which are . . . ?

"Where do they want me to work and when do they want me to be there?"

"That's easy," Bill said. "Colorado and right away."

I nodded.

"That's a problem?"

"Could be," I said.

"Listen, Jack," Bill said, and his voice dropped a little so he sounded almost grave. "I know what's on your mind and I understand. But you're looking at a one-time opportunity. These boys won't be coming back around next year."

"I understand."

"They have doctors in Colorado."

I didn't say anything.

"Okay, sorry," he said "You know that. But there has to be a way. You fly home on weekends. You get one of your kids to withdraw from school and fill in for you. These treatments won't go on forever and when there is a pause in the action, you make the move to another hospital. It has been done before. Gets done all the time."

He wasn't saying anything that I hadn't already thought. And he was right. Obviously.

Which didn't make it any easier.

* * *

The offer came and it was even better than Bill had said it would be. When I told Steve that I was grateful but would like twenty-four hours to think about it, he said that was fine but that he needed me in Denver, ready to start work, right after Thanksgiving. They'd put me up in a hotel, he said, until I'd found a house.

I thanked him.

When I told Bill, while I was cooking, he urged me again to take it. "You've got to grab it when it comes around," he said. "You don't get many second chances."

I didn't mention it to Leslie. She would have urged me to take it, too, as long as I was sure it was what I wanted to do. I told myself I didn't have to ask her since I already knew what she would say and, anyway, she had enough on her mind.

I didn't sleep much, thinking about it, and in the morning, as soon as it was late enough in Denver, I called and turned the job down.

You need a reason, I suppose, and mine went like this: There might not be much I could do for Leslie—I was just a cheerleader and a coat holder in this fight, and trying to be a good one—but I could at least pass on an easy chance to abandon her. Especially when she was at the bottom of the chemo pit.

47

It was Thanksgiving week and Leslie had rallied a little. We went grocery shopping together a couple of days before the kids arrived. It tired her out so much that she had to take a nap when we got home. I put the things away and made dinner from leftovers.

Leslie recovered, though, and the next morning, Wednesday, she got up early and started cooking. She was making cranberry sauce when I left to pick up Andy, and the kitchen was full of steam and moist cooking smells.

"How can you stand it?" I said.

"Stand what?"

"The smell. I thought it made you sick."

"What smell?" she said, smiling. "I feel great. You go get my baby girl and bring her to me."

The bus stopped at a town about forty miles away. I allowed a little over an hour and got there early. So I sat in the truck with the heater on, listening to the radio and watching for the bus. I remembered picking Andy up from the school bus and how she would wave as soon as she saw me. When she didn't wave, it meant she'd had a bad day at school.

I wondered if she would wave today when she stepped off the Greyhound and saw me.

There was talk of the economy on the radio and the usual indicators of bad times ahead. I'd heard it all before and, anyway, I worked in one of those leading indicator businesses. Nobody had to tell me it was bad out there.

The bus was ten minutes late and Andy was one of the last off. She waved when she saw me.

"Hi, Dad," she said when she hugged me. "How's Mom?"

"She's fine. She would have come but she needed to cook."

"I thought that made her sick."

"She's making an exception because it's Thanksgiving and you're home."

Andy seemed happy, but she looked thin—almost gaunt—to me. But then, it was probably how she wanted to look, and she had, no doubt, worked hard to get there. So I just said, "You look good," and took her bag.

When we were on the road home, I asked her about school and she said everything was fine. She asked how things were with me and I said they were fine. It got a little harder after that.

I sometimes wondered what Andy and Leslie found to talk about so effortlessly.

We'd ridden in silence for a while when Andy said, sounding like the little girl I'd picked up from the school bus, "Dad, how is Mom, really?"

"Don't you talk to her?" I said.

"Sure, every day. But that doesn't mean she tells me the truth."

"Oh, I think she does."

"Why?" It was a challenge.

"Well, I think because you are the one she talks to every day. And I imagine she'd consider talking to anyone—especially her own daughter—every day a waste of time if she couldn't tell the truth."

"She talks to you every day. Right?"

"Yeah. I suppose she does."

"And does she tell you the truth?"

"Sure," I said.

"So she's told you she's going to be all right and you believe her."

"I said she tells me the truth. I didn't say she tells me everything."

"Isn't that the way it's supposed to be? I mean, you're married. You share everything, right?"

Things may start out that way, I thought. But after a while, you learn to give each other some latitude.

"I'm probably the wrong person for you to be asking," I said. "If your mother is not telling me something about her condition, then I figure she's got her reasons and I respect them."

"Really? You really mean that?"

"Yes."

"Wow," she said. She folded her arms and looked out the window as though what I'd just said made further conversation impossible.

"Let me ask you something," I said.

"Okay."

"Have you got some particular reason for thinking your Mom is holding out?"

Andy shook her head slightly. "I just hear her talking to that nurse. The nice one?"

"Patty."

"Right. She was saying to Patty that she'd had this backache. And that it was a real bad one. Patty wanted to do an x-ray. They were sort of arguing about it but Mom said she'd wait and see if it got any better.

"So I got this book out of the library, and it said that when breast cancer spreads, a lot of the time it goes to the bones and one way you know is when you get backaches."

I thought about that for a while. There are so many danger signs and you are always on the lookout for them. But this one was new to me and made it seem like cancer was everywhere. Maybe even in the air.

"Has she said anything about backaches to you?" Andy said.

"No. But that doesn't mean anything. She gets backaches. She's even gone to a chiropractor for them."

"Has she been to a chiropractor lately?"

"I don't know."

We rode in silence for a while. Ten or fifteen miles. The road was climbing out of the Connecticut River valley and into one of the ski areas. The cars on the road with us had roof racks with skis attached. We drove into a light snowfall.

"You might be onto something, kid," I said. "And you might not. But the next couple of days are important to your mom, and if she's not thinking about it, then maybe we shouldn't either. If she says she's fine, and she's not talking about backaches, then . . ."

"Okay," Andy said. "I can get down with that. I'm just worried, Dad. That's all."

"Me, too, but we won't let it ruin her Thanksgiving. Okay?"

"Sure."

48

Leslie and Andy hugged in the kitchen while I took Andy's bag to her old room. By the time I was back downstairs, Leslie had put Andy to work chopping onions for the turkey dressing.

I left them and went to the office, where things felt even slower than they usually do on the day before a holiday. I put in an hour on paperwork, then left for the airport to meet Brad.

He looked older and stronger—still more time in the weight room—and his expression was even more stern than when I'd last seen him. He was beginning to look like the warrior he wanted to become.

But he smiled when he saw me and I got a fleeting look at the boy he had been.

Like Andy, he asked about his mother.

"She's doing fine," I said. "And she can't wait to see you. You can't believe how much she's been looking forward to this."

That seemed to satisfy him. He wasn't feeling any foreboding about back-aches, so on our drive home we talked about other things. His plans, mostly. He would graduate and get his commission in May.

"Will you and Mom be able to make it?" he said.

"We wouldn't miss it."

"Well, I know you want to. But . . . I mean, do you think she'll be able to handle it?"

"The whole cancer deal will be history by then," I said. I felt myself hesitate, just a little, as the thought of what Andy had said about backaches passed across my mind like a thickening cloud. But Brad didn't catch the change in my mood.

"Well, that's great," he said. "There's just one other problem."

"What's that?"

"You know how when you get your commission, you get someone to pin your bars on your uniform?"

"Yes," I said. I'd seen the pictures.

"Well, do you think Mom would be upset if I asked someone else?"

"No. Of course not."

Then he explained that there was someone he'd been seeing a lot of. She went to the University of Virginia, just up the road from VMI. They weren't getting married or anything. But it was fairly serious and he thought he'd ask her to pin the bars.

When I said I was sure his mother would understand, he seemed relieved to change the subject, and we talked about other things until we were home.

We did what we always did and what I assumed most people do over Thanksgiving. We cooked; we ate. We sat around; we talked. We went out for walks when we'd been inside too long and we came inside when we got cold. It can be good or bad, I suppose, depending on the deeper, subsurface feelings. In our house, this Thanksgiving, it was good. Fragile, maybe, but still good.

One of the dealers I worked with had sent some oysters from the Chesapeake. Brad and I opened them over the sink and served them on the half shell with lemon, black pepper, and horseradish. We had a couple of bottles of wine that Bill Winter had recommended—a Sancerre—that went with the oysters.

Thanksgiving dinner was a proper feast, with a large turkey that Leslie had basted and roasted to the color of a ripe pecan. Brad carved. Andy and I had constructed a harvest centerpiece made of gourds, dried corn, and stalks of wild cranberries. We lit candles. Brad and I wore suits. He looked uncomfortable in his, especially with his military haircut. Leslie wore her most recent wig. In the candlelight, you didn't see the fatigue and the wear of the drugs. She looked young. And happy.

We played hearts and charades. We built fires in the fireplace. We sat around and talked, and on Sunday, before it was time for Andy's bus and Brad's plane, we bought the Sunday *New York Times* and did the crossword puzzle. We almost finished it.

It was early Sunday afternoon. Andy and Brad had gone out and were waiting for me. I was in the kitchen with Leslie. She had said her good-byes and she was not coming out to the car to say them again.

"It's too cold," she said, "and besides, I'm crying."

"We all had a great time," I said. "And they'll be home again for Christmas. That's only one month. And, after tomorrow, no more chemo."

"You're right," she said. "It was a great weekend and I have nothing but good things to look forward to."

"Then why are you crying?"

"I'm crying," she said, "because I can."

In the morning, Leslie went for her last treatment with a friend who had offered to drive her. We'd had a small argument over that. I felt like it was my job to drive her and be there with her in the hospital.

"Jack," she said, "will you please leave it alone. It's not like I'm having a baby. Chemo was scary the first time. You were sweet to come, but now it's just another day at the office. One more dose of red poison. Anyway, Ann wants to drive me. I'm almost doing her a favor. She feels guilty because she's been avoiding me."

So she left the house early. After she was gone, I watched Imus on cable and drank coffee. Eventually, I got bored and went to the office. I was the first one there.

An hour later, I was called into the conference room and fired.

* * *

It was clean and quick. There were only three people in the chamber: the Ghouls and the vice president from personnel, a man named Cord.

He nodded at a chair. I sat in it and faced the three of them across the table.

"This is not easy and there is no point in dragging it out," Cord said. He was bald and paunchy. He looked like a man who lived in a world of unpleasant choices.

"We're terminating your employment immediately. As you know, the company is going through a restructuring and we are doing away with a number of positions. Unfortunately, one of them is yours."

Since I didn't know what to say, I didn't say anything.

"We had sufficient reason to terminate you for cause, but after some discussion, we've decided against that."

"Cause?" I said. "What cause?" I had been at the company three times as long as Cord, who knew nothing about the things we made or the customers we sold to.

One of the Ghouls spoke up. "An unusually high number of days out of the office lately," he said, sounding bored. "An unwillingness to work with your superior on an urgent report having to do with the company restructuring because it would interfere with your plans. Not exactly the cooperative attitude this company needs from its executives in tough times."

"You've gotta be kidding."

"Hardly."

Elena had told them, obviously. I was surprised and then wondered if I should have been.

"Then," the other Ghoul said, "there is the matter of your meeting with people who plan to launch a company that will be a direct competitor."

How, I wondered, had they found out about that?

"So we could have terminated for cause," Cord said. "But we won't. Now, I'll explain the severance package."

I listened but not very attentively. I got the part about three months' salary and medical insurance and transferring my retirement account. Then they moved on to the next part.

They wanted me to return to my office, where somebody from security would monitor my packing and then escort me from the premises. I would not be allowed to access my computer to copy files.

For some reason, I resented that more than any other part of it. Being treated like a Goddamned thief. And by this crew.

The packing didn't take long. My office was only the place where I did my work and somebody else paid the rent and owned the furniture, so I didn't keep a lot of personal stuff there. A couple of photographs, not very recent, of Leslie and the kids that I put in a box along with a couple of books and some odds and ends. I was out of the building and pulling away from the parking lot in less than fifteen minutes.

49

I didn't know where to go or what to do. Home was out of the question, but there wasn't really any other place where I spent time. I felt unmoored.

I drove around for a while with my head full of fragmentary, incoherent thoughts. I picked some shirts up at the laundry. I went to a breakfast place and drank a cup of coffee that I couldn't taste and read a newspaper that made no sense.

The only consistent impulse I felt was to hurt someone. I imagined myself going back into the office with a baseball bat or a shotgun and leaving a trail of destruction. I couldn't quite picture myself actually shooting anyone but I understood, for the first time, how people got there.

I'd learned, long ago, that the best thing for me when I felt this way was some hard exercise. So I went to the gym. It had been a while. Since the whole cancer thing had started, I had felt like it was indulgence, working on my own body while Leslie's was deteriorating.

I skipped the usual soft warm-up on the stairstepper or the treadmill and went right to the weights.

I noticed, between sets, that I was the only man in the place. Which made me work harder. I stayed on the bench, doing set after set, dropping the weight between sets and squeezing out every last rep, until my whole body was trembling and I felt a steady, deep burn in my chest. It was almost as satisfying as those images of the mayhem I saw myself doing to the office and that conference room where the Ghouls and Cord sat in judgment. After two hours on the weights, I was too tired to feel the anger anymore. I was shaking but it was with exhaustion, not rage.

It was now late morning. I took a long shower, dressed, and called Bill Winter.

"You have maybe the worst sense of timing of anyone I know," he said.

"Tell me about it."

He wasn't free for lunch, he said. "Meet me at the house later."

I ate lunch at a diner, then went to a movie. I couldn't remember the last time I'd watched a movie in the middle of the day.

Strangely, it was Bill who was drunk when I got to his house. Maybe not drunk, exactly, but you could tell he'd had more than one or two glasses of wine. I'd only seen him like this once or twice, and then late, at parties.

"I'd say you should have listened to me," he said, "but that's probably already occurred to you."

"Yes," I said. "So thanks for not mentioning it."

"I'm drinking single-malt," he said. "You want some?"

I said I'd pass. I didn't have anything to celebrate and there was something about the picture of me, unemployed and sipping Lagavulin while Leslie was working the last dose of chemo through her system . . .

"Suit yourself," Bill said, and took a careful sip from a brandy snifter.

"You know, first time I got fired," he said, "I went out and got roaring. It was one of those deals. The market took a dive—you remember, nineteen eighty-seven—and I was just part of the herd of young studs working on the Street. They canned more than a thousand of us. The brokerages were hurt and bleeding that week but the bars did fine. I managed to get into the last fistfight of my life that night. Came out of it with a broken nose and two black eyes for my trouble. I couldn't even go to job interviews for a month."

"What did you do?"

He shrugged. "I lived off the severance till I could show my face. But it was going to take longer than a month for the market to come back from that particular massacre. So I sold shirts at Paul Stuart for a while. Moved to a cheaper apartment. Canceled the lease on the Porsche. The usual. When these things happen, you ride them out."

He took another sip and asked me about the severance.

"Cheap bastards," he said when I'd described it. "But then, we knew that. The medical could be a problem."

I'd already thought about that, but so far my thinking hadn't gotten much beyond more cancer, more treatments, no insurance, and no money.

"You'll figure something," Bill said. "And I've got a friend who understands these things. I'll tell him about you and e-mail you his number."

There was no chance that I could still catch on with the men from Colorado, Bill said without my asking. I hadn't asked because I already knew.

"I called before I left the office and talked to Jay. You know, they were a little chapped that you turned them down in the first place. Now . . ." He shrugged.

"Sure," I said. "I understand."

"Sucks, for sure," Bill said, "but I did ask him about the possibility of some consulting. They have a lot to learn about the nuts and bolts of the business and you're in a decent position to be their teacher."

"I appreciate that, Bill."

"Well, it ain't entirely altruism," he said. "You're good and I know that. I'm an investor in this thing and I'm looking out for my stake. So if you do some consulting for them, do me a favor."

"What's that?"

"Consult good."

"Oh, I will. Promise." I was having second thoughts about that drink.

"You're going to be all right," he said. "You're going to have some bad nights. But you're going to be all right."

He shook his head mournfully.

"You okay?" I said.

"Yeah. Compared to you, anyway."

"What is it?"

"I got the papers today. So I guess I'm officially a three-time loser. That's why I'm getting after the single-malt."

"I'm sorry to hear it, Bill."

"Yeah . . . well."

He drained the snifter and refilled it.

"Don't be feeling sorry for me," he said. "I can do a better job of that myself."

"Right."

50

I was home sitting in the study, working on my résumé, when Leslie returned from Boston and her treatments. Her friend, Ann, was worried about her condition and came in with her.

"I'm fine, honestly," I heard Leslie say. "Anyway, Jack is here if I need anything."

They were in the kitchen but the sound of their voices carried.

"You're sure?"

"Absolutely. But thank you for the ride. And the company."

"Don't be silly," Ann said. "I'm just glad I could do something. Even if it wasn't much."

"It was a big help. Jack would have come with me but he needs to be at the office. Anyway, it was fun to visit."

"Take care of yourself," Ann said.

"I will."

I heard the door close as Ann left. I walked out to the kitchen, where Leslie was leaning against the counter with her eyes closed and her arms crossed in front of her so she looked like she was hugging herself. She had taken off her wig and there were gleaming beads of sweat on her forehead. She looked weak. She also looked like she was in pain.

When she heard me, she opened her eyes, straightened up, and smiled.

"Free at last," she said.

"No more chemo," I said.

"That's right. No more chemo. To hell with cancer."

"Are you okay?" I said. "How do you feel?"

"Never better," she said. "I told you, remember?"

"Remember what?"

"I told you I was going to beat this thing if I had to fight it inch by inch. Right now, I feel like a mountain climber and I made the top."

She reached into a shopping bag and brought out a bottle of champagne. "So now we celebrate, no matter how much it makes me puke."

"You're sure . . . ?"

"Yes," she interrupted. "I am absolutely sure. I've never felt more like partying in my life, even if I do feel like hell. I even got an x-ray today and found out my back isn't hurting because of cancer."

"What is it?" I said, feeling a rush of relief.

"Who knows? Stress, maybe. And now that will go away."

"You hadn't told me about your back," I said. "I knew something was wrong . . ."

"I know, Jack. I got tired of worrying you, tired of the whole thing. And now it's over. Except for the radiation."

"Yes."

"And that's a walk in the park. A piece of cake."

"Right."

"So we need to celebrate."

"Maybe we should wait."

"Not happening, Jack. You may have to drink most of this champagne, but we are opening it and we are going to celebrate the end of chemo, even if I gag on the first sip. You chill it and I'll go change and maybe lie down just for a minute."

I nodded and she looked at me like she was noticing me for the first time.

"What?" she said.

I shook my head. I felt, suddenly, like I was raining on her parade. Just like me to get fired on the day she finished chemo.

"Come on, Jack, tell me. What is it, baby?"

I might as well have been telling her about a change in the weather—a heavy rain that meant we'd have to postpone something we'd been planning. Her face showed only the mildest concern, like she was trying to work out who needed to be called about the change of plans.

"Well, what a bunch of low-life creeps," she said. "But then, I've always known that."

"Yeah, well . . ."

"You're better off out of there, Jack. You're way too good for them."

"Kind of you to say."

"Look, I know it's a shock. And your pride is hurt. It's never a nice thing to be fired. But look at it as an opportunity. Remember that sappy slogan you used to see everywhere? 'Today is the first day of the rest of your life.' Well, turns out that's what it is for both of us. I'm through with chemo and you're shed of a crummy job. We really do need to celebrate."

I didn't know what to say.

"Look at it like one of those old 'bad news/good news' jokes," she said. "The bad news is you got fired from your job. And the good news is . . ."

"I got fired from my job."

"Right."

"And tomorrow I'll start looking for a new one," I said.

"But tonight, we drink champagne."

I heard something in her voice; the spirit I remembered from when we were a couple of kids and she was up for anything. If she was anything at all, back then, it was enthusiasm. When I heard that old music I looked at her closely. I was hoping to find that seductive vitality, but what I saw was deep fatigue. Her face was gray and drawn and her eyes were glazed and had lost their precision. It was as though she had exhausted herself—spent her last reserves—trying to pump me up. The enthusiasm wasn't faked, maybe. But it was willed.

"Sit down," I said. "No, go lie down. I'll chill this champagne and be right back."

"Are you sure . . . I mean, maybe this isn't the night for celebrating."

"Depends, entirely, on how you feel."

"I'm up for it," she said and forced a smile.

"Then we celebrate. Go on. I'll be right back."

She was in her nightgown, looking thin and brittle, when I brought the champagne and two glasses into our bedroom. She was propped up against the pillows and I handed her a glass and poured. There was barely two inches in the glass when she stopped me.

"All I can handle," she said.

When I filled my own glass, she raised hers and I touched it with mine.

"The end of cancer," I said.

"And the beginning of something else."

She managed to get the champagne down. Then she handed me the glass and gave me a feeble smile.

"That's about all the celebrating I'm good for, baby. Sorry, but I took one of those killer pills and I'm almost gone."

"Good. You should sleep."

"So should you. Drink some more of that stuff first. It'll take the edge off. But don't stay up brooding, okay?"

"Okay."

"Promise?"

"Sure."

"Good. I'll see you in the morning. You can even stick around for breakfast."

For the next two weeks Leslie went downhill. She was still up and dressed every day, but it was plainly a struggle. She would work at her computer and make some calls, and most days that would leave her looking drained and on the edge of some kind of meltdown that never happened.

I would fix something for lunch and she would try to eat. Then she would take a nap. Later, I would make something bland for supper. I'd gotten to where the rice pudding was effortless, and some nights that was all she could handle.

Otherwise, I did the usual things an out-of-work man does. I sent out letters, résumé enclosed; e-mailed everyone in my address book; made calls. Waited for callbacks. Worried.

I talked to someone I knew at a company that was solid in the industry and he said, "Man, I wish you'd called last year. I would have hired you in a heartbeat. But this year we're shedding people like skin. I just don't have the slot or the money. Maybe when things turn around, *if* they turn around . . . "

I got that, or some variation of it, just about every day.

I was sending memos to the men in Colorado and they were paying me what Bill Winter said I should be charging. I had some hope that they still might call to offer the job that I'd already turned down. Then, the next minute, I'd feel certain they were going to call and cut off the consulting. It ran hot and cold, that way.

Meanwhile, Leslie went on losing energy by the day. Almost by the hour. Her naps got longer and she had a harder and harder time eating. But then, ten days before Christmas, things started turning around. She went out on some calls, and when she came home she had several bags of groceries in the car.

"We're making fruitcakes," she announced.

"When?"

"Just as soon as I finish my nap. And I sleep fast."

I put the groceries away while she was sleeping. I was reading the paper when she came back into the kitchen, almost precisely fifteen minutes later.

"How about a glass of sherry," she said. "That, and a kiss for your bald-headed Christmas babe."

We worked on the fruitcakes until bedtime, with just a few minutes off to eat some cold leftovers for dinner. It was something we had done every Christmas since we'd been married. Her way, I suppose, of staying in touch with North Carolina and her roots. She said it always made her think of the Capote story about the old lady and the boy who made a fruitcake for President Roosevelt. We'd keep one fruitcake for ourselves and give the others away as gifts.

We sliced the sticky fruit, broke up pecans, mixed the eggs and cream and sugar, put the mix into bowls, and put the bowls over pans of water in the oven to steam. Then we mixed up another batch while we waited for the first one to come out of the oven and then be tested with a broom straw. A sweet, warm aroma filled the kitchen; a smell of whiskey and butter.

We listened to the Neville Brothers doing Christmas music and we each had a second glass of the cheap sherry that Leslie had brought home.

"I'm going to feel that tomorrow," she said. "But what the hell. It's Christmas, right? What good is Christmas if you can't use it as an excuse to get drunk?"

"Absolutely," I said.

"Drink as much as you want, Jack," she said. "Don't hold back on my account."

"I'm fine," I said. I didn't feel like I ought to be drinking at all, but I was enjoying the mild buzz from the sherry.

"You're entitled to drink as much as you want," she said. "You more than anyone."

"Right."

I brewed up some tea instead, and we drank it with honey.

By the time the last batch of fruitcakes was ready for the oven, she was exhausted.

"Go to bed," I said. "I'll stay up until these are done."

"Thank you," she said.

"Please."

"This was fun, Jack. Most fun I've had since my last dose of chemo."

"*That* was fun?"

"Maybe I could phrase it differently."

"No. I get it. And this was fun," I said. Which was true.

"Christmas just like the old days," she said. "Only I've lost my hair."

"Merry Christmas," I said.

"Merry Christmas to you."

She grew stronger, almost visibly, in the days leading up to Christmas. One afternoon she went out with the dogs, was gone over an hour, and came back with a bag full of spruce boughs and garlands of creeping cedar, which she used to decorate the house. She put Christmas cards and candles on the mantel and made a wreath for the front door. When I asked about the tree, she said, "When the kids come home. We'll go out and cut down our own, the way we did in the good old days."

I wondered, sometimes, if all her old days were "good old days." Cancer, or something, seemed to have made all her memories happy. The real test, I supposed, would come later. Would she look back on this year, sometime down the road, and think of it as "the good old days"?

Possibly.

"I'm going to cut out one thing this Christmas," she said one day. "You can only do so much when you are walking around with your body full of cancer-killing drugs."

"What's that?" I said.

"Presents," she said. "I just don't have the energy to shop. I don't think anyone is going to hold it against me."

"Christmas without presents," I said. "I like it."

"We don't need presents," she said. "It's just junk. Please don't buy me anything."

"Okay."

"Promise?"

I said Yes, wishing I could go out and spring for an emerald.

"It's going to be such a wonderful Christmas. Presents would just clutter it up."

52

The kids arrived two days before Christmas and we drove out on a dirt road to a broken-down farm where the owners were hanging on by raising chickens and Christmas trees. The man who took my money was missing some teeth but he seemed happy. When we left, carrying the bow saw and dragging a sled, he wished us a merry Christmas.

"Merry Christmas to you, too," Leslie said.

The snow was old and dirty, barely deep enough for the sled to glide along behind us as we trudged up a long hill. We could make out the tops of the trees, planted in careful rows. There were a few footprints and sled trails from the people who'd gone before us.

It was cold and getting colder, with a wind that was noticeably rising.

"Man," Brad said, "the hawk is definitely out."

Leslie and Andy walked arm in arm, close together. They both wore ski hats and had the hoods of their parkas pulled up. They looked like monks in festive cassocks.

It felt good, I realized, to be out. I'd been spending most of my days inside, at the computer or on the phone, futilely looking for work. I had the saw in my hand and thought, idly, that it wouldn't be so bad to work in the woods for a while. Swap the bullshit for the cold. Seemed like a fair trade.

"What kind of tree do we want?" Leslie shouted over the wind when we were at the top of the hill.

"What've you got?" I said.

"I got some Scotch pine. Got your red spruce. Some blue spruce. And a little cedar."

"Blue spruce," I said.

"No way," Andy said. "Blue isn't a Christmas color. I want red spruce."

"Scotch pine," Brad said.

We all looked at Leslie.

"Cedar," she said. "What did you expect?"

It was one of those old family routines. We always argued about the Christmas tree. We'd done it in earnest one year, long ago, and the kids had gotten into one of those arguments where they started yelling about how much they hated each other. Now it was just a gag and we ran with it.

"Anorexic," Brad said about one tree.

"Wonky," Leslie said about the next one.

And so on, until the cold forced a compromise. The metal frame of the saw felt cold through my glove. It took me a couple dozen strokes to cut through the tree's trunk. Brad lashed it to the sled and we started back down the hill, dragging it behind us. I wondered, as I had for the last three or four years, how much longer we would do this.

We spent the rest of the day decorating the tree. We used a couple of ornaments the kids had made when they were little: a lopsided star that Brad had cut out of poster board and wrapped with tinsel, an asymmetrical snowflake Andy had made by folding and cutting paper. I hung them on conspicuous branches.

We drank mulled cider and hot chocolate, played Christmas music, and put a few wrapped presents—Leslie had relented a little and allowed us all to buy one inexpensive gift—under the tree. We used the automatic shutter setting on my camera to take some pictures of ourselves standing in front of the tree. I'd been thinking about getting one of those digital cameras to take the pictures for this year's Christmas album. Now, I didn't want to spend the money.

Inch by Inch

The storm arrived and the snow was so heavy we almost didn't make it to church for the midnight service, which was another one of our Christmas traditions. The church was full, in spite of the blizzard. The service consisted of the usual Bible readings, from Luke—*Glory to God in the highest and on earth, peace, good will toward men*—and the singing of the usual hymns—"O Come, All Ye Faithful." I didn't sing, but the music—and maybe the message—did something to me. I felt . . . well, at peace.

Then, near the end of the service, when we all sang "Silent Night" in the thin light of candles, I almost lost it. For some reason, I remembered a story I'd read somewhere about the soldiers in the First World War coming out of their trenches and singing that hymn together in no-man's-land.

The storm passed through sometime before dawn, so Christmas was one of those still, cold, sunny days with the land buried under a foot or more of fresh, unblemished snow. For the first couple of hours of the morning, the branches of the conifers were piled with snow, and now and then one of them would give under the weight, leaving a small, puffy, white cloud on the motionless air.

We bundled up and took a walk, then made waffles for breakfast and opened the presents. It was a meager haul compared to other years, but nobody mentioned that. The most inspired gift was from Andy to Leslie: a gift certificate for the works at a fashionable hair salon in Boston.

"Good for at least a year, I hope," Leslie said and ran her hand over her bald head. She seldom covered it around us any longer. "I need time if I'm going to have anything for them to work with."

"Good for two years," Andy said. "Read the fine print."

"Thank you," Leslie said, putting a hand to her eyes. "I'm really touched."

We cleaned up the wrapping paper, went for another walk, called the grandparents, and watched videos of *Scrooged* and the original *Christmas Carol*.

It was a good Christmas and Leslie was undeniably happy. And that, I told myself before I went to sleep, was the whole point.

53

The kids left right after New Year's Day and Leslie left a couple of days later. She would be living in a small apartment the hospital owned. She got it almost rent free, which was all we could afford, and would be going in every day for her radiation treatments.

"For the next three months," she said, "I'll be the bald-headed lady who glows in the dark."

She would drive home on weekends. That was the plan, anyway, unless she was too tired from the radiation, which she'd been told was a real possibility.

But Andy's dorm was only a few blocks from the apartment where Leslie would be staying. They would see each other every day. And if Leslie was too tired to come home for a weekend, I could drive down and stay with her.

Actually, there wasn't any reason why I couldn't go down to Boston and stay there full-time. Somebody needed to look after the dogs, but otherwise, I didn't have a job and there was no place I had to be every morning, Monday through Friday. First time for that since I'd finished school.

The idea, of course, was that I would spend all that time alone in the house on a job search and doing any consulting I could scare up. By the time Leslie's treatments were done, the severance would have run out. I needed to have something lined up by then, so the pressure was on.

But I didn't feel any particular sense of urgency when I went back inside on the cold and overcast morning that Leslie left for Boston with her car full of clothes and the things she needed to stock the kitchen and bathroom of her apartment. I felt the other thing, entirely—a kind of lassitude and loneliness.

I spent the day at the computer and on the phone anyway, without feeling much conviction about it. I was just getting through the hours until Leslie would call and tell me that she had moved in and was ready to start the next battle in her war with cancer.

I felt guilty for not being there with her. Guilty for being at home, baby-sitting a couple of dogs, while other people were out there in the marketplace, working and earning a living. Guilty in general.

Leslie's call came in the early evening.

"You know what?" she said.

"What?"

"I am so with it."

"Why's that?"

"Because I have a tattoo."

"You're kidding."

"No. They had to outline the area on my breast where they're going to aim the radiation. They made these little dots. Kind of cool, don't you think?"

"If you say so."

"I do. I mean, I thought I was a pretty conservative lady, but now, here I am, this hip chick with a bald head and a tattoo. I'm thinking about a little body piercing."

"Please."

"Just kidding. Anyway, my body has been messed around with quite enough, thank you. When all this is over, I want it to be left alone for a while."

"Not much longer," I said.

"Three months," she said. "Ninety days. I can do that standing on my shiny, bald head."

"Right."

"And how are you and the dogs?"

"Just fine. We had a great day."

The dogs may have had a great day, I thought. I knew I hadn't. But I lied anyway. It seemed like the least I could do.

The days dragged and the nights weren't any better. Sometime in the middle of that first week, I called Monk. It was midnight our time, barely cocktail hour in Alaska.

"My man," he said. "I've been thinking about calling you. How's Leslie?"

Monk knew how to rank things. He would ask about me later.

"She's fine, Monk. Finished the chemo in time for Christmas."

"That's good," he said. "And is she doing the radiation now, the way I said she should?"

"Just started. She goes for the next ninety days."

"Good. That stuff will get in there and fry those cancer cells for sure. You know, there wouldn't be any cancer at all if we could just radiate your whole body. We'd kill all the cancer cells. Only problem is, we'd kill the patient, too."

"Yeah, well sometimes it does seem like overkill."

"Jack," he said, "there is no such thing when you're talking cancer."

"Okay," I said. I'd heard it before.

Monk, however, was going to make sure I heard it again.

"Be glad she's going for the whole right side of the menu," he said. "Surgery, chemo, and radiation. If leeches and bleeding were options, I'd be recommending them, too. Just hang in there. It'll be over soon."

"I know."

"How about it? You holding up okay?"

"Yeah. I'm fine."

"Come on, tell me. It's your old buddy, remember. You sound kind of low. You just lonely, or is it something else?'"

We talked a little longer and, inevitably, my own woes came out.

"Shit," Monk said. "Ain't that a bitch? You okay in the short run, here? For money, I mean?"

"Yeah," I said. "We're fine."

"Really, man . . ."

"Everything's okay," I said. I was irritated but not at Monk. "Just means I need to find a new job. It could have come at a better time."

"Yeah," Monk said. "I know what you mean. But have you ever noticed how none of the things that are a real pain in the chops seem to happen at a good time?"

"I see your point," I said.

"Meanwhile, your wife doesn't have cancer anymore."

For some reason, it made all the difference to hear that. All my life, it seemed, I'd needed to be reminded of what my father had told me constantly, right up until he died: "Keep your eye on the ball."

54

Leslie's first weekend at home was quiet and slow. She took walks and naps. I cooked. We watched a little television and we read books. On Sunday afternoon, she went back to Boston.

I couldn't handle hanging around the house all day. I could make the calls and send out the letters and write the memos for my consulting deal in about two hours. That left a load of time and it hung heavy. So I got a couple of jobs—tending bar and limbing trees for a man who had a logging contract on a couple hundred acres not far from the place where I'd passed up a shot at that trophy buck.

It had been a while since I'd done that kind of work—pouring drinks or running a chain saw. But I liked the noise and the cold and the gas fumes far more than the quiet of the house, the buzz of the computer, and the silence of the telephone that did not ring. I came home with sawdust in my hair and grease on my hands; then, two hours later, I'd be making drinks at a place called Stone Steve's.

Actually, I mostly poured wine and opened bottles of micro. But occasionally, someone ordered a martini or a manhattan or something a little trickier.

I liked tending bar, too. There aren't many situations where you can just lay back in the weeds and observe people being people. You're sober and everyone you're dealing with is at least drinking, if not half in the bag with their inhibitions down. You see, and hear, some interesting things.

My clientele consisted of young people who had jobs and needed companionship. No kids and very few couples. Steve's might have been called a "singles bar" at one time, except that these people were just a little bit past that. They weren't single in the strict sense. Divorced, most likely, or, as one of the waitresses said, "working up to it."

Now and then I would recognize one of them, usually someone from the office. They would, inevitably, say "Hello," then quickly put some space between us and concentrate on not making eye contact. I'd heard there was more downsizing still to come, and they no doubt saw their own futures when they looked at me across the bar, busily polishing glasses and drawing drafts.

When Leslie came home for her next weekend—too tired, again, to do very much—I told her about my new jobs.

"I hate the logging," she said, "but I think the bartending is great."

"Why?"

"I don't know. I guess I like it that you're getting out and seeing people."

"Even if most of them don't see me?"

"Or see two of you," she said.

"Right."

"I don't know about the lumberjack part."

"I'm careful."

"I know . . ."

"I like it, actually."

"Of course you do."

"I could come to Boston."

"No," she said. "You need to be here, to do your calls and stuff. I can come back on weekends and, anyway, I've got Andy."

"How is she?"

"She's very sweet to me. She comes by or calls two or three times a day. We cook dinner or go out almost every night."

"Good."

"But she's got boy trouble."

One of those things you don't want to hear about. Hard enough for a father to imagine his little girl having anything to do with some boy. Much worse to know the boy is making her unhappy.

"Bad?"

"I don't know. She won't tell me much."

"Anything we can do?"

"No."

That made it three out of four, I thought. Leslie had cancer; I was out of work; Andy was involved with a bad man. I wondered how Brad was doing.

I told myself that it wouldn't take much to fix everything. We just needed to hang in a little longer. Leslie would finish her treatments and get a couple of positive checkups, I'd land a job, and Andy would ditch her boyfriend.

Life would be coming up Cadillacs.

And it might even happen. Six months or a year ago, it had all seemed on track. But I suppose that's what cancer does to you. Everything about life seems suddenly very damned contingent.

55

So we fell into a new routine. Leslie would leave for Boston on Sunday afternoon and stay all week. She would go into the hospital for radiation every morning and we would talk on the phone every evening, usually after I was finished in the woods and before I left for the bar.

I had flowers delivered to her apartment twice a week by a florist who gave me a good price. Leslie made some sounds about how it was too expensive, but I won that one.

After her treatment on Friday, Leslie would drive home. She would be tired when she arrived—she was always tired—so she would take a nap. In the evening I would fix something for dinner. She would see friends over the weekend. We would take walks, watch television, listen to music, or read in front of a fire. On Sunday, after lunch, she would go back to Boston.

A routine, then, and a quiet one. The treatment, it seems, suppresses a lot more than the immune system.

"What do you want to do," I asked her, "after the last blast of radiation?"

"What do you mean?"

"You know, to celebrate being cured."

"We don't call it that," she said. "I'll be a *survivor.*"

"Yeah?"

"Right. It's like this. You're monitored for five years—closely—to make sure some stray cancer cell hasn't escaped and infiltrated another part of your body like some solitary, anonymous terrorist carrying a bomb into an unsuspecting crowd. But you know, I don't see why they bother. Nobody makes it through a metastasized breast cancer."

I didn't have anything to say about that. So I just thought about how, with the end in sight and things looking as promising as we could have let ourselves hope, there was this feeling, almost, of anticlimax. A kind of letdown.

I could read Leslie's moods—you don't have to be emotionally acute or insightful if you've been married long enough—and I could sense she felt this way. We'd both imagined that it was going to be like she had started up a long, tough mountain and was nearing the summit or had run a long, grueling race against lots of other competitors with people watching and cheering. But it wasn't, really.

Turns out, it was more like she'd gone, without much choice in the matter, on one of those hard treks that pioneer women once made along the Oregon Trail, where we'd seen that melancholy marker not long after her surgery. You followed ox teams pulling wagons for hundreds of hard miles. You saw friends, even family, sicken and die. You endured. And at the end, for all your efforts, the reward was . . . you got to work hard building a new house and a new life in a strange new land.

It was right, I thought, to feel like you were a survivor and there was some nobility in that. Even if there were no prizes and no sense of triumph.

I tried to make the weekends special, but there was this feeling hanging over them, of just getting across the last couple hundred miles on that much longer trail.

We'd celebrate later, I thought, when she wasn't always so tired.

One night, near the end of my first month, Elena LeFevre came into Steve's. She was with a friend—a woman—and I saw her barely a second before she saw me.

She looked surprised. Then she looked away.

I went on with my work, making drinks and drawing beer. I imagined I could feel her eyes on me. I didn't mind it when my friends came in but I was discovering that it was different with my enemies.

We weren't especially crowded, but I did what I could to stay busy. It was a way to avoid dealing with the customers, except to give them their drinks and take their money. After a while, Elena came to my end of the bar.

"Well, hello," she said. She had her head tilted just slightly, the way you do when you're appraising something you might buy. There was something a little malicious in her smile.

"Hello."

"I didn't know you were working here."

"I am, though. What can I get you?"

"Belvedere, rocks. Two of them."

I made the drinks and put them in front of her. She gave me another appraising glance.

"How much?"

"Eight-fifty each. Seventeen bucks."

She put a twenty on the bar, picked up the glasses, and turned around. She didn't say "Keep the change," but she could have.

"Thank you," I said, trying to use the same bland, professional voice I used with strangers.

"Sure," she said without turning around.

Before she left, twenty or thirty minutes later, she came back to my end of the bar.

"I'd like to talk to you," she said.

"I'm working."

"I can see that," she said. "Do you get a break?"

"Not tonight. I'm on alone."

"Do you work tomorrow?" she said, and there was something softer now in the way she said it.

"Yes."

"What time?"

"Seven."

"Then will you meet me for a drink at six-thirty? I'd really appreciate it."

I looked at her and didn't say anything.

"Please."

"All right. Sure."

"See you then."

56

She was late by five minutes. In the office, she'd always been on time.

"Are you having anything?" she said.

"No."

"Would it bother you if I did?"

"No."

She signaled the waitress and ordered vodka on the rocks. "I was surprised to see you working here," she said. "Are things really that bad?"

"Pretty much all over," I said. "You must see it."

She nodded. Her drink arrived and she took the first sip. She did it in a way that made me think about ordering one myself. But I had a long night ahead of me and I had to run a chain saw in the morning. I felt strangely grateful for that.

She touched her hair, which was thick and dark and styled so that it seemed to draw attention away from her face as much as frame it. I wondered how much she had invested in all that hair.

"Is there anything I can do to help?" she said.

I looked at her. In disbelief, I suppose, and thinking *Give me a break.*

"I know people," she said. "I could make a phone call or two."

I didn't say anything.

"Like you say," she went on, "things are tough all over. But there might be something somewhere."

I still couldn't come up with anything to say.

"You're very good, Jack, and I wouldn't have any trouble saying that to anyone. Because you *are* very good."

"Kind of you to say."

She smiled in a feeble sort of way, took another sip of her drink, and touched her hair. Again.

"It wasn't my fault, you know."

"Oh."

She shook her head. "Ron—and the Ghouls, too, probably—made the decision. The way I understand it, they'd decided it was either you or me. They thought you had the advantage with the people below and I was better with the people above. I guess they wanted someone they could keep on the reservation."

"I see," I said.

"They liked our plan," she said. "Accepted just about everything in it."

"So are you running the place now?"

There was some quality to her smile—irony, bitterness—I couldn't quite pin it down.

"No. I'm leaving."

"The company?"

"And this town."

I wondered if it was her decision or if the Ghouls had gotten her, too. But I didn't feel like asking.

"Where are you going?"

"First," she said, "I'm going to Martinique to purge myself with sun. And then I'm going back to New York. Three more days, then I'll never see this place again. Just three days."

"I'm sorry it didn't work out," I said. The job, I meant. Or thought so, anyway.

"Why didn't you return my call?"

"Huh?"

"That weekend. I left a message but you didn't return my call."

I nodded.

"You got the call, though?"

"Yes."

"For the best, probably," Elena said.

"Yes."

She stood up and said, "Good luck, Jack. If I hear of anything before I leave, I'll let you know."

Funny thing, I liked her again.

57

A day or two later, Leslie called to tell me that she would not be coming home for the weekend.

"I'm just so tired, Jack. I'm going to rest. Maybe Andy and I will go to the movies and eat Chinese."

"Sounds like a good plan," I said.

"You don't mind?"

"No," I said, "of course not."

"But you *will* miss me?"

"Absolutely."

"Good."

She asked how things were going with me.

"Okay," I said, "but nobody called to offer me a seven-figure salary with a car and a driver thrown in."

"Imagine that," she said.

"You know, I could come down there and join you and Andy for the movies. We could all go to dinner."

"It's a long drive, Jack. And that will mean I *have* to go out, even if I don't feel like it. Stay there and do something fun. I'll be home next weekend."

"Okay," I said.

"Love you, baby."

"Good-night," I said. "Love you, too."

I had an empty weekend and I felt a need to move. Almost like an animal—a big cat, maybe, or a bear—with a nature to roam. It was the same feeling that, when you're young, pushes you to drive across America without stopping. So Saturday morning I got out my cross-country skis and waxed them, then drove out to a trail that led back up and into a big wilderness section of Forest Service land. There were old logging roads all through the piece.

I had to herringbone to get up to the flat sections, and it was hard work. Hard enough to break a sweat. After that, it was smooth going through big maples, beech, and ash along a wide, level trail. It was 15 degrees, maybe colder. A blue wax day.

The snow was fresh and unbroken through most of the woods, except where a small animal or a deer had left a trail. I had to work to get any momentum, kicking and gliding and leaning on the poles. The snow seemed to resist, just slightly, then give way like a stubborn knot. A packed trail would have made better skiing, I thought, but for some reason, I preferred this. Maybe it was the sense that, except for the occasional fox or deer, I was the first one down this road and had it pretty much to myself.

I skied a few miles to the site of an old marble quarry that jutted out on a ledge overlooking a long valley running north and south with a river and a highway down the middle.

I took my skis off and leaned them against a large block of marble that must have been one of the last ones blasted out of the mountainside before the quarry shut down fifty years ago. The money had run out before they got this slab to market.

I'd heard somewhere that marble from this place had gone for headstones at Gettysburg. It made you think.

Inch by Inch

I took off my pack and got out a thermos filled with coffee and a sandwich I'd made from bacon left over after breakfast. I drank the coffee and ate the sandwich while I looked down at the valley. It was a clear day and I could see the traffic on the highway and the buildings, shops, and church steeples in town. I finished the coffee and put the lid back on the thermos. I put my pack and my skis on and started back the way I had come.

It was still early, three or four hours before dark, and I wasn't ready to go back to a house with just the dogs for company.

There were other logging roads, branching off from the one I had taken. I knew some of them, but it had been a while since I had been up here, and then there were some trails I had never been down. I decided to take one and see where I came out.

There were blowdowns across the trail. I could jump a few, but I had to sidestep over most of them. It was slow going, and after an hour or so I hadn't gone much more than a mile. The trail had begun to neck down and also to climb a steep section of the mountain. I tried sidestepping, but the trees kept cutting me off or trapping me. I would have been all right on snowshoes but skis were not getting it done.

"Time to turn around," I said aloud, "and remind me again why we came this way." My voice sounded alarmingly loud in the still woods.

So I started back, following my tracks. I'd gone a couple hundred yards when I saw a spur off the road that looked like it might have been a landing where lumberjacks had cold-decked logs they would skid off the mountain in the spring. It also looked like a way to get around a nasty stretch of blowdowns, so I took it.

The new trail did get me around the blowdowns, but it did not wrap around and pick up the old trail like I'd thought it would. In another couple hundred yards I was on a totally new trail and not sure of my direction. I hadn't brought a compass or a map. Hadn't thought I would need them.

I was lost . . . sort of. I could always turn around and backtrack, I thought. Or I could simply keep working my way downhill, taking the cleanest-looking trail whenever I came to a junction. Eventually I would make it down to the valley. If I was too far from where I'd parked, I could knock on a door and call for someone to come get me. Bill Winter, maybe. He'd be amused that I'd gotten myself lost.

Backtracking would mean going uphill and it would take time. Following the path of least resistance down the mountain would be easier, but it might take even more time. The sun had reached the point where the light changes in quality and you can feel night coming. The temperature had dropped, it seemed, a full 5 degrees in the last thirty minutes.

I had to make up my mind what to do and get started doing it.

I hate to backtrack and always have. So I started downhill, looking for the widest, cleanest trail to take me to the valley.

I had been lost before but never for very long and never in the winter woods. I kept telling myself that I wasn't *really* lost, since I could always backtrack, unless a new snowfall covered my trail. There were a few fat flakes falling from a thin layer of overcast. A front might be on the way through, but I couldn't tell how serious it was. I hadn't checked the weather channel and didn't know if I was looking at a blizzard or a dusting. Either way, I had an hour or two before any heavy new snow and a little more than that until the sun went down. Also, the moon was full and if the sky stayed clear, I could use its light to find my way down the mountain. I remembered seeing the moon on the rise the night before, two hours after sundown. So if I had to use the moon to get home, I would be in the dark woods, unable to move on skis, for three hours or so.

But I was thinking ahead of myself and also trying to move way too fast. I had edged up to the verge of panic and was flailing through the woods, knocking spruce boughs out of the way with my poles and trying, almost, to use the skis like ice skates and sprint my way home.

Slow down, skipper, I told myself. *You'll break a leg if you don't watch out.*

I remembered another time when I had been lost in the woods, in the summer, and without realizing it had started running. No telling how far I might have run if I hadn't tripped over a root. Later, when I told a friend about the experience, he said, "That's what people always do. They panic and run. You hear about them running off cliffs." He'd been to EMT school and worked for the local rescue squad, so I figured he knew. I remembered what he had said and I stopped and tried to get myself under control. If you are really lost, he'd said, then the best thing you can do is just stop and stay where you are and wait to be rescued.

Good advice, I thought, but nobody knew what I was doing or where to come looking for me. I might be lost, but I wasn't missing yet and might not be for days.

You should always tell someone where you're going, I remembered reading somewhere, so that if you do get lost or hurt they will know where to look for you.

Mistake one.

There were others. If I had to spend the night in the woods, I would have to get by with what I was wearing and what I had in my pack. That consisted of the thermos—now half full of coffee—an extra parka, some matches, and a tube of plastic wood that I used as a fire starter. No signal flares and no cell phone.

With the sun dropping closer to the horizon, the light had gone flat and it was hard to make out the shape of the ground or choose the cleanest line downhill and the clearest path through the trees. I told myself to pick my spots and take my time. Be deliberate.

But going slow wasn't a perfect solution. I had dressed for speed, not warmth. One pair of fairly thin socks and uninsulated boots. Light, polypro underwear and fleece gloves that made for a better grip on the poles but didn't trap a lot of heat. Standard parka and wool stocking hat. I could move freely and I could shed excess heat. But when I wasn't moving fast—or at all—I got cold.

If I had to spend the night in the woods, I thought, then I might lose some fingers and toes. Or worse, maybe. If a big front did move in, bringing a storm with it, hypothermia was not out of the question. I could freeze to death out here, I realized.

I had pushed my goggles up over my forehead and was trying to pick a line in the leaden light when I hooked a ski tip on a small tree and went down hard enough to see stars. I didn't break anything, but I was on the ground long enough that, when I stood up, I was shuddering. It was the reflex shudder of a body losing heat. Capillaries were squeezing down and shutting themselves off to conserve heat and keep the central core warm. I'd read that somewhere and remembered it now.

I brushed the snow off and started back downhill. I tried to look simultaneously up ahead for a trail and close by for obstacles. I was on fairly flat ground that was thick with old blowdowns and new saplings. I thought about taking off the skis, but the snow was too deep. I put both poles in one hand and used the other to grip whatever tree was closest and pull myself along. It was slow going. If I'd been panicked before, I was frustrated now, almost to fury. I couldn't have been more than a mile, straight-line distance, from my truck. But I was trapped in this maze.

My entire goal was to get back to the truck before dark. But I didn't make it.

58

I couldn't move any farther in the woods until I had some light. Three more hours, and if it clouded over, maybe a lot longer than that.

I'd been cold for the last hour or more and now I felt much colder. The inside of my nose was frozen, my fingers and toes were numb, and I was shuddering more than ever.

I found a large, flat rock and swept the snow off it. Then I broke branches from a blowdown—an old, brittle spruce—and piled them like a pyramid on the surface of the rock. I got the tube of plastic wood out of my pack and squeezed a line on one of the spruce limbs like I was putting toothpaste on a toothbrush.

I unscrewed the top from the little waterproof container I used for carrying matches. It held half a dozen of those old strike-anywhere matches. I took one out and flicked it across the surface of the rock. But my fingers had no touch and I used too much pressure and broke the match in half, losing the head in the snow.

I had five matches left and I remembered, involuntarily, the Jack London story I had read when I was a kid: the one about the prospector who dies when the snow buries the little fire he has built to warm himself after falling through the ice. The prospector wasn't that far from his cabin when he died out in the big emptiness of the Yukon. That was the pity and the tragedy of it. If I froze to death a few miles from the safety of my quasi-suburban home with central heating and a Goddamned Jacuzzi bath . . . well, that wouldn't be tragic, I thought, it would be pathetic.

My fingers were shaking as I fumbled for the next match, and I nearly dropped the waterproof container, and all the matches, in the snow.

"Come on," I said. "Come on. You can do this."

I held the match firmly, but not too firmly, and dragged it across the face of the rock.

Not too hard.

I could feel the friction and hear it and then sense the ignition. I immediately put the head of the flaming match on the wormlike trail of plastic wood. The epoxy caught right away.

In a few minutes I had a fire, and I started breaking more branches off the blowdown and adding them to the blaze. Then I ran out of branches that broke easily off the trunk of the dead spruce. The bigger branches took more strength. It was hard work, but it kept me warm.

I looked around, in the flickering light of my fire, for more blowdowns. There were a couple, and I broke branches from them and piled them next to the fire. Then I stopped to get my breath and to warm myself in front of the fire. In a minute or two, my face felt warm and dry. The back of my neck, though, was damp and cold. I was still shuddering but less than before.

I wrapped my arms so that my hands were under my armpits and I was hugging myself as I looked into the fire. The spruce burned fast and hot. The flames were bright yellow and they moved and shifted around rapidly. Even lost in the woods, there was something irresistible about a fire, and I watched it like a small animal in the spell of a snake.

It was an old thing with me, going back to when I was a kid out in the woods on a camping trip, spooked by bats and owls hooting in the night. I would put off going in the tent and crawling into the sleeping bag until I couldn't stand it any longer, just so I could keep gazing into the glowing coals. It was like a narcotic.

And, like any other narcotic, I guess, it made you think profound thoughts and feel like you had somehow grasped truths that otherwise gave you the slip. You felt like you knew things even if you didn't know what they were. Fire made you wise.

Or made me believe I was, anyway. Wise and, somehow, unafraid. Like maybe it had burned away all the nonessential stuff and left only the hot, fundamental core. It was a feeling that went away, of course, when the fire went out. Just like when the dope wore off and the high was replaced by a gnawing hollow.

So I looked into the fire and I didn't feel miserable and stupid anymore. I wasn't a bumbling-middle aged man now; I was a young scout on the trail of truth. But I was also hip enough to that idea to smile about it and say the word "bullshit" through numbed lips.

It came out "buuuhsheee."

Still . . . as long I kept looking into the flames and the accumulating coals, my mind went where the fire took it.

I thought about things, and saw them, in ways that I hadn't for a long time and maybe not ever. It wasn't totally hallucinatory since I was aware of what was happening. But I wasn't in control, either. I wondered, for a moment, if it was the thing that happens—the thing that they say happens, anyway—when you are dying. The part about how your whole life passes in front of you. Maybe I was dying, freezing to death in a domesticated woods less than ten miles from home, and I was just imagining the fire and the warmth.

But no . . . when I put my hand close to the fire, I could feel the heat, and if I tried to get too close, my hand came back in a hurry, on its own. This fire was real

It wasn't my life that was passing before me, then, but the parts that the fire had picked out for review.

Funny how most of them included Leslie, and they were almost all what you'd call happy. The fire must have thought I rated a break.

I remembered reading a book about a man who spent more than five years as a POW in Vietnam. He had an answer, when he got home, for people who wanted him to talk about it.

"I only remember the funny parts," he would say.

And the really weird part is, while most people thought he was putting them on, there *were* some funny parts. Really funny. Like having wine tastings in the Hanoi Hilton. Or classes in opera and etiquette. Just imagining the picture of these skinny, haunted, unshaven guys standing in the gloom of a damp cell whistling an aria from *La Traviatta* or talking about the merits of a particular Bordeaux—there was something funny about it. Sort of like the picture of a guy lost in the woods a little way from home, trying to keep warm and save his fingers in the heat of a fire made from branches off a blowdown and telling himself he's thinking wise and profound thoughts. That would seem funny, too, provided the guy made it home.

Looking into the fire, I remembered, with clarity, things I hadn't thought about in years. Passages from my life with Leslie that, when I remembered them, seemed to come to life again. Maybe that's what cancer does. It can be your own or belong to the person you love, but either way it makes you remember the funny parts and jettison all the rest.

59

So I stared into the fire and, feeling its warmth, rode on currents of memory that carried me back to the time when Leslie and I had just met. We were in those early throes of a love affair where you cannot get enough and are calling each other four or five times a day at work and spending just about every minute outside the office together. I'd sort of forgotten those days. I knew I had lived through them but didn't remember what they had been like.

The fire, it seemed, brought them back to life.

It was summer and one of those long hot spells had gripped New York like a fist. Air-conditioning seemed like a blessing and you did anything to keep from going out into the street or, God spare you, down into the subway, which felt like Hell's own mezzanine. If you could possibly get out of the city on the weekend, you did. But we were young and we didn't have the money for a beach rental. We got invitations from friends now and then, but nothing for what was shaping up as the hottest weekend in years.

Then, on Friday afternoon, Reg walked into my office.

He was dressed in cutoffs, sandals, and a T-shirt, and he was baked brown as the skin of a potato. I hadn't seen him in five years.

"Well, Jack," he said, "you look like a bloody undertaker in that suit. But at least you haven't gotten fat."

"Where did you come from?" I said.

"England." Reg was British. Called himself a "Limey."

"I know that," I said. "I mean, where did you come from just now?"

"England, actually," he said. "Sailed over on a dreamy little forty-one-foot ketch. Took eleven days and made a perfect landfall."

I'd met Reg one summer when I was working around boats and thinking I always would. I'd given up on that dream, but Reg obviously never had.

"Where's the boat?"

"Tied to a pier on the East River. I'm on my way up to Long Island Sound. Thought I'd drop in on you first. See how you're getting on. So, do you have a wife to go with that ridiculous suit or are you free to go sailing?"

When I told him about Leslie, he said, "Well, then, I expect she'll have to come sailing, too. Matter of fact, you two take the boat for the weekend, why don't you? I have other business. Just don't put it on the rocks, will you, Jack? I've only just started paying for it."

So Leslie and I sailed with Reg, that afternoon, up to Fire Island, where we anchored. He showed me where everything was and then he went ashore by dinghy and left us with the boat. He had an ex-wife in town, he said, who was renting a place.

"There's a child of mine, too," he said. "I'm really here to see him. Nobody sails three thousand miles, tacking most of the bloody way, to visit an ex-wife."

He'd see us again Sunday, he said, in time to get us back to town for work Monday morning.

"What a beautiful boat," Leslie said when Reg was gone. "And we have it all to ourselves. Can you believe it?"

"Do you know how to sail?"

"Hey," she said, "I'm a Carolina girl. Three years at Camp Seafarer."

"Oh, sorry."

"But I've never sailed anything this big."

Inch by Inch

I had crewed bigger boats but never sailed one this size alone. Still, we were young and cocky, it was a beautiful day with a mild sea breeze, and there was a small diesel to get us out of trouble. Leslie took the tiller while I pulled the anchor and set the mainsail.

"Enough canvas for you?" I said.

"I'm in no hurry," she said.

She took off the T-shirt she had been wearing over a two-piece bathing suit. It was black and not cut to be scandalous or revealing, which made what it did show of her athletic body even more provocative to me. I kept looking back at her, in the cockpit, with her arm draped casually over the tongue of the tiller and her hair blowing in the wind. She was tanned and the muscles of her stomach were flat and firm. The cleavage that was revealed by the black bathing suit took my breath away.

It seemed like some sort of dream that I was alone with her on a boat, sailing a warm sea. We weren't in the tropics, with miles of empty green ocean around us, but we might as well have been.

I could never have imagined her, then, as the mother of my children and cosigner of my mortgage and all the rest of it. Couldn't have imagined her as anything other than this almost unbearably desirable woman confidently sailing a boat and wearing a bathing suit that made it hard to look at her and impossible not to.

We sailed until nearly last light, then carefully maneuvered back to the area where Reg had left us. There was another boat a quarter of a mile upwind, but we felt alone. I gave the anchor line plenty of scope.

We had a moon rising from the sea, and when the sea breeze died, there was no relief from the heat, so we stripped and dove off the bow of the boat into the warm water of the sound. We swam, close together, touching each other underwater until we were too excited to stay in any longer and we climbed over the stern and fell into the cockpit where we made love.

We showered on deck and searched the boat for something to eat. Then we lay on towels up forward, still wearing nothing, and we drank wine and watched the spokes of moonlight dancing on the rippling surface of the water.

We spent that night, and the next one, like that. Drinking wine, sleeping, making love, and studying the moon and its light. During the day, we sailed and we napped and we swam. It was only two days, but while it lasted, it felt like everything was happening outside the realm of time, as though I were imagining it or dreaming it.

It came back to me now, in the cold woods, under the spell of a hasty fire. I could see with clarity the breathtaking shape of her body in the moonlight when she took off the black bathing suit. I could feel her touch under the water. It even seemed like I was breathing the scent of salt water, but it was probably just dried perspiration from when I had been struggling to make it out of the woods before dark.

That memory led to others, not all of them erotic. There was a dinner we ate at a *tapas* bar in Barcelona. That was after we were married but before kids. We spent three or four hours there, drinking wine and sharing plates of small fish and squid and skewers of rabbit and beef.

There was an image of the two of us, with our new baby asleep in a basket, taking the train back to New York to visit friends and to let them see how it had worked out for us, moving to the country.

Leslie in the kitchen making pasta while I fed two children their suppers.

Four of us hiking up into the woods, not that far from where I was stranded now, and camping out for a couple of days.

A trip to the Islands, where we all learned to scuba dive.

Graduations.

Puppies.

Christmases.

Inch by Inch

Staring into the fire was like digging through an old box of random, aging snapshots; the chaotic record of one little family's life together before time, or something else, closed the book.

But the later images were just that—snapshots—while the hours on that boat, on those two hot nights in July, were a movie that kept running, over and over, as I added more spruce limbs to the fire, shuddered and stamped my feet, and watched the sky, begging for a moon.

That had been the beginning of it. And this felt like the end. With me cold and lost in the woods at night and Leslie a couple hundred miles away, a prisoner of hospitals and doctors. That marvelous, breathtaking body had betrayed her and the hair that had trailed her like a mane when the boat was underway was rotting in a compost pile.

Strange, but while I knew what she looked like now—had seen her just days earlier—that image would not play for me. When I saw her through the prism of fire, it was always the way she had looked on that boat that weekend in July.

60

By the time the moon finally came up, I was stiff and drowsy. Part of me wanted to lie down on the rock, next to my fire, and go to sleep. It would be so much easier, I thought, to find my way out of the woods at dawn.

No way, skipper, a voice inside me argued. *Lie down and sleep, and you might never get up.*

The moon was sleek and bright. It threw enough light, easily, for me to find my way down the mountain. Especially if I could cut a wide, clean logging road.

Come on, skipper. Let's get moving.

It was hard to leave the fire.

I was stiff and my eyes were unaccustomed to the dark. When I took my first steps I felt like I would either fall or walk into something, and it seemed like it took five minutes for me to go twenty steps. I told myself that it was likely to be a long night.

But the flexibility came back to my legs and I got my night vision. Enough moonlight was reflected off the snow to make the trees and the rocks stand out in clear relief, and I was soon gliding on the skis again instead of walking on them. But it was still slow going and I was worried that I wouldn't make it out before my fingers and toes were frostbitten.

I'd been moving for an hour and it was getting close to decision time. Press on, or stop and build another fire and try to thaw out a little. My hands and feet felt like single, solid units at the ends of my arms and legs, too thick and numb to be flesh. It wouldn't be the end of the world, but I didn't want to lose a single toe. I didn't want to even have to see a doctor about it. That seemed important. Very damned important.

"Five more minutes, skipper," I told myself through heavy, immobile lips. "Five more minutes, then we'll stop."

That's when I saw the logging road. It was wide and clear and packed down where the snowmobiles had been running.

"About time my luck changed," I thought. I kicked hard into one of the snowmobile tracks and started downhill, fast enough to feel the wind on my frozen face.

And my luck, it seemed, had changed even more than I thought. This was the main road and in ten minutes, maybe less, I was back at my truck.

"Thank you," I said when I slid under the wheel and the engine popped once, then started. I'm not sure who that was addressed to, but God would be my guess.

"Unbelievable," Leslie said. "Simply unbelievable."

"I had a hard time believing it myself," I said.

"Jack," she said, "if you had frozen to death up in those woods, I would never have forgiven you."

"I know. That's what I was afraid of."

"I mean, there I was laid flat in Boston, all worn out from being bombed by gamma rays, and you're out by yourself, getting lost in the woods at night. What were you thinking?"

"Not much."

"No. I guess not."

We were drinking hot chocolate and looking into the fire. It was Friday night and she had been home for an hour or so. She looked very tired and it seemed like talking was work. But she was happy. Or seemed so, anyway.

"It would be some kind of bad deal, wouldn't it," she said, "if at the end of this year the one who wound up dead was you. I mean, *I* am the one who is dying, Jack. You're poaching on my turf."

"You aren't dying," I said quickly. I'd never heard her say that before.

"I know, baby. I'm just teasing you. I saw my surgeon the other day. She said she figures I have a ninety-percent chance of no recurrence."

I thought about that, and the way I saw it, there was a ten-percent chance the cancer *would* recur. Too high for comfort. But right there was the difference between us. She looked at the ninety. I saw the ten.

"So don't freeze to death in the woods. I've invested a lot for that ninety percent. I'd like you around. I figure I've earned it."

"Okay," I said. "Deal."

We didn't do much that weekend. She didn't have the energy. The next weekend she seemed a little stronger, which was a good thing since we had to go to a funeral.

Bill Winter had had a heart attack while he was asleep in a chair. His daughter, visiting from school, found him. He was, I suppose, the perfect candidate for a coronary. Type A and proud of it, and he'd been under more pressure than he'd let on. But then, he wasn't the sort to admit that he felt any pressure at all. It just wasn't his style. I was shocked, of course, but more than that. He'd helped me and I'd been looking forward to repaying the favor somehow, and now all I could do was stand in the small crowd at the cemetery and listen to the familiar words: *Dust to dust* . . . We were hitting the age, I thought, when funerals weren't remarkable events anymore but something you could count on, even if you couldn't schedule them like New Year's parties and graduations and would never, in a million years, get used to them.

After the service, people came up to Leslie and told her how good she looked and how much they had missed her and been thinking about her. She smiled and thanked them and I think she was glad to see people, even under those circumstances. We went out that night with another couple. Leslie had fun even though she got tired and we went home fairly early.

The next morning, before she left for Boston, she said, "You know, it is almost over."

"I know. And that's great."

"I feel like I a dodged a bullet. Maybe."

"You did."

"Well, there is still that ten percent."

"Yes . . ."

"But I figure that's just the chance you take. You could be struck by lightning, right?"

"Right."

"Or get lost in the woods and freeze to death."

"Right again."

"So what's next, Jack?"

"What do you mean?"

"I mean, once I don't have cancer anymore, what's the next thing?"

"Nothing."

"*Nothing?*"

"Well . . . whatever there was before there was cancer."

"Everything just the same?"

"I guess."

She thought about that for a while, and a sort of dreamy look came over her face. It was one of those moments. She was going to say something; I knew that. I waited, wondering what it would be.

"Well," she said, "maybe you're right. Everything will be the same . . . only different."

"Exactly."

"Okay," she said. "I can live with that."

61

When the last dirty scraps of snow had melted, we began going out and working together in the yard. One afternoon, I took a wheelbarrow down to the wood line where I had piled all the cuttings from the fall cleanup. It was compost now and looked dark and fertile. I used a pitchfork to load it and looked at it carefully, like I expected to find something I'd lost. I was looking for the hair that Andy had sheared off with nervous fingers, but there was no sign of it. It had rotted completely away, along with the eggshells, coffee grounds, and grapefruit rinds I'd added to the pile over the winter.

I turned the compost into the vegetable garden. Leslie watched and said, "Any sign of it?"

"Your hair, you mean?"

"What else?"

"No," I said. "None at all."

"Good," she said. "But it is weird to think we'll be eating tomatoes that grew out of my old hair."

She reached up and touched her new hair. It was still not long enough to brush, coming in curly and ragged so she looked young and boyish.

A kind of momentum came back into our lives. Calls came in for Leslie and she stayed busy. I was either on the road for the company in Colorado, doing some selling, or working from home, doing consulting. We had enough, for now, to get by. Brad would be a military officer soon and Andy was heading west for the summer, as soon as school was out. She'd landed a job at a dude ranch.

Leslie had said, "Please don't marry some cowboy."

"I should be so lucky," Andy said.

We were sitting out on our small stone patio one evening, cooking on the grill. The air was cool and dry and sounds carried. We could hear cows mooing as they made their way to the milking barn at a farm almost a mile away. The world seemed ordered and . . . something else.

"Safe, probably," Leslie said when I asked her for the right word. "Some people might say 'boring,' but I'm ready for some of that."

"Me, too," I said.

"I have to go to the hospital," she said. "Next week."

I felt something. It passed like a sudden, cool gust.

"Why?"

"Routine checkup. Don't worry. I'm fine."

How did she know? I wanted to ask, but I guessed that she would say what she usually said. That she just *did*.

"Can I drive you?"

"No."

She said it so firmly that I did not respond.

After a moment or two, she sighed and said, "I appreciate the offer, Jack. Really, I do. But you know what?"

"What?"

"It's *over*. History, you know. And that's how I want it. This is just one of those little routine details, like going to the dentist to get the plaque cleaned off your teeth. You don't drive me when I have to do that and then take me out to lunch after."

"Okay."

"I'm going to put this in one small closet, where it belongs. I know I'll have to go to the fund-raisers and wear a pink T-shirt when I run in the Race for the Cure. I can open the closet and get the T-shirt out when I have to, but otherwise I'm drawing a line. You know what I mean?"

"Sure."

"I'm very lucky. Blessed, even. One year crawling through this tunnel inch by inch. And now I'm out of the other end. I'd just as soon not look back."

I smiled.

"What?"

"Nothing. I just remembered that Satchel Paige line."

"What is a Satchel Paige?"

"He was a baseball player. A pitcher. Maybe the greatest ever. But he was black and probably in his fifties before he ever pitched in the big leagues. He was still good then. He had these rules for longevity. Stuff like, 'Go easy on the vices; the social ramble ain't restful.'"

"I like that."

"And, 'Avoid fried meats, which angry up the blood.'"

"Even better."

"Yeah. But the most famous rule—the one everybody quotes—is 'Don't look back. Something might be gaining on you.'"

"Perfect," she said. "Just perfect. From now on, that's my rule, too."